PRAISE FOR *MR. BREAKFAST*

AN AMAZON BOOK OF THE MONTH

"[Carroll's] prose is spare, polished and quick-moving, sometimes lightly comic, always immensely engaging . . . *Mr. Breakfast* is pure pleasure to read . . . It will surprise you, make you laugh and scare you—and then, just when you think it's over, add several extra twists." **—THE WASHINGTON POST**

"[Carroll] has been winning awards for his elegantly spooky magical-realist fantasies since his 1980 debut, *The Land of Laughs.* His first novel since 2014 plays with ideas about fate, choice, art, and love . . . Every bit as inventive and engaging as the best of his earlier novels, and still with a sinister edge, this is more dream than nightmare, and a pure delight to read." **—THE GUARDIAN**

"*Mr. Breakfast* is worth the wait . . . a tale of regret and reincarnation, of second chances arriving perhaps too late. Its narrative strands are folded inside one another and the whole thing is couched in pristine prose. To Carroll, the mundane can yield unexpected delight and danger, making everyday lives fascinating." **—THE FINANCIAL TIMES**

"Carroll's prose . . . imprints deep into your psyche, amplifying the beauty and absurdity of everyday life while highlighting the metaphysical in the seemingly mundane." **—THE LOS ANGELES REVIEW OF BOOKS**

"Entertaining and thought-provoking." **—THE BOSTON GLOBE**

"Carroll works comfortably and confidently within his fantasy and simply tells a good story." **—COMPLETE REVIEW**

"You won't miss the humor inside this book, or the longing, or the real beauty of the prose . . . *Mr. Breakfast* is a book to pick." **—THE BOOKWORM SEZ COLUMN**

"This is a superior fantasy novel . . . The humanity of the entire cast shines through." **—THE WASHINGTON INDEPENDENT REVIEW OF BOOKS**

"Few recent works of fiction in any genre have touched on the vagaries of life, love, and art more movingly or with deeper understanding. An intoxicating, deeply affecting novel by the influential fantasist." **—KIRKUS, STARRED REVIEW**

"Another winner from one of our best fabulists . . . the novel thrilled me; it made me reflect on art, love, choices, and regrets; it left me with tears in the corners of my eyes and a smile on my face. What more can a reader ask for?" **—TOR.COM**

"A compulsively readable, introspective tale about the road not taken . . . At its heart, this is an arresting and imaginative meditation on life. Perfect for fans of magical realism with a free-flowing style like that of David Mitchell and Toshikazu Kawaguchi." **—LIBRARY JOURNAL**

"Both wistfully melancholy and downright joyous." **—LOCUS MAGAZINE**

"As always with the exceptionally imaginative Carroll, he creates complex worlds for his hero to inhabit and with clever crossovers between realms that are carefully thought out and fun to explore. Carroll's attention to details is impressive, and the unexpected prevails." **—BOOKLIST**

"[Carroll] gives readers so much to consider about love, art, disappointment, loss, the wondrous possibilities of life, and the vast unknowables of the universe . . . This really interesting and weird novel challenges and delights." **—BOOKREPORTER**

"It's not much of a stretch to call Carroll a modern master of magical realism. Except that's to pigeonhole him and, like David Mitchell or Haruki Murakami, his work defies categorization . . . there really isn't anyone else quite like him." **—SFX**

"Sharing the DNA of movies like *Sliding Doors* and *The Weatherman*, Jonathan Carroll's latest novel is a cinematic exploration of nostalgia, regret and self-reflection . . . a tender work of literary fantasy; absorbing and provocative, yet free from the cynicism of a Hollywood redemption arc. *Mr. Breakfast* is a charming and thoughtful tale, an introspection on reckoning with the choices you make and how they can weigh and balance with personal values and the many opportunities life brings." **—SCIFINOW**

"*Mr. Breakfast* is ultimately a novel about happiness and all the ways we find it elusive . . . I wanted to know more at every turn, yet I entirely trusted the writer to tell me all I needed. That sense of needing more is always a key litmus test of any novel for me, and *Mr. Breakfast* passed easily." **—BRITISH FANTASY SOCIETY**

"This is both a characteristic book—a part of the Carroll mosaic—and a unique one. I love the refractions as early scenes are reconsidered in light of later ones. I slowed down in the last third, to savor the gorgeous intricacies. I love the humor—the sly humor, and the dumb jokes and the surreally-simple/simply-surreal word combinations that are always Jonathan Carroll's signature."

—JONATHAN LETHEM, AUTHOR OF THE
NEW YORK TIMES-BESTSELLING *MOTHERLESS BROOKLYN*

"A beautiful, brilliant meditation on art, love, inspiration and what makes life worthwhile."   —NEIL GAIMAN

"A well-drawn world and characters in a completely original and unpredictable setting . . . I don't know a more enjoyable or intelligent writer of his kind."

—MICHAEL MOORCOCK

"Like Murakami, Brian Eno, or David Lynch, Jonathan Carroll is entirely sui generis, someone whose work is so fresh, weird, and original, it stands in a class of its own. Maybe the most striking thing about this lean, remarkable novel is Carroll's caffeinated curiosity about everything, his roving eye for everyday wonders, for the effervescent in the banal. *Mr. Breakfast* is a small book of big ideas, a set of Russian nesting dolls with an entire universe glowing at the center."   —JOE HILL, BESTSELLING AUTHOR OF *HEART-SHAPED BOX*

MR. BREAKFAST

A Novel

JONATHAN CARROLL

MELVILLE HOUSE
BROOKLYN • LONDON

MR. BREAKFAST

First published in 2023 by Melville House
Copyright © Jonathan Carroll, 2022
All rights reserved
First Melville House printing: November 2022
First paperback printing: May 2023

Melville House Publishing
46 John Street
Brooklyn, NY 11201

and

Melville House UK
Suite 2000
16/18 Woodford Road
London E7 0HA

mhpbooks.com
@melvillehouse

ISBN: 978-1-68589-088-9

ISBN: 978-1-61219-993-1 (eBook)

Library of Congress Control Number: 2022945979

Printed in the United States of America

1   3   5   7   9   10   8   6   4   2

for
Celina Pająk

Nothing will tell you
where you are.
Each moment is a place
you've never been.

—MARK STRAND

We don't really know it, but we sense it: there
is a sister ship to our life which takes a totally
different route.

—TOMAS TRANSTRÖMER

When words become unclear, I shall focus with
photographs. When images become inadequate,
I shall be content with silence.

—ANSEL ADAMS

"Do you want to talk about Patterson now? We don't have to if you're not in the mood."

Ruth Murphy's face went through a whole Olympics of different expressions—anger, sadness, resignation—before she spoke. "Patterson the joker, right? The joke*ster*, the clown, the idiot. That's the Graham I knew. Back then, what wouldn't the man do for a laugh? I assume you know about the time with the prosthetic arm? They were going to arrest him. They had him in handcuffs, for God's sake! But he was so over-the-top goofy with the cops he made them laugh too, so they let the fool go. *That* time. There were others, and they didn't end so happily." She knew she wasn't being fair or telling the whole truth because there were so many other things she had loved about Patterson. But now she was old and alone, and old love unfulfilled can sometimes fester.

The interviewer said gently, "But that was in his career as a *comedian*—long before he became famous and disappeared. You were together a long time . . . "

"Three years. We stayed together because I *loved* him. You can love someone and still think they're an idiot. I want to show you something."

In the old woman's lap was a battered, sun-bleached manila envelope. Opening it, she slowly slid out a large photograph. One side had a large crease, and overall the picture had not been well cared for. She handed it to James Arthur, the interviewer. He took one look and nodded—of course he'd seen it before. Hundreds of thousands, perhaps millions, of people had seen it before.

"That's a very well-known picture, Ms. Murphy."

"I *know*," Ruth said irritably, having heard the condescension in his voice. "But it's my line."

"Excuse me?" Arthur straightened his back and tried to control the disbelief in his voice.

"He used my line—I said it. Or rather, I *wrote* it to him in a note, right after we broke up. Turn the picture over and read what's on the back."

The man did, and saw written there in handwriting that was instantly familiar to him:

"To Ruthie—who gave me the beginning with a Brownie. Thank you for that, and for so much more. Great Love, Graham."

"Whoa, amazing! It's hard to believe. I'm sure you know how famous this photo is—it's on par with anything by William Eggleston. Personally, I think it's better."

Ruth grumbled, "I didn't say I *took* it—that was all Graham's doing. The picture, the way he framed the image, the lighting, he found the location . . . it was all him. But the *line* itself was mine. I even remember writing it to him on a postcard."

"Patterson would never say where the billboard was. It's part of the mystery of the photograph."

She touched her white hair, creating a little dramatic pause before spilling the beans. "Hallet, Nevada. Somewhere up in the Eureka district. Graham said it was originally called Hell It's Nevada but they changed the name in the 1930s because the town was getting rich and the citizens wanted to make it sound more respectable. But when the silver mines nearby went bust in the 1950s, the place started dying and never stopped. In its heyday, everyone in town hung out at Mr. Breakfast. It was apparently Hallet's social center."

"Wait, wait—I'm writing this down. How do you know all this?"

Ruth Murphy moved slowly back and forth in her chair, trying to find a comfortable position. At least, one she could share more comfortably with her arthritis. The last days were closing in on her, and she knew it. She had no legacy, a son she hadn't seen in two years, no business to pass on, and no life's work she had created that would continue to exist after she was gone. Nothing to show the future world there had once been a woman named Ruth Murphy. No, she knew the only thing that might bring her a few footnotes in some biography or a line in an appendix was the fact she had lived with Graham Patterson before he became *Patterson*.

James Arthur handed the renowned photo back to her. She looked at it thoughtfully, pursing her lips.

It showed a large run-down, vandalized, and badly boarded up salmon-colored roadside diner set alone on some bleak desert stretch of highway that looked like it could just as well have been on the moon. The first word to come to mind on seeing the image was *forlorn*. The diner had a long-faded red-and-white sign over the front door. It said "MR. BREAKFAST," although two of the letters had fallen sideways over time, making the building look even sadder and more depressing. At the front of the diner's empty parking lot was a giant weatherworn standalone statue of a smiling chef in a high toque holding up a tray with the name of the diner across the top. Below it, on the marquee sign where specialties of the house or community greetings like "Welcome Lions Club Members!" might once have been listed was a single sentence:

SOLITUDE CAN BE A MOODY COMPANION

In an early influential article about Patterson's work, one art critic wrote what was so arresting about this photograph was *because* of the eerie way it was composed, it made a viewer feel the building itself was still somehow alive. The message on its giant sign was akin to a street beggar's handwritten sign asking the world for help. Though, in the case of Mr. Breakfast, the place *itself* was saying, "I don't want to be alone anymore."

"Do you like the picture?" Ruth Murphy asked James Arthur.

"'Mr. Breakfast'? Oh yes, very much. It was the first Patterson I ever saw, so it was the picture that got me hooked. Don't you like it?"

The old woman sighed and thought a bit before answering. "I have mixed feelings. I can appreciate it as a work of art, famous image and all, but I also remember what was going on in Graham's life then, and how much confusion he was in at the time he took it."

———

It wasn't supposed to happen like this. You buy a new car and it runs. It runs great for a few guaranteed years without anything going wrong. After that, but *only* then, is it allowed to break down—not in the first month of ownership. Not with only 2,695 miles on the damned machine, and most definitely not when you've just base jumped off the cliff of your old life into the great foggy unknown.

Could anything *else* go wrong in the Graham Patterson universe? His career—up in smoke. His love life? Down the toilet. His prospects for a rosy future? More likely to fit his fat body through the eye of a needle at that point.

The day after he bombed so badly at the comedy club in Providence, Rhode Island, Graham Patterson went to a car dealer and bought a brand-new, lipstick red Ford Mustang convertible right off the showroom floor. A check for five figures? Boom! Done. Next, he went to a camera shop and bought the Nikon he'd been lusting after for months because he wanted a photographic record of the trip he was about to take. He had a few thousand dollars left in his bank account afterward, which would get him across the country to where his patient and very successful brother Joel was waiting with a job, if he wanted it.

What Patterson really wanted was to be paid to make people laugh, but it was never going to happen. He accepted this fact now, and he had finally resolved to give the dream of being a famous comedian a decent burial during the trip. He'd been trying for years to make it, but after so long, knew in his heart it wasn't meant to be. It was time to accept failure and make new plans for the rest of his life.

His father used to say, "There comes a point . . . " Patterson had reached that point in Providence, the quiet murmur of the audience in reaction to his best comedy routine the final devastation. Added to this humiliation were the looks of indifference, impatience, and even derision on the faces of people who'd come to laugh but did not. To be fair, there had been *some* chuckling here and there, an amused snort or two and a few snickers at his best jokes, but big loud "ho ho!" laughs at Graham Patterson's carefully crafted, torturously worked over act? *De nada,* baby. *Nichts.*

So he buried his life's dream and drove away from that cemetery in the new convertible, which took him as far as North Carolina before it died, too. Luckily, the problem was only a defective fuel pump. It was covered under the warranty and could be fixed in an afternoon.

While waiting for the car to be repaired, Patterson decided to grab a bite to eat and take a walk around the town. Two pulled-pork sandwiches and a large Royal Crown Cola later, he felt a tad better about the shape of his predicament.

A few blocks from the sandwich shop on a small, nondescript side street, he passed a tattoo parlor called Hardy Fuse. Thinking about it later, he didn't know if he stopped to look in the window because of the odd name of the establishment or because of the photos on display in the store window. Patterson was no tattoo connoisseur or even much of a fan, but these were the most beautiful he had ever seen. Some were realistic, some abstract, but no matter where they were on the body, all of them were drawn and colored in such an arresting, singular way that it felt . . . it almost felt like the tattoos were speaking a whole new visual language to Patterson's eyes and sensibilities. He had never seen anything like them before. He had to go into the place and investigate.

A bell above the door tinkled thinly when he opened it. Once he was inside, a low woman's voice with a heavy Southern accent sang out, "Sorry, but we're closed."

Patterson hesitated, wondering why the door was open if the store was closed. A moment later the voice sang out again, "Just kiddin'. Hold on—I'll be right out."

Standing still, unsure of what he was going to say when this woman appeared, Patterson looked around—at nothing, really. There was little in the store to look *at*: a bare counter, a cash register, two scarred wooden chairs on either side of a cheap wooden coffee table. Some beat-up *National Geographic* magazines were scattered across the top of it.

"Hello. How can I help you?" A small, pleasantly plain woman who appeared to be in her forties walked out from the back room of the store. Short black haircut, jeans faded and ripped at the knees, and a sleeveless fuchsia t-shirt that said "HEARTY FUSE" in large white letters across the chest. This confused Patterson, because he remembered the spelling on the store window was "hardy."

"Are you *hearty* or *hardy*?" Patterson the wise guy asked, the jovial character taking over as he often did when in a tight or awkward spot. He'd learned over the years being funnily forward or sweetly aggressive with strangers usually amused them in situations like this.

The woman picked right up on what he was talking about and smiled. One of her front teeth was gold. "Well, sometimes it's one, sometimes t'other. It's like sometimes you're in *this* mood, and sometimes *that*? Since I'm the boss and sole employee here, I decided to keep both. Are you here to get some ink?"

Patterson pointed to the shop window. "I'm here because while passing by outside, I saw those photos in your window and was knocked for a loop—they're *beautiful*."

She nodded her agreement—she knew they were good. "Want one?"

He wasn't sure he'd heard her right. "Excuse me?"

"You want me to do one on you?"

Never in his life had Graham Patterson wanted or even considered getting a tattoo, although he liked some he saw on other people. But now that she asked and he'd seen examples of her great artistry, the thought intrigued him, and why not? Maybe this should be part of his new life—the new Graham Patterson, inked. "Can I see some of the others you've done? I mean, besides the ones in the window?"

"'Course! Let me get my books." She put out her hand to shake. He noticed it was very small and chubby, like a baby's. "My name is Anna Mae Collins. What's yours?"

"Graham—Graham Patterson."

"Well, Gray-yam, I'm going to show you some things now that'll put new batteries in your flashlight. Have a seat." She went to the back room again and reemerged holding two thick ring binders. Laying them down on the table, she gestured for him to take a seat. "I'm going out to get some coffee. You want one? While I'm gone, you look through my books and maybe find something in there you might want on your skin for-evah."

He loved her slow Southern drawl and the fact she trusted him, a complete stranger, to stay put and not snoop around her place, or worse, while she was out.

As if she knew he would need time to look and linger over the choices, Anna Mae was gone quite a while. Patterson was amazed by what he saw in her books. The artistry, colors, the combinations *of* colors, the imagination and *execution* of that imagination . . .

Once, when things were going well between them, he and Ruth Murphy had taken a vacation in Mauritius. The thing he remembered most about the trip was the moment he stepped out of the plane at the Mauritius airport and smelled the night air. The first whiff was so gorgeous, so overpowering, but best of all so utterly *foreign* he just stood mesmerized in the doorway of the plane with eyes closed, sniffing. Seeing Anna Mae Collins' tattoos for the first time felt a little like that.

"Your work is unbelievable. Where did you *learn* to do this?"

Anna Mae put a Styrofoam cup of black coffee in front of him and sat down in the other chair. "Here, there, everywhere. Art school, London, a *mambabatok* in the Philippines, Marseille, but I spent the most time in Japan . . . I wanted to know how to do it right, so I found out where the masters were and went to them. Took me seven years, and then I came back home. It was hard at first making ends meet, especially in this business, but people got the word about my work, and now they come from all over. Did you find something you liked in there?"

"I did." Patterson had marked the page in one of the albums with a red plastic toothpick he had in a pocket. Turning to it, he pointed at one of the photos. Like the Russian *matryoshka* dolls, where one figure sits inside a larger one, which sits inside an even larger one, and so on, the tattoo he had chosen was of a bee inside the stomach of a frog inside the stomach of a hawk inside the stomach of a lion. What was most extraordinary about the image, besides the stunningly exact, almost photographic detail and coloring of each creature, was how *small* the tattoo was: insanely intricate interwoven imagery inside a space no larger than a pack of cigarettes, yet he saw clearly each figure and could only marvel at how perfectly every one of the creatures had been rendered. It reminded him of those oddball artists who paint pictures on the inside of matchbook covers, a rice kernel, or the head of a pin.

"*This* one. I'd like to have it right here." Patterson patted his left bicep.

Anna Mae leaned in close over the page, studied the picture, and nodded. "Interesting choice. Two sessions, I'll need two sessions to complete it. How long're you staying in town?"

"Just today. I'm having my car fixed."

"Stay the night. My mother runs a real nice bed-and-breakfast three blocks from here, and as a cook, she is out of this world. We call her the Queen of Tomato Soup. You'll be glad you stayed, both for my tatt and her cooking. You in a hurry to get somewhere, Gray-yam?"

Patterson was not in a hurry to get *anywhere*. His destination was California, but he knew once there he'd either have to take the unwanted job in his brother's fruit and vegetable exporting company or start looking around for something else he could do. Neither option excited him. So hell no, he wasn't in a hurry. He slyly asked, "What's Mom cooking tonight?"

Anna Mae nodded once and said ,"Very good. Let me give her a call right now and ask. Then we'll get started here."

———

Surprisingly, Mrs. Collins turned out to be from Vienna, Austria, and even after forty years in North Carolina still spoke with a strong German accent. That night over dinner, she told a story that resonated with Patterson.

The last time she visited Vienna, people were talking about a court case drawing national attention: A man had been arrested and charged with writing in Italian the graffiti *"Mondo Prestato,"* which meant "Borrowed World," an estimated ten *thousand* times on every conceivable surface in the city—the walls of buildings, benches, the sides of trucks, cars, and buses, windows, urinals, garbage cans, sidewalks . . . This went on for months, until he was finally caught after a concerned friend turned him in to the police. When asked why he did it, the tagger reportedly said, "Because we're always borrowing what others see and saying it's our own. It's got to stop!"

Years later, Patterson's highly controversial photograph "Borrowed World" caused a furor at the Venice Biennale when the gigantic original print was severely defaced with acid by a man dressed as a nun.

But Patterson loved the way the picture had been vandalized and insisted the damaged copy be used whenever the photo was displayed in any museum.

The photograph depicts three teenagers facing the viewer: two girls and a boy, all looking intently at the screens on their cell phones. It is night, so the glow from the phones lights all their faces an identical cold gray-white. Because the rest of the photograph is so dark and shadowy, it takes the viewer a moment to realize behind the kids is a car rammed so hard into a tree its front end has lifted off the ground. The driver's door has swung open, but there is no sign of a driver or passenger. Has this accident just happened, or is it ancient history? Is the picture staged? Why are these kids ignoring the crash? Were they driving the car? Are they calling the cops? Why are all their faces so impassive? Why are they out here in the middle of a dark nowhere staring at telephones when behind them . . . ? And etcetera.

———

In Mrs. Collins' kitchen, Patterson took the first photographs with his new camera. One of them, "The Queen of Tomato Soup," later reworked endlessly, would eventually get him his first gallery show.

As a girl, Ursula "Uschi" Collins was badly burned when a New Year's Eve fireworks display went horribly wrong and many of the explosives shot straight into the crowd instead of up in the air. Uschi's right hand and arm were particularly disfigured and discolored. But she was right-handed and showed no embarrassment or shyness using it.

She and Patterson hit it off immediately. After spending the afternoon in the tattoo shop with him, Anna Mae introduced Patterson to her mother as "a three-ring circus all under one hat" because she knew how much her mom loved to laugh. Uschi particularly liked his jokes and showed her appreciation with both a rowdy cackle and large helpings when serving him a helluva good meal. Naturally, the first thing she brought to the table was her famous cream of tomato soup. Patterson had his new camera out by then and was taking pictures of everything while they talked, just to get used to it.

As she placed the white bowl of soup down in front of him, he thanked her and snapped a picture of it. He did not look at the picture until much later. But the first time he saw it, his breath caught in his throat. The most strikingly poignant thing about the photograph was the soup was almost *exactly* the same color as her scarred arm and hand. The stark white of the bowl was the only contrast between the salmon pink of the cream of tomato soup and the gnarled hand holding it. The comfort of soup contrasted with the catastrophe of the hand, yet the colors were almost identical. The resulting absolutely accidental photograph was macabre but beautiful, as domestic as it was disquieting.

The next day at her shop, Anna Mae had been working steadily for an hour when she lifted the tattoo machine off Patterson's arm and wiped his skin with a cotton cloth. "Why are you getting this now? You're practically middle aged."

Patterson had been daydreaming while she worked. He never got used to the pain from the buzzing tattoo needle, but his skin became sort of inured to it the longer the work went on. It allowed him to zone out while she did her stinging magic. "*Why?* I don't know—I think it was more spur of the moment than anything else. I never wanted a tattoo before, but when I saw the pictures in your books it was like, I gotta have one of those."

"But why *this* design in particular?" Her voice was neutral. She put the machine against his arm again and went back to work.

"Do you want the truth?"

Surprised by the question, she lifted the device off his arm so she could look him in the eye. "Absolutely!"

"It's the one I liked least."

Totally thrown off guard, Anna Mae laughed. They had been talking for a long time by then, so she knew all about Patterson's failed career as a comedian, failed relationship with Ruth Murphy, and quixotic decision to drop his old life completely, buy a racy new car, and head out for parts and hopefully adventures unknown. "Explain it to me, willya, Gray-yam? When I don't like something I don't want it near me, much less written under my skin forever."

He took a deep, sorrowful breath. "Up till a few weeks ago, too many nights ended with me drinking in shit bars alongside guys with names like Dublin Paul and Epic Johnny. I kid you not with those names, by the way. Then I'd go home to an apartment decorated in terrible taste by a woman I adored and had failed completely. Half drunk, I'd sit there alone and wonder why no one laughed at the jokes I wrote." Patterson stopped, and his mouth tightened. Pain and sadness radiated off him like heat from a Texas road in August. "I've never been good at getting to the heart of things, like the bee in your tattoo. Right down to the center—the *core* that nourishes everything—first the frog, then the hawk . . . I've never been able to get to *my* core, Anna Mae. I've never been able to see or feel, to *create* from the middle of my soul. Never. Maybe on my best day, once in a while I've gotten to the frog, but no farther. I realize it now.

"It was the first thing I thought when I saw the tattoo and knew in an instant I had to have it, like some kind of *memento mori*. Know what I mean? It'll always be there to remind me the whole point of anything is try to reach your core and work out from there. To *start* from the bee."

Two days later while driving, Patterson was stung on the forehead *by* a bee. No warning, no *bee lands, you swat, it gets mad and comes back in for the kill-shot sting.* Nope—just a sudden OW! on what felt like the middle of his forehead. Wincing, his eyes jumped up to see in the rearview mirror what happened. There was a damned bee on the top of his face. Kamikaze mission accomplished, it fell dead onto his leg. Patterson carefully picked up the body and put it on the passenger's seat. He snorted at the irony. "I guess I just started from the fucking *bee,* all right. Damn it *hurts!*"

Patterson hadn't been stung by a bee in years and couldn't remember the last time it happened. But he knew he needed to get the stinger out if he wanted the pain to go away. It was midday and there was almost no traffic on the highway in either direction. Fortunately, he sped by a sign saying a roadside rest was two miles up the road. He pulled in there a short while later. After stopping the car, he twisted the rearview mirror toward him again to see exactly where the thing was on his face. The stinger was almost smack in the middle of his forehead. It came out pretty easily, and after wiping it off his finger on a tissue he grimaced and shook his head.

The land all around him was flat. This was Illinois, and crops grew in every direction as far as the eye could see. His was the only car at the rest stop. There were a couple of picnic tables to the left of where he'd parked. To the right, a small cinderblock building housed toilets for men on one side and women on the other. He had been driving for hours and felt like getting out of the car for a good long stretch and a piss.

Patterson liked these roadside rests, liked the busy pound and rush of cars and trucks whizzing past on the turnpike nearby. He liked the idea of people past and future sitting at the now empty picnic tables having a bite to eat and a small intermission while on the drive home or to who knows where. Lousy gas station white-bread sandwiches in hard-to-open transparent triangular plastic envelopes. Or great food, cooked at home and packed with care and love in preparation for the long trip ahead. Paper napkins, white plastic forks and knives that never worked well because they were too flimsy and bendable. Small red-and-yellow envelopes of ketchup and mustard, cans of warm soda fizzing ferociously and bubbling up fast over the sides when you popped the top. He liked the image of the family dog jumping eagerly out of the car to take a long whizz and sniff everywhere at this unfamiliar territory. For a dog, such a place far from home was like landing on another planet—all these new smells and things to investigate.

Patterson stretched both arms up and down over his head a few times, then tried bending over and touching his toes—wishful thinking that stopped when he got about a third of the way down and his straining back cried no. He sighed, knowing no matter where he ended up on this trip, he'd have to lose at least some weight. Which was worse—exercise or cutting back on eating whatever he wanted, whenever he wanted?

An enormous silver and blue sixteen-wheel truck blew by on the highway trailing a high whine of tires and spillage of gasoline fumes, hot rubber, and dust. For no reason at all other than a spur-of-the-moment appreciation for the size and power of the great machine, Patterson waved at the truck. Then, pumping his arms like a race walker, he strode briskly back and forth across the length of the empty parking lot a few times to get the blood flowing around his body. Then his bladder demanded—go now or else.

There was no door to the bathroom, just a cinderblock wall he had to go around to get to the open doorway. Sprayed crudely on this wall in fluorescent orange paint were the words "Please wait here to be seated." Patterson smiled. The last time he'd seen that sentence was on a brass sign on a maître d's desk at an upscale restaurant in Hyannisport, Massachusetts.

To his surprise and delight, inside the building smelled *fantastic*. Not the normal horror of a public toilet or the harsh fake pine and chemical reek so many of them have after they've been cleaned. This rest room out in the middle of Nowhere, Illinois, smelled amazingly like the fresh outdoors; even better, it smelled like the outdoors after a magnificent sky-cracking summer thunderstorm washes the world clean, leaving it fragrant and glistening. Patterson couldn't get over the beautiful smell in this cinderblock bomb shelter of a toilet that was otherwise basic, minimal, and dark.

He took a long pee, rinsed his hands at a banged-up stainless steel sink, and walked out of the building.

As soon as he stepped outside, he saw the truck. He made two fists, closed his eyes, and hissed a happy "Yessss!" Parked down the way was a Ford Raptor pickup truck in exactly the same shade of red as his new car. To Patterson, the Raptor was the most kickass 4WD, 411 horsepower, drive-it-straight-up-the-side-of-Mount-McKinley macho truck around, bar none. He'd fantasized about owning one for years but frankly didn't have the nerve—or presumption—to buy the monster because he'd feel like a pathetic weekend Rambo phony behind the wheel. Rides like this belonged in the rough hands of Montana cowboys, ex-Navy Seals, Alaskan ice road truckers, or Texas oilfield workers, not an overweight ex-comedian whose only claim to toughdom was a brand-new tattoo that still made him wince with pain if he moved his arm the wrong way.

Still, a fellow could window-shop. Never having seen a Raptor up close, he went to check it out. So delighted by the opportunity to get near his fantasy truck, he didn't pay much attention to the owner sitting way over on top of one of the picnic tables and talking on a cell. The man's head hung down, obscuring his face as he spoke into the phone. The one thing Patterson *did* notice out of the corner of his eye was the guy had a Mohawk haircut, which he kept stroking like a pet as he spoke.

Hands behind his back, the comedian peered into the cab of the truck. What he first saw were the objects on the passenger's seat: a rust-colored jean jacket and an instantly recognizable wooden box. Seeing those two things made him frown and wrench back his head like he'd been slapped. Fifty feet away, in the trunk of his own car, were these same objects. *Exactly the same.*

The jean jacket had been a birthday present from Ruth Murphy a year before they broke up. It was one of Patterson's most treasured possessions. She'd originally bought the Japanese selvedge denim jacket in beige, then had it dyed his favorite color—that precise coppery rust— by a specialist company in Manhattan. He loved jean jackets and had several. But the thoughtfulness and generosity inherent in her having one made specifically in "his" color was a gesture beyond compare. He had certainly never seen another like it—until now.

The wooden box he owned, identical to the one inside the truck, was another story, and a vinegary one. Originally it had contained a Lichtenberg Figure wristwatch that cost about nine thousand dollars. Now *his* own box was empty, but Patterson had brought it along on his cross-country trip to remind him that life sometimes demanded you take big chances now, or else.

Graham Patterson's best friend was Steven Bergman. His roommate in college, Bergman went on to become one of the premier eye surgeons in the country. As a result, he was rich as Croesus. A handsome, charismatic man, he had never had the slightest romantic interest in either men or women. When asked about it, Bergman shrugged and said indifferently, "I was born without *that* gene." The confirmed bachelor lived modestly but very well. He owned little, but everything was the absolute best, whether it was clothes, whiskey, furniture, watches . . . His great passions were travel to unusual places and extreme adventure. Whenever possible, he flew off to remote jungles to do things like live in trees with endangered species of monkeys, or to Himalayan mountain peaks, where he'd drink yak-butter tea in snow caves with Sherpas, often getting dysentery, exotic diseases, or food poisoning and losing ten pounds along the way. Straight as an arrow and serious as a mortician, Bergman had almost no sense of humor. But for some mysterious reason, Graham could always make his friend laugh and the doctor loved him for it, although he never cut Patterson any slack when he believed he had fucked up.

A few years before, Steve had called one day and said he'd been thinking about Patterson. He thought it would be really game-changing for Graham's career if the comedian got a Mohawk haircut and dressed formally in a suit and tie whenever he performed. Patterson thought he was joking, but Bergman was not. He'd been thinking a lot about his friend's middling success as a comedian and decided the lack of real success was likely because Graham didn't have a singular shtick—he was only another guy telling pretty good, but pretty vanilla jokes. Ergo, his entire image required a total reboot. Patterson's routine needed edge and bite—served up with a risky, take-no-prisoners attitude. A crazy bold haircut would make an immediate visual statement, which should be paired with both a contrasting impeccably conservative suit and sharper, much more dangerous jokes—humor aimed for the throat and gasps of recognition rather than just yuk-yuk chuckles and chortles, material that willfully offended some people but enlightened and informed others with their original insight and observations.

Patterson heard his friend out but then immediately said a firm, "*No.*"

Bergman asked, "Why not?"

"Because that guy is not me, Steve; you know it as well as I. I'd feel like an idiot walking around with a Mohawk haircut and wearing a business suit, especially on stage. What if I told *you* to shave your head and operate in flip-flops, lederhosen, and a pith helmet?"

Bergman's voice turned icy. "My career is not balls-deep in quicksand and sinking deeper by the month, Graham. Every time you perform these days the venues get smaller; soon you'll be doing bat mitzvahs in Secaucus.

"I'll make you a deal: Next month you have the gig in Brooklyn. Just get the haircut. Get the Mohawk, wear a suit and tie, and add at least six minutes of new, completely chancy material to your routine. Go in the direction I just suggested. Get *gritty*; make jokes that stab and provoke rather than tickle."

"And what if I do?" Patterson had no intention of doing any of this but wanted to hear what Bergman had to offer in return.

"You love my Lichtenberg watch. I'll give it to you if just this once you perform the way I suggested."

"Steve, your watch is worth like eight thousand dollars—"

"*Nine*, plus change. But I'm completely serious—do it my way one night, only one performance, and the watch is yours."

"You're crazy."

"No, I'm your friend and trying to help. If you take my advice, you can take my watch."

When they were students, Bergman once said, "Most people would rather *die* than make big changes in their lives." Back then, Patterson thought his pal was just trying to sound dramatic and deep. But as years passed and he experienced more of how people behaved and actually lived their lives, he realized how true the statement was. And he thought of the line again minutes before going on stage weeks later in Brooklyn, dressed as he always dressed when performing and telling the same jokes he'd told at his last few shows.

Afterward, the manager of the club came over to Patterson and handed him a large gray cardboard box. The reaction of the audience that night had been pretty good—some strong laughs throughout his set—so the comedian came off stage on a high, feeling good and pumped up by the decent round of applause he'd received.

"What's this?"

"Dunno. A guy handed it to me, said it was for you, and walked away. Handsome guy—looked like an actor."

Patterson took it to a table at the back of the club (there were no dressing rooms). He ordered a glass of rum and sat down with the mystery package. The top was sealed with a single strand of tape, so it came open easily. Inside was a light cherrywood box with two parallel black lightning bolts carved diagonally across the top. Patterson recognized it because Bergman had shown it to him months earlier: This box held his Lichtenberg watch.

"*Holy shit!*" Twisting his head from side to side to see if Steve was nearby, Patterson couldn't believe it. He hadn't even known Bergman was coming tonight. The doctor had said he'd be out of town at a conference. He was giving Patterson the watch, but why? The comedian hadn't done any of what Bergman had suggested—he still had all his hair, and instead of a suit and tie, he was wearing an eight-year-old black cashmere sweater and jeans. For a moment, a chilling thought raced across his mind—what if Bergman was very sick, and the watch was a parting gift to his best friend?

But that scare quickly evaporated when he opened the box—and saw nothing inside except a yellow Post-it Note covered in Bergman's careful Bauhaus block letter handwriting:

I CAME WITH THE WATCH AND LEAVE WITH THE WATCH.

YOU CAN HAVE THE BOX.

Months later when his act bombed yet again in Rhode Island, Patterson thought about how differently things might have turned out if he'd taken Steve's advice and gone drastic in his act. When packing the new car for the big trip west, he had decided to bring the Lichtenberg box along as a kind of sour souvenir of a road not taken.

But now the box sat next to his custom-dyed jean jacket on the seat of a stranger's truck. They must have been stolen while Patterson was in the toilet. The owner of the Raptor had broken into the trunk of his car and taken the box and jacket.

Patterson *was* heavy and out of shape, but he did not mind confrontation at all. And if it led to some kind of physical scrap, he was okay with that, too. As a kid, he constantly got into fights for both good and bad reasons. Like a pilot light on a gas stove, he'd carried the flame into adulthood. Often when someone rubbed him the wrong way, he would be up in their face in seconds.

Marching straight across the parking lot, he ran a few lines over his tongue to say to the thief. *Why is my stuff in your truck?* No—too mild. *Hey fuckface, what are you doing with my shit?* Too vague.

He was still working on a better line when he clearly saw the thief's face for the first time: Graham Patterson with a Mohawk haircut.

Identical.

A mirror version of himself with a crazy haircut sat on a picnic table four feet away.

He froze and gaped, stunned down into the absolute cells in his blood. This other Graham Patterson continued talking on the phone but now looked directly at him. No reaction—no recognition or ac-knowledgement. From the impassive look on the guy's face, it appeared he didn't even see the real Graham. There was no *whaaat?* or *what the hell* anywhere in the man's eyes, facial expression, or body language, even though his exact double stood directly in front of him. He only squinted straight ahead, concentrating on the phone call. Raising an arm, he stroked his narrow patch of hair again. The sun glinted off something there—his wristwatch. *The* wristwatch—a Lichtenberg Figure, nine thousand bucks on Mohawk's wrist.

"I'm somewhere in Illinois. Why? Because I needed to get away for a few days, Steve, it's as simple as that. People were coming at me from every side, wanting things. I started shutting down; it scared me. All the offers—TV specials, movies—they're great, but sometimes life needs to slow down so you can fuckin' *breathe*. I decided to take a little solo road trip to get some perspective."

There was a pause.

"*Hey*, if anyone knows about pressure, it's you. Didn't you say you sometimes do three operations a day? What?" He listened a while and, smiling, looked down at his wrist. "Yeah, I'm wearing the watch! I always wear it. It's been my good luck charm since the day you gave it to me. I even took the damned box along, that's how superstitious I am about it. Whenever I take the watch off at night, I put it back in the box so it won't get mad at me for not treating it right." He listened again and nodded. "Yeah, my agent *is* going nuts, but too bad, I just talked to her. She's made a mountain of money off me this year, so she needs to cool her jets now and give me some space. Anyway, I'll be back in two days."

All his life, whenever Patterson got really upset scared or confused, his bowels would start grumbling, and he had about ten minutes max to find a toilet or else. There was nothing he could do to stop or control the gut—volcano. After a few mortifying accidents in his past no matter where he was or what he was doing, he knew to find a toilet fast.

The combination of seeing this Mr. Mohawk and hearing what he said on the phone finally hit Patterson, and his gut said *move now.* No matter how much he wanted to stay and listen to Mohawk talk to *his* best friend, Steve Bergman, about living the life he had always dreamed of having, he couldn't. Hurrying back across the lot to the toilet, he passed the big red truck along the way. The macho Ford Raptor his successful other self owned. The one with *his* favorite jean jacket and watch box on the passenger's seat.

Once inside the public bathroom, he barely noticed that beautiful fragrance again in there. Hurrying into the single stall, he got to work just in time. While sitting there, he could feel his heart pound inside his chest like a five-pound hammer on an anvil. It felt as if he had been running hard somewhere, but astonishment and fear drove that beat now—nothing else.

How was it possible? How could it *be?* Patterson believed in God, but not in *this*—not doppelgängers, spooks, alien beings, ESP, visitors from The Beyond, or any other nutty stuff. None of it held even a millimeter of real estate in the "yes, it might be possible" part of his mind.

In contrast, Dr. Steve Bergman *did* believe. He was intrigued by all things weird because he had witnessed a number of genuine wonders in his world travels. At various times over the years, he had given Graham books by Charles Fort, Mircea Eliade, P. D. Ouspensky, Carlos Castaneda, Madame Blavatsky, and others to read. But Patterson thought it was all hooey. "If these people or things do exist and are so powerful, why are they always playing hide and seek with us? Even flying saucers, for Christ's sake. Why don't they land in Times Square and say *here we are*? And why do we need mediums or psychics to hunt ghosts or call the dead to invite them to show their faces? How come they're all so *coy*, Steve?"

Today, coy had stopped. Five minutes ago in the middle of life, Graham Patterson had almost shit his pants after coming face to face with . . . himself. Even better, face to face with a second GP who was apparently living a version of the life Patterson had always dreamed of—excluding the Mohawk haircut.

When his colon gave the all clear, he buckled up and walked out of the bathroom half defiant, half afraid. He had a head full of questions matched by a stomach full of fears. He must get to the guy and talk to him, ask him what . . . no, ask him *who* the hell he was and what was going on.

But after striding around the cinderblock wall to the outside ("Please wait here to be seated"), he saw the red pickup truck was no longer there. Snapping his head to the left, he saw the other Graham Patterson was gone, too. Taking a few steps out into the middle of the empty parking lot, he looked both ways quickly. The man was nowhere to be seen. Mohawk and his red Raptor were gone.

When Patterson returned to his car, he opened the trunk and saw the jean jacket and wooden box were exactly where he had left them.

—

The place was named The Slingshot Club and Patterson was pleased to be there, although there was nothing special about it other than it was the only comedy club in town.

After what had happened that afternoon, he was completely freaked out. Driving too fast to the next town, he rented a room in the first motel he came to and lay on the bed staring at the ceiling, his mind racing a million miles an hour, until the room got so dark he could barely see.

Luckily for him it was a university town with a busy commercial district catering to students that included a comedy club. The woman at the motel desk said it was pretty much a hit-or-miss kind of place—sometimes the comedians there were great, other times cringeworthy. But Patterson loved comedy clubs, good and bad. He loved the high energy of the crowds and pumped adrenaline of the performers, the tightrope-tension and anticipation you felt every time someone new came on stage and began their act. It was immediate and exhilarating. He thought it must be sort of like what a parachutist felt the moment she jumped out of a plane into the sky ten thousand feet above the ground. In the case of the comedian, his "parachute"—the only thing to save him from certain (stage) death—was good jokes. For years, whether performing or sitting in the audience, comedy clubs had been Patterson's refuge. He felt at home in them and, when he had performed well, redeemed.

A sign over the bar said the club was famous for its hot wings and craft beer, so Patterson ordered them while waiting for the first act to appear. But when the waitress put a large red plate full of wings, celery stalks, and blue cheese dip in front of him, he frowned. Because the redolent food didn't smell like chicken wings at all, but rather freshly cut *wood*. Normally a beautiful fragrance in itself, here, wafting off buffalo chicken wings, it was completely weird and wrong.

However, when it came to food, Graham Patterson rarely stood on ceremony. "What the helling it" now, he picked up one of the wings and took a small bite, not knowing what to expect of the woody smelling wing. Delicious! Tangy and hot, with the perfect balance of spices to tingle the tongue and mouth but not murder his taste buds. But the chicken *did* smell like just-cut wood. Strange.

The beer was good too, and for the next hour Patterson ate, drank, and listened to a few mediocre but energetic comedians give their best. It was a Tuesday, and the room was half full. Around ten thirty when people were starting to leave, the club owner took the microphone and enthusiastically said, "We have a surprise for you now, ladies and gentleman. It's not open mic night, but I thought we should make an exception for the next guest. It's surprising to see him in our neck of the woods, but a great honor he dropped by our club. Please welcome *Graham Patterson!*"

The room exploded. Mohawk Patterson walked onto the small stage to raucous applause, cheers, and whistles—a hero's welcome. People were absolutely thrilled the famous comedian was here. Dressed in the same jeans and black polo shirt he wore that afternoon in the turnpike parking lot, he grinned and waved sheepishly to the audience to calm down, thank you very much, but that's enough clapping. Across the room, the other Patterson saw light glint off Mohawk's large, familiar wristwatch.

"Thank you, thank you everyone. It's very kind of you, and thanks to Adam for letting me have the floor here for a little while. Okay, but now please don't ask how I got here tonight—"

Some wiseass clown in a corner of the room immediately shouted, "How did you get here tonight?"

Mohawk replied in a calm voice, "I rode in on the back of your IQ. Luckily for both of us, it was a short ride."

The crowd ate it up. Even Patterson snorted at the insult, appreciating the way it was instantly delivered in a deadpan, not very interested voice rather than a nasty shout-back or slap in the face. He remembered being heckled in clubs. Sometimes he came up with clever retorts, but not as often as he would have liked. Certainly none as quick and surreal as the one his alter ego had just flicked out as fast as static electricity.

Mohawk went on to perform a brilliant fifteen-minute set. "Christian weightlifting—anyone ever heard of it? No? Well then let me tell you about it . . . " The monologue that followed was a brainy madcap, searing rant about male machismo, religion, and hypocrisy that segued beautifully, *seamlessly,* into politics and finished with an inspired "where the hell did *it* come from?" bit about sex with a radiator that had some in the audience gasping in shock while others stood up and applauded, laughing. It was original, risky as hell, and magnificent. It was also exactly the kind of material Steve Bergman had suggested Patterson do instead of his same old ho-hum routines, which far too often had audiences looking around for a waitress to order another drink or getting up in the middle to go to the toilet.

Most disturbing about the set, though, was *all* of the topics Mohawk brought up Patterson had in his notes to write jokes about but had never gotten around to before the fateful night in Providence when he had said The End to his moribund career. He distinctly remembered the afternoon he read about the cult of Christian weightlifting on the internet and knew he *had* to use it somewhere in his routine. It wasn't hard to put two and two together and see that Mohawk, this wildly successful version of himself, had followed Steve Bergman's advice. It appeared to have rewarded him with everything he'd ever dreamed of in this job.

The famous comedian bowed now, did a two-hand wave at the crowd, touched one hand to his chest over his heart as a sign of thanks, and left the stage. He bumped fists with the still-clapping owner standing nearby and went right out a side door.

Patterson got up, dropped two twenty-dollar bills on the table, and left the club by a different door. This time he *would* catch the guy. He had no idea what to say, but he knew he must do it or go mad.

He needn't have hurried. Glancing around the parking lot behind the club, Patterson saw the red Raptor parked under a lamp in a far corner. Mohawk was leaning against the front of the big truck, lighting a cigar. One more similarity between the two men: Patterson loved cigars. Bergman got him hooked on them years before by providing the best. Patterson was quickly spoiled into snobbery. His favorite cigar was a *Padron Maduro*, but they cost a fortune. He bought one only every few months when he was feeling very sad, very happy, or very self-indulgent, which was rare and probably better for his health. But if he could have afforded it, he would have smoked them all the time.

Wound tight as a violin string now, he crossed the lot toward his mirror image. But the closer he got, it was clear Mohawk didn't see him. When he was *right there*—a few feet away and in plain sight— the other Patterson showed no sign of knowing anyone was near. He kept smoking, staring into the distance or down at his feet.

"Hey?" Loud, but not too loud.

No reaction.

"Excuse me?"

Mohawk took the cigar out of his mouth, turned it around in his hand, and blew on the glowing tip, firing it up to an even brighter orange.

How could he not hear? They were right next to each other.

"Hey you, Graham!"

Nothing.

Emboldened, Patterson walked up to Mohawk and tapped him on the chest with a finger. But his finger and whole hand disappeared completely *into* Mohawk's chest like a hand sliding into water. Patterson screeched as if scalded. Snatching back his hand, he looked and saw it was all right, nothing had happened.

"What the fuck . . . what the *fuck!*"

Mohawk smoked on in peace, completely oblivious to what had just happened.

At wit's end, Patterson impulsively stuck both hands out and grabbed for the other's shoulders to shake shake shake him and have some *contact.* There had to be a way to make sense of what was happening. Part of him thought if I can just touch this guy . . . if I can just get *through.* But again his hands disappeared into Mohawk's body. Patterson pulled them back and stood there sort of panting, making strange high noises in the back of his throat.

"Mr. Patterson? Excuse me?"

The voice came from behind Graham. Turning, he saw two men close by hesitantly staring at Mohawk.

"Yes? Hello." Mohawk picked a piece of tobacco off his tongue.

"I'm sorry to bother you Sir, but could you sign this please?" One man held out a white baseball cap.

"You want me to ruin your hat?"

"Oh no, you won't ruin it, believe me! We both love your work. I have the DVD of your last special—"

"*Bread and Bitter?*" Mohawk smiled, taking the cap and a Sharpie pen from the man.

"Yes. I love it." His friend elbowed him in the side, and the guy said quickly, "I mean *we* love it. We've watched it a few times and keep finding new stuff to laugh at."

"That's very kind of you. What's your name?"

The man hesitated, then said, "It would be great if you would sign it to Lock and Key."

Mohawk looked up at him and cocked his head. "Are you guys Lock and Key?"

"Yes, we're together: His name is Kirk and I'm Lockwood—Lock, so you know we kind of—"

Mohawk cut him off. "Gotcha. To Lock and Key it is." He signed the hat, clicked the top back on the pen, and returned them. "Now, can I ask you two something?"

The couple looked at each other with surprise in their eyes—what could the famous man want to know from *us*?

The real Patterson stood there while this conversation went on, realizing to his disbelief none of these three people saw him. First he put his hands through Mohawk's body, and now this—*invisibility*? Because he was closest to one of the men, he reached over and touched his shoulder. As before, his hand sunk into the other's body as if he were putting it into liquid.

"Hey!"

Nothing.

"Hey, I'm talking to you!"

Nothing. The couple were all eyes on Mohawk, waiting for his question.

On impulse, Graham jumped up and down like a lunatic, waving his arms and shouting at the top of his lungs. None of them reacted to his loud craziness. Patterson stopped, drooped, his lower jaw hanging open, bewildered.

"How long have you two been together?"

Lock and Key looked at each other and grinned shyly. "Three years. We got engaged in May."

Mohawk shook his head in admiration "Three years. Wow. So tell me, how did you make it work? What's kept you together all this time, besides of course all the fabulous jungle sex I'm sure you're having." He said it so sweetly and funnily there was no way they could take offense. Both men smiled and again glanced at each other to see how to answer the comedian's unexpected question.

A few steps away from the trio, Patterson frowned, also wondering why Mohawk had posed such an unexpectedly intimate question to these young strangers.

The braver of the two men asked, "How come you're asking?"

"I ask every couple I meet who are really committed to each other, no fooling around, you know what I mean? One day someone is going to answer the question in such a way that a big light bulb will go on inside my brain—bing! And I'm going to think 'So *that's* how romance is done! No wonder I've been doing it wrong all this time.' Because I am *terrible* at love, you guys. Terrible."

Patterson, the real Patterson, *was* terrible at love.

"Paper towels," the young man said quickly, grinning as if something wonderful had just happened.

Mohawk looked at him the way you do when someone sounds vaguely insane. "*Paper towels* are the secret to your relationship?" He glanced at the other man, who was now staring at the ground but beaming from ear to ear, as if both embarrassed and in on some great secret joke.

"Yes. Kirk has this weird thing for paper towels. I don't know where he gets it from. He uses them like crazy on everything and basically refuses to use dishtowels or anything else in the kitchen. For as long as we've been together, I've been saying to him 'Why don't you save some trees and use less of them?' In other ways he's great about recycling and really cares about the environment, but not with paper towels. With them, he's a nut."

Looking up quickly, Kirk whined, "*Lock* . . . ." and made an exasperated face at his partner.

Mohawk waited for him to continue, not knowing where this was going.

"We argued about this forever, and sometimes it got pretty ugly. Never major fights, but some bad things were said. I told him it's not the paper towels, it's the *waste*. He listened every time, but then completely ignored me. It's a ridiculous little thing, I know, but it's always irritated me, and he knew it. Right?" He looked at the other man, who nodded, smirking.

"Anyway, one night a few months ago he washed his hands at the sink and tore some paper towels off the roll on the counter. Right *next* to them were cotton hand towels I'd just washed and stacked there. I put them exactly in that spot so he'd use them and not the paper ones. As usual, though, he ignored them and did what he always did—reached for the paper. I was going to spout off about it for the eightieth time when all of a sudden I had one of those light bulbs you mentioned before go on in my head. I thought 'Just let him *have* the paper towels. Stop being a stubborn idiot about this and let him use all the damned paper towels he wants until his last day on earth.'

"A second later I said exactly that to him. He smiled so big, it was huge. He came straight across the kitchen, hugged me, and said 'I can't tell you how hearing that makes me love you more. You said to yourself it's who he is, no matter how weird or eccentric, so ignore it.

Just leave him alone about it now, let him be who he is.' I really love you for that." Lock looked at Kirk, who, clasping his hands together as if in prayer, nodded again enthusiastically.

Mohawk pursed his lips, the story sinking in. "*Paper towels*. It's a good story. I'll have to remember it. Thank you for telling me."

His thanks were clearly heartfelt. For a few moments, the couple was silent and embarrassed, not knowing exactly what to say. Finally, Lock shifted the autographed cap from one hand to the other and put out his right.

The comedian took it and shook hard. "The best of luck to you two. I wish you a *lifetime* of paper towels."

Spontaneously, Kirk stepped forward and embraced him for a few seconds before stepping back and covering his mouth with a hand, as if a little ashamed at being so forward with a stranger. But the famous comedian bowed his thanks for the sweetness. The couple waved goodbye and walked off across the parking lot.

A few feet away, Patterson shook his head watching all this. No young stranger had ever unexpectedly embraced *him* like that after a show. All his other self had done was ask the couple a rather personal question, and suddenly he had two new friends for life.

Mohawk relit the cigar that had gone out while he spoke with Lock and Key. Then he reached into a pocket with his other hand and took out a cell phone. He started to tap in a number, made an unhappy face, and stopped. Whoever he was about to call, he decided not to and put the phone away.

"Paper towels." He said the words sadly, as if they were the perfect solution to a long ago problem but now it was too late.

A silver panel truck entered the parking lot at the far end. It moved slowly toward them, the driver impossible to see in the diffuse coppery overhead light. Both Patterson and his double watched as the truck approached. Oddly, it pulled up *very* close to them and stopped. Patterson could see the driver now—a pretty smiling woman who looked to be in her thirties, her hair a kind of short boy's cut. The window on the passenger's side slid down. She called out, "Mr. Patterson?"

Without thinking, Patterson answered "Yes?" but then remembered he was invisible as long as his other self was here too. The woman was addressing Mohawk, not him.

"Hi. Yes." Smiling, Mohawk took a step toward the van, then stopped abruptly.

The woman had a gun in her hand and was pointing it at him. "Get in the van."

Mohawk put up both hands in surrender "Look, I—"

"Get in the van *now* or I'll shoot you in the eye." As if to prove her point, the woman calmly moved the pistol a few inches to the side and fired. There was some kind of silencer on it, so the shot was very quiet—a *pfft* more than a bang. Both Mohawk and Patterson gasped and jerked.

"Get in the goddamned car."

As soon as he was in, she accelerated. The last thing Patterson heard her say was "shut the door" before they took off, though the van pulled out onto the street and moved away at a normal speed—no screeching or speeding.

Graham Patterson was not a brave man, but neither was he a coward. He knew he had to do something, so he started back across the parking lot toward the door to the comedy club. But what could he do? What was he going to say if he spoke to someone, or called 911? *"I just saw myself kidnapped"*? Or "Call the cops—I've been kidnapped by a woman with a gun but I'm here too telling you this story"? The insanity and impossibility of the situation made him slow, then stop altogether halfway across the lot.

"What am I supposed to *do*?" he asked out loud to the emptiness around him.

The door to the club opened, and someone walked out into the parking lot. It was a woman, and, to his astonishment, Patterson *recognized* her—Anna Mae Collins, the tattoo artist. He stood there, overwhelmed by all the events of the last few minutes.

"Mr. Patterson! Confused, I assume?" Smiling, she walked right up to him as if they had an appointment to meet there in that empty Illinois parking lot, nine hundred miles from her home in North Carolina.

"Anna Mae, what are *you* doing here?"

"Graham, it's time for your first intermission, and I'm here to answer all your questions. You know—about your double with his Mohawk haircut, and what just happened to him, and . . . well, whatever else you want to know. But let's go back inside and talk about it over a drink. I saw the bar has a bottle of Bunnahabhain whiskey, and that is my all-time favorite."

Pinecone

Anna Mae Collins took a small sip from her third glass of whiskey, smiled with eyes closed, and shook her head at how perfect the stuff tasted. "You really should try this, Graham. It's sooo good."

"I don't like whiskey."

"I know, but you're missing something."

As if enjoying his worry and discomfort, Anna Mae wouldn't answer any of Patterson's questions until this third glass had been placed in front of her by the waiter. "He's all right for now, if that's what you're fretting about."

"Who?"

"Mr. Mohawk—your other self. But let's call him Graham 2. It's easier." She took another sip. "Show me your tattoo. Have you been putting the cream on it like I told you? And keeping it out of the sun? Show me."

"What? *Why?*"

"Show me and I'll tell you. There really is method to my madness, believe me."

Patterson took off his denim jacket and sweater. Beneath, he wore a short-sleeved white t-shirt. The tattoo Anna Mae had made days before low on his left bicep was vivid and bright.

She was sitting on his left side, so when he exposed it she leaned in for a closer look. Seeing something there must have satisfied her because she nodded approvingly and sat back in her seat. "Excellent. Remember the book of tattoo samples I showed you when you came into my shop?"

Patterson nodded.

"Do you know how many different designs are in that book, Graham? Three hundred and seventy-four."

He shrugged. "What does that have to do with any of *this*?" He tried keeping his voice under control, away from frustration and anger, but it was difficult. If she really *did* know about everything that had happened to him since they last met, why the hell was she talking about tattoos now?

Anna Mae pointed at his arm. "In the years I've been doing them, *very* few people have chosen that specific design—the tattoo you wanted? The last one was Mark Curry a few years ago."

Taken aback, Patterson frowned. "Mark Curry? The *billionaire* Mark Curry? You did him?"

"Yes. He wanted it on his right arm, in about the same place as yours." Sliding back in the seat, she took another sip of whiskey. The expression on her face was both amused and curious. She wondered what he would ask next.

"And this has something to do with me—that Mark Curry and I got the same tattoo?"

"Yes, it has everything to do with it." She held up a hand and counted off on her fingers. "You both chose *that* one, both agreed to spend the night at my mother's B and B. *And,* come to think of it, both of you drank her tomato soup. You even took a picture of it." Anna Mae beamed. "Do you know what Mark did before he started his business? Worked as a stock boy at a discount store called Lazy Larry's in Pacific, Missouri. Quite a jump from that to where he is today, right?" She pointed to Patterson's left arm. "Now it's your turn."

"What? What are you talking about?"

"I said it's your turn—"

"I heard you the first time, but I don't understand the connection. Please, Anna Mae—just *tell* me."

"Better than that, Graham, I'll show you." She lifted a hand and moved it toward him. When it was a few inches from his bare left arm, she opened her fingers wide. Contracting them several times, she moved her hand backward and forward, backward and forward . . . as if trying to pull something off or *out* of Patterson's arm.

He watched in silence. His eyes jumped from her hand to her face to her hand . . . why was she making this odd gesture?

"Anna Mae—"

"Shhh—watch now."

He felt nothing when it happened. No sting, no burn, pull, or pain, no sensation at all in the area of his lower arm where the figure was. But as she moved her fingers and hand in and out, Graham Patterson's tattoo—the bee inside the frog inside the hawk inside the lion—rose gradually from beneath his skin until it was out and off his arm, hovering in the air inches below her hand.

Horrorstruck, Patterson made an involuntary croaking sound down deep in his throat.

Eyes narrowed and lips pursed, Anna Mae gently took hold of the now three-dimensional tattoo and placed it on the table by her whiskey glass. Reaching with thumb and index finger carefully into the center of it, she separated the bee from the other figures, pulled it out, and lowered it to one side. Next, she took the frog out of the tattoo and put it next to the bee, then the hawk, and finally the lion a short distance away from the others. Four solid figures in a row, separated from each other by a few inches.

Mesmerized by what she'd done and what he was seeing, Patterson could only stare at the figures on the table. Anna Mae let him have some seconds to look and absorb the picture before she spoke.

Pointing to the bee, she said, "*This* one is your life now." Next, she pointed at the frog. "The frog is the life Graham 2 is living—the 'Graham Patterson famous comedian with the Mohawk' life." She stopped talking and looked over to see if he fully grasped what she was saying. He didn't move or speak, but his eyes were riveted to her face. "The hawk is Graham 3—the life you *would* be living if you'd stayed with Ruth, married her, and had children together." She pointed to the lion. "And the king of the jungle there is your future: the life you'll live after you decide which of these three you want forever."

"Graham, you now have the opportunity to visit these other two lives and observe them, like you've been doing today with Mr. Mohawk. When you're ready, you'll choose one of your three and live it until you die. The moment you *do* decide which you prefer, you'll forget you ever had a choice, and the tattoo will disappear.

"But I must say this too, and you gotta listen carefully: I have no idea what will happen to you in the future no matter *which* of those lives you choose. It might be good, it might be disastrous. You might live to be a hundred—or get cancer tomorrow. You saw what happened to the comedian in the parking lot. I don't know what his fate will be, or yours, in whatever life you choose. Honestly—I know nothing about your life from now on.

"My job was to make the tattoo after you chose it and explain it to you now. The same thing happened with Mark Curry and the others I tattooed. If you have questions, I can only answer those that pertain to my instructions. I really don't know anything else. It's obvious that's the way they want it."

"Who's they?"

She closed her eyes and shook her head. "I don't know."

"Why me?"

"Because you chose this specific tattoo. No other reason. My art on your arm was your winning ticket." Anna Mae smiled. "You're not like some kind of superhero who needs to be woken up and shown his powers. It's only because you chose a specific tat out of all the others in my book."

Patterson wasn't having it. "But come on—who is behind this? Who has the kind of *power* to do the things that've happened to me today, Anna Mae?" He coughed a bitter laugh. "This shit's insane!"

"I don't know, Graham—I *honestly* don't. And to tell you the truth, I don't want to know.

"Here's my story. Years ago, I was in Japan learning a method called *irezumi* from my master—who's long dead now, by the way. He saw I was talented and, after years studying with him, said he would teach me how to make your tattoo. Even if no one ever requested it, as its guardian I would be taken care of for the rest of my life *if* I was willing to be one of the only artists in the whole world who could make it. What did I have to lose? Of course I said yes."

Grimacing, Patterson slapped the table. "*By who?* Who was behind it? Who would take care of you?"

She shook her head. "I told you twice now—I don't know. He taught me how to make the tattoo and what to say afterward to whoever chose it. That's why I'm here now.

"You saw my store. I'm well known in the tattoo community now, and people come from out of town just for me. But no matter how good you are in this profession it's hard to make a living at it, especially if you're not in a city. And I hate cities. But my bank account is always full, no matter how good or bad business is in the shop. So I'm fine with the arrangement, even not knowing much about it.

"Look, forget about me. You need to know some things I *do* know, and I have to show them to you now. So save your questions till I'm finished, okay?

"Reach down, pick up the bee, and put it on top of the frog."

Uncertainly, Patterson did as he was told. When he touched the bee it felt solid, like it was made out of stone or metal. Picking it up, he put it on top of the frog as gently as he could. The two figures pulled to each other like magnets.

"Good. Now put the hawk on top of the lion, and then the other two on top of *them*. Don't worry—it'll work."

He did as he was told. When all four figures were stacked, they immediately blended together into his original tattoo.

"Take it and put it back where it was on your arm."

Before doing it, he couldn't resist looking around the room to see if anyone was watching, but they weren't. He lifted the tattoo off the table and touched it to his left arm. It entered the skin as quickly as water into a dry sponge. In an instant it was back where it had been originally, looking no different.

"Okay, now you're ready. When you were young, did your family have pets—a dog or cat, maybe?"

"We had a dog. Why?"

"What was its name? Everybody remembers the name off their first dog."

Confused by why she was asking the question, Patterson answered slowly, "Pinecone."

She made a face. "That was the name of your dog? *Pinecone?*"

"Yes, my little sister named it. We got the dog when she was seven. She liked pinecones."

"Fair enough—then Pinecone it is. Here's how this works: You're allowed to visit each of your parallel lives three times and return here a fourth and final time, if you need it. All you have to do to go from one life to the other is touch your tattoo now that I've prepared it, then say 'Pinecone' and the number of the life you want to visit. In an instant, you'll be there.

"This life you're living now is Graham 1, Mohawk is Graham 2, married you is Graham 3. Whichever one you want to visit, touch the tattoo and say Pinecone and the number. That's all. You can stay in any of these lives as long as you like. But if you want to change, do the same thing—touch the tat, say Pinecone and the number of where you want to go next. Are you with me so far?"

Patterson nodded.

"Good. Now, as I said, you can visit each of your lives three times and stay as long as you like. But you will only be an observer of lives Graham 2 and 3. You *cannot* participate in either of them in any way when you're there. After those three visits are finished, and a fourth to bring you back here if you need it, you'll have to choose which one you want to stay in permanently.

"The second thing to know is however long you *do* stay in any of the lives, when you change to another you'll be that much older.

So you're forty-two now, right? If you go to Graham 2 for five years, when you come back here you'll be forty-seven years old, like your other self."

Patterson touched his forehead, closed his eyes, and blurted out, "Anna Mae—none of this is bullshit? It's all real?"

"Real as the blood in your veins. But you're skeptical, and I would be, too. Do you want a demonstration? You'll have to use up one of your visits, but you can stay there as long or as short as you like, remember."

"*Wait!*" Patterson threw up a hand to stop her from continuing. "Tell me again—where am I now?"

"In your own life, Graham 1."

"Which means Mohawk doesn't exist here and what I saw in the parking lot before never happened in *this* life? I was in the life of Graham 2 when it happened?"

"Correct."

"If I touch anyone *here,* my hand won't pass through them like it did out there?"

"Right—because this one here is your life *now,* Graham. When you visit either of the other two, you're only an observer. You can't participate in anything going on in them—only watch."

He took a deep breath and *whooshed* it out fast, as if clearing his whole head of all that had been thrown in there in the last minutes. "How did it happen before without my doing anything, my going into Graham 2's life? I was in the parking lot on the turnpike taking a leak, and suddenly there he *was.* Or when he showed up here at this club? I didn't make those things happen."

"No, it was *them.* They were easing you into this change. Do you remember the smells? The really nice ones that didn't fit the places where they were? Like the beautiful smell in the turnpike toilet or the food you ate here earlier? It was the beginning, done real gently so you wouldn't freak out. At the rest stop they slid you into the life of Graham 2, then back to 1 after he left and you drove to this town. The moment Graham 2 walked into this club, you were in his life again—until you saw me out in the parking lot just now."

"May I?" Without waiting for permission, Patterson picked up her glass of whiskey and took a sip. Wincing, he wiped a thumb across his lips. "Do I always have to come back here first, or can I move from Graham 2 to Graham 3?"

"Whatever way you want to do it, but only three times each, re-member, and a fourth to get back here at the end to this life, if it's necessary. The moment you *do* make your final choice and go to live in that life, you'll have no memory of any of this. You won't even have the tattoo anymore."

Patterson could not help asking again, "But *why me?*"

She smiled understandingly and shrugged. "I don't know. Honestly, I don't. Except for the tattoo you chose. I think it might be as simple as that. We are our choices, you know?"

They were silent a while. Anna Mae was about to finish her whis-key, but decided against it. She looked at Patterson and remembered the time she'd had this same conversation with Mark Curry. The two men had such different reactions to their situation. Curry never doubted for a minute what she said. She'd barely finished giving him the lowdown when he asked a few logistical questions, touched his tat-too, said the name of his first dog, and was gone. No hesitation—only excitement and eagerness to witness his parallel lives. If Curry was like a racing greyhound raring to burst out of the starting gate, Patterson came across now as a timid turtle, warily pulling his head back into his shell in fear of what might happen.

"Graham?"

"What?"

"You don't *have* to do this. You can say no. It's your decision."

"I *don't?*"

"No! You can choose not to and go on living this life right up till the end of it, whenever that may be."

"And I wouldn't get punished or penalized or anything?"

"Nope. I didn't."

The room, the air, the *world* around Graham Patterson froze solid a moment.

His eyes widened. "*You* didn't. This happened to you, too?"

"Yup. My tattoo's here." She patted her stomach down low on the right side.

"Son of a *bitch!*"

Anna Mae smiled. "But I was never interested in the offer. Soon as I discovered truly beautiful, visionary tattoos and how to craft them, I knew it was what I wanted to do with my life—nothin' else. I didn't need to see or sample any alternative me living a parallel life. It's why I spent so much time traveling around to the different countries—learning everything I could from the best teachers I could find and practicing the art *after* I got my tattoo.

"Early on in Japan, my master asked which of his designs I'd like him to make on me. If you think you had a lot to choose from in my example books, he had *forty years* of designs, Graham. I picked ours. The master didn't react dramatically or anything when I did. Only nodded and said he named that one *the breakfast tattoo* because each of the creatures has just eaten one another. They're all sitting in each other's stomachs. He didn't say anything more at the time, only that we would talk about me getting the tatt after I'd finished my apprenticeship.

"I stayed there and studied with him four years. Toward the end of the time, he told me the real story behind it and asked if I would like to learn how to make it myself and become one of its keepers. He was passing me the torch because he was dying. But I didn't know it at the time.

"It was a very great honor, but what I loved almost more was the look on his face when, after he'd put it on me, I said I didn't want to see my alternative lives. There was nothing else I wanted to do more than become a tattooist like him."

She was about to continue, but Patterson interrupted. "How did you know I would be here tonight? How'd you get here?"

She smiled but shook her head: no—not your business.

"Is it part of being the guardian—you can't tell me anything about it?"

Same smile from her, same silence.

"You were never curious, Anna Mae? Never even wanted a *peek* at what your other lives might be like?"

She gave a quick half-hearted, up-and-down shrug with one shoulder. "When you find what you're looking for, you stop looking. At least, I do. Far as I'm concerned, it can be something as small as the right kind of pencil or as big as a life."

On hearing those words, Patterson felt an almost physical lurch of despair in both body and soul. Because he realized he was at the absolute opposite end of the satisfaction spectrum from Anna Mae Collins. There was almost nothing in his life he loved, liked, or wanted to hold onto forever. If some kind of metaphysical, force-five psychic cyclone had blown through him then, destroying everything he'd accomplished or attained, he wouldn't have cared. In his mind were news images of earthquake or tornado survivors picking forlornly through the scattered wreckage of what remained of their homes, discovering a single family photo or dirty child's stuffed toy in the rubble and looking glad, grateful even, to have found this small token of their life before. He didn't have something like that he cared about.

He took a deep breath and said, "I want to do it."

She pretended to clap for him. "Well, okay. Then whenever you like—you know how it's done."

"Wait! I have another question. Let's say I go to these other lives but after only one . . . trip to each, I want to come back here and stay. Can I do that?"

"Yes, it's fine. You can stay wherever you want *whenever* you want. There's really no trick involved here, no devil or other sinister force behind it trying to *dupe* you into doing anything foolish or fatal. It's really not like that, Graham. Think of it as having won some kind of weird, wonderful lottery or Golden Ticket, but instead of choosing a bunch of lucky numbers, you chose the breakfast tattoo."

Looking hard at her, Patterson reached a hand over and was about to touch his arm when he stopped. "I don't . . . I don't know which one I should go to first."

She pursed her lips. "If I were you, I'd choose the safer one first. Instead of jumping into the deep end of the pool, work your way in from the shallow part. Someone just kidnapped Graham 2. There's no telling what happened to him. On the other hand, it's pretty safe to assume married you isn't in any kind of danger." She was quiet, then, opening her mouth to say more, hesitated a beat. "But you know what, Graham? The hell with it. We can fear life's mysteries or embrace them. More often than not the choice is ours—we just don't want to admit it because when things go bad, we don't like to take the blame. Right now, the choice is yours, so I say go for whichever life intrigues you most this very second."

Her words lit a fuse inside him. Without hesitating another second, Patterson looked Anna Mae Collins in the eye, touched the tattoo on his left arm, said "Pinecone" and then "Graham 2."

Nothing happened.

So ready and excited to be transported into a whole other who-knows-where world, he was stunned. Had the woman tricked him? Was it all a big lie, the joke's on you, sucker?

"What the *hell*? What happened?"

"You said it wrong! Say just the word and the number—not Graham 2 or Number 2—say *Pinecone 2*. Wherever you decide to stay *forever*, you must say Pinecone 2 *here*. That's the only difference. To stay temporarily, it's Pinecone 2. You say Pinecone 1 when you want to return to this life. When it's forever, you say Pinecone 1 *here*, or whichever number life you choose to be permanent. Try it again."

"Pinecone 2."

———

The next instant, even before he could blink or breathe in, Patterson was sitting across a battered white Formica table from two teenage boys. Seeing them, his breath stopped. Because despite what just happened to him he recognized both of them immediately, although he had not seen either in almost thirty years.

One was enormously fat. His name was "Giant" Romeo Mrvic. The other was Butch Harris, the scariest person Patterson had ever known. What made Harris even creepier was he was exceptionally handsome, almost beautiful. Back in Crane's View, New York, the town where Graham grew up, Butch and Giant Romeo were best, albeit unlikely, friends who essentially terrified all the kids in town for years.

When he wasn't eating, Romeo was thinking up creatively horrible things to do to whoever was on his shit list at the time. Anyone could be added to the list for the smallest infraction, often for things you didn't even know *were* infractions, like happening to be standing in front of him in a line for tickets to the movies. The World According to Giant Romeo Mrvic was not a fair or forgiving place. The problem was he was so obese he couldn't physically do some of the awful things he thought up, but Butch happily did them for him. Harris had the face of a movie star, brain of an iguana, and the conscience of a psychopath on LSD. The synergy between the two teens was ominously perfect, and perfectly ominous.

Luckily for the youth of Crane's View, Butch enlisted in the Marines as soon as he turned eighteen and was killed in the First Gulf War. The friends' psychic connection seemed to work almost supernaturally even when they were thousands of miles apart, because around the same time Butch died, Giant Romeo had a massive cerebral hemorrhage while descending the long steep flight of cement stairs to the Crane's View train station. By the time his huge tumbling body bang bang *glumped* to the bottom, he'd left his last earthly breath about ten steps back up the staircase.

But lo and behold, here the boys were on the other side of a dinged and scratched table, very much alive again, both staring vulpinely at Graham Patterson. It was only after some time passed did he recognize his surroundings, so shaken was he by these two familiar ghosts right in front of him.

They were in Sal's Pizza, the joint where all the Crane's View kids hung out when Patterson was young. Now the forever familiar, beautifully rich smell of baking pizza perfumed the air around them, although when he looked toward the counter, no one was there. In fact, no one else was in the joint but the three of them.

"In case you were wondering, we're all dead," Giant Romeo said in a pleasant voice.

"Why?" Patterson asked.

"*What?*" Butch mumbled, furrowing his brow.

"Why am I dead? I know why *you* two are, but why am I?"

Butch shrugged, uninterested in explaining what had happened. He looked at Romeo to do the grisly honors.

"The van they kidnapped you in? Five minutes ago the dumb bitch driving tried to get across a railroad track right before the train came—"

"No luck, Chuck," Harris interrupted, waving an exaggerated goodbye to Patterson and snickering.

Romeo nodded. "They'll have to pull what's left of you out of there with tweezers and a vacuum cleaner."

Bizarre and impossible as his situation (and location) was, Patterson could only shake his head in disgust and moan angrily. "Son of a bitch—*that's* how I would've ended up in that life—at the peak of my success? Kidnapped, then pancaked by a train?" Through the mental mud and toxic smog of his outrage he remembered something—the tattoo. The three visits to the three lives he could choose from. The life of Mohawk-wearing Graham Patterson was obviously D.O.A. now, so it was time to move right on to the next.

As Patterson was reaching to touch his tattoo, Giant Romeo groaned, "Wait! Wait wait wait! You haven't heard the best part yet. Don't do anything till you hear what I gotta tell you."

Was this a trick? Was fat Mrvic trying to stall him from leaving for some evil reason?

Patterson crossed his arms. "I'm listening, but be quick about it."

"Aren't you wondering why *we're* here?" Romeo threw a fat thumb at Butch and then pointed it at himself.

Patterson said nothing.

"Welcome to the Afterlife."

Patterson said nothing.

"Whenever someone dies, they send a familiar face to meet them in a familiar place so they're not completely freaked out by the transition."

Patterson shook his head. "You guys weren't *familiar*—you were monsters. You used to scare me. You scared *every kid in Crane's View!*"

Romeo rested his big head on hands as thick as loaves of rye bread. "Whatever. I'll take that as a compliment. Anyway, we do as we're told here, and we were told to come for you. Why? Because you *do* know us, and you remember Sal's Pizza. Hey, you can even have a slice while we're talking. Remember how delicious they were? God, the Pizza Hawaii with those big chunks of pineapple on top . . . You want one now?"

"No, pineapple on pizza is disgusting. Just get to the point." As if to speed things up, Patterson started reaching for his tattoo again in case Mrvic was beating around the bush.

"You're about to get reincarnated, Graham. Or this version of you is. Aren't you interested in knowing where your next life'll be? You can do it. If you stay a wee bit longer, you can see where you're going to go next. Who knows—it might be fabulous."

"How come *you* two weren't reincarnated?"

Butch spoke, all grumpy. "*Why?* Because they say we're fuckups and gotta stick around here doing this meet-and-greet for as long as they tell us to. You think I *want* to be a tour guide to little pissers like you, Patterson? If I were still alive, I wouldn't give you the smell off my shit—"

Romeo shook a warning finger at his friend. "Calm down, Butch. Remember what happened the last time you mouthed off here."

Harris's beautiful eyes widened in genuine alarm. He looked quickly from side to side, checking to see if anything horrible was coming for him again. Yes, he damn well *did* remember what happened last time . . .

Romeo turned his attention back to Patterson. "Look, Graham, at least let me explain how reincarnation works. It'll only take a little while. Then you can decide if you want to stick around here and see where you go next."

What seemed like no more than seconds later, Patterson, looking like he'd just been punched in the face, slowly shook his head at everything Giant Romeo had said. "That is total *bullshit*! I don't believe it."

Mrvic lifted one of his bread-loaf hands and, with a languorous flick of his wrist, said, "Watch!" There in the Land of the Hereafter, the dead teenager showed dead Graham Patterson everything he had said about reincarnation was true.

———

James Arthur frowned. "Excuse me, but could you repeat what you just said please?"

Ruth Murphy sipped from her cup of now cold tea and cleared her throat. "Love and tools have one important thing in common: In any hands they can do the job. But only in really skilled ones do they create beauty. Graham wasn't very good at love, but he made a lot of beauty with a camera, which was *his* tool."

The biographer wrote this all down as fast as he could in the teal colored "bullet journal" notebook perched on his knee. Teacup in hand, Ruth stretched her head forward to see what he was writing. It all looked like indistinguishable scribbles to her.

"Is that English? I can't make out a single word."

He smiled. "It's a version of shorthand. It lets me get down almost everything people say and not just a vague semblance."

She nodded and sat back in her chair. "Did you ever see Graham's picture called 'Shorthand'?"

"Yes, Ms. Murphy, I'm pretty sure I've seen all of his work. I mean, all of it that's been made available to the public. I've heard from various sources there are several Patterson photographs the public's never seen." Arthur said this while still writing, so he didn't catch the expression on the old woman's face until he glanced up a moment later. That expression—mischievous, knowing, "I-have-a-secret"— said everything.

Understanding in an instant, he slowly lowered the pen to the table. "You've seen them. You've actually *seen* those missing images?"

She nodded. "Well, sort of."

"My God, when? Where?"

"'Tin Eye,' 'Older Caveman,' 'Giant Romeo,' 'Tying Water in a Knot,' and 'Pinecone.'"

Confused by what she'd said, Arthur shook his head.

"Those are the titles of the pictures no one's seen. There are only five of them. Everything else has disappeared, or Graham destroyed them."

"Please could you repeat the names again?"

She did, and he wrote them down. Once finished, Arthur was hesitant to repeat the next question but had to be absolutely sure.

"And you *have* seen them?"

"Yes. Sort of"

"All five?"

"Yes, I have, Mr. Arthur."

"Where? Where are they? Did Patterson show them to you?"

"No, I never saw Graham again after we broke up. He wanted to meet years later, but I said no. I was done with it. He hurt me very badly, and I knew seeing him later, even a lot later, would only make some part of me bleed again. I wrote this to him in my last letter: 'You can't have me anymore. You don't deserve me.'"

"So, um, how did *you* see these pictures?"

Ruth Murphy raised her head and closed her eyes. She remained like that a long time without saying a word. After a while Arthur wondered if something had happened to the old woman—a heart attack? Stroke? *Death*? She was so still and quiet.

"They're in here."

"Excuse me?"

She tapped the envelope in her lap with a finger. "Prints of the five pictures are in here. But you can't see them."

The biographer was a very well behaved, sensitive, and discreet man. Good at his job because he read people well and usually asked the right questions at the right time, always trying his best not to offend, trap, or trick a subject into saying things they would later regret if they read them in his finished article or book.

Right now, however, he was bursting to demand why Ruth Murphy wouldn't let him see the famous missing Patterson photographs. If she was telling the truth and they were *right there* in the frayed envelope inches away, some primal, *ur*-aggressive, altogether un-James Arthur part of his soul wanted to reach over and snatch it out of her liver-spotted hand. For God's sake, he was writing the definitive biography of Graham Patterson. How could she even *think* of withholding such important, potentially game-changing material from him?

Then she did a most surprising thing—without saying another word, Ruth Murphy handed him the envelope and said, "Look inside."

Completely taken aback by this sudden reversal, he hesitated. Hadn't she just said he couldn't? But now Patterson's old lover was offering them without his having to protest or even say a word. What the hell had happened? What changed her mind?

James Arthur didn't care. He was about to see the legendary lost Patterson photographs he'd read and heard about for years. Excitement and anticipation took up all the space in his head at that moment. Maybe later he'd ask why she had changed her mind, but not now. With nervous hands, he reached into the envelope and pulled out all of the sheets inside.

On top was the signed copy of "Mr. Breakfast" Ruth had shown him earlier. He slid it behind the others and went on to the next one. It was blank. Confused, he turned it over in case the image was on the other side. It wasn't. Both sides of the photographic paper were blank. He looked at her. She stared back, but her face said nothing.

He slid the blank sheet behind "Mr. Breakfast" and went on to the third. It was also blank, as was the fourth. He was about to say "I don't understand," but instinctively his hand was already shuffling to the fifth paper. When he looked down and saw what was there, he froze.

Ruth Murphy saw the abrupt change of expression on his face and her mouth half opened in surprise. "You see something? *You see something there?*"

He nodded, still taking in the image. Looking again and again at everything there, every detail, then the big picture, then the details again, over and over.

"*Really*? You see it?"

Eyes never leaving the photo he nodded. "Yes."

"Turn it over. Turn it over and tell me if you see something on the back."

He did. One word was written there in sloppy scrawl. "Pinecone."

Ruth Murphy had not been excited about anything in years. That fact had even crossed her mind more than once—growing old means nothing excites you anymore. But she was excited now. Breathing too fast, she put a thin hand to her chest to calm her heart from beating—from *galloping*—too fast. "Tell me what you see there. Describe the picture for me."

James Arthur cleared his throat and tried to tame the smile on his face. The discovery of the picture, the utterly surprising subject matter, and the fact it was a Patterson few people had ever seen before . . . He was overjoyed at everything in that moment of his life.

"A woman is eating a giant jelly donut. There's white powdered sugar all over her mouth. She looks like a delighted child. Staring straight at the camera and laughing, she's obviously indifferent to how silly and wonderful she looks.

"But the best part of the picture is a few feet behind her, out of her line of vision: A bull terrier dog is sitting nearby staring up at her with absolute hatred and envy. It's hilarious. I don't think I've ever seen a picture of an animal with such a human expression on its face. This one is pure jealousy."

Eyes closed, Ruth listened but nodded at everything he said. It was true—he *did* see what was on the paper.

"It's a great photo, Ms. Murphy, but nothing like any Graham Patterson I've ever seen before. It's funny and . . . *sweet.* Not at all like his others, especially the famous ones that are usually so stark, full of stillness, shadows, and sad echoes . . . " Arthur looked up from the photo to see if she understood what he was talking about. "It *is* a Patterson, you can tell that in an instant, but it goes in a completely different direction. A whole new side of him I've never seen before, a new *eye* at work, but it is definitely his eye. Do you mind if I ask where you got them?"

She touched her chest again, patting the left side above her heart. "Look at the last sheet—see if you can see anything there."

He did, but it too was blank on both sides. He shook his head. "Nothing. It's only white, like the others."

She nodded "I would think you'd be most interested in why you can't see those other four pictures. They *are* there, too."

Instead of answering, the biographer looked at the sheaf of six papers in his hand and slowly shuffled through them again: Mr. Breakfast, blank, blank, blank, woman with the donut, blank.

Something crossed his face, a sudden jolt in his expression that the old woman saw before he was even aware of doing it. The kind of twitch-squint one makes when the sudden stab of a sharp stomach cramp slashes across the gut like lightning. He shuffled through the sheets of paper yet again: Blank, blank, blank, woman with the donut, blank. Only this time he wasn't really looking for anything there. The gesture was unconscious, as his flailing mind tried to buy time while crazy new thoughts and impossibilities made his head feel like it was going to burst. "Other people were here before me, weren't they? You showed these to them, too." He said it as a statement more than a question because he knew it was true.

She nodded while trying her best to keep a neutral face.

"They all wanted to know about Patterson?" Another nod from her, but with a small grin this time. She couldn't help it. He was getting there.

"Did they want to write about him? Did someone else want to write his biography?"

"Yes, one did. She told me she was very famous—her name was Cabot, I think."

Shocked, James Arthur's hands dropped to his lap. "Pernilla Cabot came *here* and wanted to write Patterson's biography?"

"Yes, that was her name. An unpleasant woman—*much* too pleased with herself. I showed her these pictures, but she didn't see anything. I wasn't surprised. Then she left. Is she really a famous writer?"

Arthur puffed his lips in wonder. "She *was*. Won a Pulitzer Prize for biography before she died. How long ago was she here?"

"A few years, right after I moved in. I don't remember exactly because it was not a nice visit. She was brusque and rude. I don't like rude people. She thought I was tricking her with those photos. All but accused me of lying when I said images *were* there and they could be seen by the right people."

"Who else came? Who else wanted to write about Patterson?"

"Somebody from a French magazine. I think it was a photography magazine, or maybe it was fashion. Anyway, they wanted to do a big piece on Graham and maybe expand it later into a biography. So I showed them the photos, too. They didn't see anything. Just you, Mr. Arthur, but you only saw 'Pinecone.'"

"Why? Why is that?"

She pointed a finger at him and shook it. "Ah! Now you're getting somewhere. Why do you think?"

Instead of answering her question, James Arthur found "Pinecone" and looked at it again. "Why can I only see this one? Why *not* any of the others?"

For the first time that afternoon, Ruth's voice was playful. "This conversation suddenly has a lot of 'whys' in it, have you noticed? Maybe you have to do some detective work before the other ones come into focus for you."

She was giving him a big hint from Patterson's last letter to her and was eager to see how the writer would react. But then, to her dismay, her right thumb began to cramp and turn inward toward the palm. She fought it, but as usual it felt like the finger had a stubborn mind of its own.

This happened often now, always when she began to tire. It was almost like her body's way of saying "that's it—time to shut down." She took magnesium pills for the cramping. It helped somewhat, but there was no pill for goddamned old age. She had always had so much energy. When younger, she would stay up late, wake early, and go go go all day long on a few hours of sleep and too much coffee. These days she had about as much vigor as a dying pigeon with one slowly flapping wing. As important as this conversation had become, she knew very soon she'd start to fade, and her thinking would become cloudy. For both their sakes, she needed to tell James Arthur certain things before that happened.

"I said before, I never saw Graham again after we broke up. But he wrote me often, usually postcards from places all over America. Not long before he disappeared, I got an envelope in the mail with these photos in it and a letter."

"What did it say?"

"That I was to show them to whoever asked, but never to advertise or basically make public I had them because of what you just saw—or *didn't* see. If anyone ever *did* see something there, even only one like you did, I was to send them to a specific place."

Arthur licked his lips and shook his head. "Patterson disappeared years ago. Everyone assumes he's dead."

Ruth Murphy rubbed her aching hand and nodded. "It doesn't matter. In the letter he said any person who was able to see any of these photos was to go to this address anyway. That is, if they really *were* interested in him or his work. I guess he assumed if they went to the trouble of tracking *me* down and then saw any of the pictures, they wouldn't hesitate to go."

"Where is this address?"

"In North Carolina—a tattoo parlor in North Carolina."

"*Tattoo parlor?* Why there? Do you know anything about this, Ms. Murphy?"

"No, not a thing. Just the address. I'm going to have to stop now because I'm tired." She hesitated a moment and looked down at the envelope in her lap. "Would you like to take this with you?"

James Arthur couldn't believe what she was offering. "The photographs? You're *giving* me those photographs?"

She smiled and nodded. "Yes, but under one condition. If you're ever able to see the rest of these pictures, I want you to come back here and tell me what you see. You have to promise me."

"Yes, of course. But I'd like your permission to come back anyway and talk to you some more about this, if that's all right?"

"We'll see, Mr. Arthur, we'll see. I'd like to know what's up with the tattoo parlor. Do you think you'll go?"

Arthur touched a hand to his chest over his heart. "I'll drive down there next week. I can't tell you how serious I am about this project, Ms. Murphy."

"Then good—I'm curious to know why he wanted you to go there. When you're back, get in touch and we'll make another date. In the meantime, give me your hand, would you? I'm not good at standing up these days."

In the parking lot afterward, of course the biographer had to open the envelope again and look at the photographs. As before, he was only able to see "Mr. Breakfast" and "Pinecone." The other four sheets of paper were blank. Returning them carefully to the envelope, he put it inside the leather messenger bag on the passenger's seat.

The bag was an appropriate place for them. One of the only pictures of Patterson in his later years was of him standing in front of a small, primitive-looking outdoor *taverna*. He had lived for a summer on the Greek island of Kalymnos with a woman named Antheia Lambrinos. In the photograph, credited to Lambrinos, Patterson is wearing sneakers, baggy cargo shorts, a black t-shirt, and horn-rimmed sunglasses. He is smiling, looks thinner but fit. On a strap across his chest is a very beautiful leather messenger's bag James Arthur fell in love with the moment he saw the photo, only in part because it was owned by his hero. Arthur tracked down the company that made it (Elephant Lane—a small outfit in London). To both his delight and dismay, he learned the bag in question was still being made and was one of the company's most popular models. On the homepage of their website was the photograph of Patterson in Greece with a caption beneath it stating "Renowned photographer Graham Patterson with his Elephant Lane messenger bag."

But Arthur was in for a rude shock on learning the astronomical price of the bag, "made with the finest leather tanned in Sweden by Tarnsjo Garveri." As far he was concerned, the leather might just as well have been tanned on Neptune for the price they were charging. But he loved it, and because Patterson had owned it, he splurged and bought one. Now the bag held those five legendary photographs few people had apparently ever seen. For that matter, James Arthur hadn't seen four of them either, but he would do everything in his power to fix that. Starting with the trip to North Carolina.

———

"*That* was fast." Coming out of the toilet at the comedy club, Anna Mae Collins stopped and grinned on seeing Graham Patterson sitting once again at her table across the room. He was writing furiously in a pocket notebook, and she assumed whatever it was had to do with what he had just experienced "over there," although he'd only been gone ten minutes.

Whenever Patterson got nervous, talked on the phone, or had a few minutes to kill, he found a pen and paper and drew alphabets. He'd been doing it since he was a boy. Some people doodle faces, nudes, puppies, or random numbers and squiggles. Patterson drew alphabets. They were never the same because he loved playing with the different shapes and sizes of each letter. Usually he lingered over each one, trying to figure out a new way of creating it, making every letter as different as he could from the last time he'd drawn it. If you'd told him over the years he had drawn thousands of M's or R's, he would not have been surprised.

"Hello. stranger, you're back soon."

Without looking up from the paper he said, "Would you get me a whiskey, please?"

Anna Mae was about to comment about how she thought he didn't drink whiskey. But then she glanced at his hands.

Patterson's thumb, index, and middle fingers were normal, as was the back of his left hand. But his fourth and fifth fingers were inhuman, from another world and frightening to see. Both were a vibrant and deep swirling carnival of colors—like a puddle of water with an oil slick on the surface. The two fingers were also curled, the skin on them thick, reptilian.

"*Jesus!* What happened to you over there, Graham?"

Patterson continued to draw. He shook his head, not willing or able to tell her yet. She sat down slowly, unsure what to expect next. The last time she had done this—with Mark Curry—it had been so simple: She explained in detail the breakfast tattoo and what it meant. He disappeared five minutes later into one of his other lives. She never saw him again except on television or in newspaper articles describing his newest mega-deals. She assumed he had found something in one of those other lives that he brought back here and used to make his vast fortune. Good for him. Looking at Graham now, the only thing he appeared to have brought back was a monstrous, colorful half claw.

She couldn't stop staring at Patterson's left hand with its two brilliantly colored reptilian fingers. What had happened in his other life to transform him in less than a half hour? Why wouldn't he say? Then again, did she really *want* to know?

He mumbled, "You didn't tell me."

"Tell you what, Graham?"

Slowly he lifted his head and glared, his resentment palpable. After a few moments of staring lasers at her, he made a disgusted face and looked down again.

"Tell you *what*, Graham? Please, I really don't know what you're talking about."

He was drawing an R. It didn't look good, so he drew another. Then, halfway through yet another, his hand stopped, and he looked up at her again. "But wait a minute—you didn't do it, did you?"

"Do *what*?" Despite her anxiety, she was frustrated by his cryptic language.

"You didn't take the deal. You didn't *want* to know what your other lives would be like."

She nodded this was true, not knowing where he was going with it. "So you couldn't know." He sounded relieved.

"Know what, *Graham?*"

Putting the pen down on the table, he rolled it back and forth beneath his hand as he spoke. "In my other life—the one I went to just now? I was dead, Anna Mae. Half an hour after leaving the parking lot in the van, I was killed."

"Oh, for God's sake!" She cringed and clutched the edge of the table with both hands.

"That's not the worst part. After death, we're reincarnated. It's real, absolutely real. Believe me, it's true. What happens, though, is we don't move on to some higher plain or cosmic next level. We don't get born as something different in the future or move on to some higher plane.

"No, we go *back* to one of our *earlier* lives and live it again, or at least experience it again, for some reason. I think that's what happens—but I can't be sure because I wasn't there long enough to find out." He held up his hand with the colorful fingers and pointed to it. "This was me a zillion years ago. Back in the dinosaur days, or maybe even before then. I don't even know what I looked like completely because as soon as it happened and I realized *what* had happened to my body, I saw my arm, or paw, or whatever it was.

"Then I could feel . . . I could feel my mind—*this* mind, my human one—slipping, sliding away—going back to being that creature again, I guess. At the last second before my brain was gone, I was able to say *pinecone* and get back here." His sentences got faster and faster as he told the story, as if he needed to get the whole thing out in one gust.

"Why . . . why are your fingers still that way?" Anna Mae lifted her chin an inch toward his hand.

He looked at it and licked his lips. "I don't know. Maybe I got out of there too late and they're permanent: a little souvenir of Graham Patterson the successful comedian, dead man, and lizard."

A waiter passed, and Anna Mae gestured to him to bring two more whiskeys. While they waited for them, Graham told her about meeting dead Romeo Mrvic and Butch Harris on the other side and his conversation with them.

"He tricked me. After I died, the fat bastard tricked me into staying over there just long enough so I'd be stuck and *have* to go back to one of my early lives, which he knew was horrible, which just happened to be a fucking *reptile* or whatever the hell it was. I think Romeo's job was to explain how reincarnation worked and convince me I was going to miss something wonderful if I didn't at least take a look. And if he was lucky I'd stay there long enough to lose my brain and *stay* a tie-dyed gecko. Thank God when it happened I had enough presence of mind to be able to say the words and get the hell out of there."

The drinks came. Putting them down, the waiter saw Patterson's left hand on the table and did a double take. It was such an unexpected, bizarre sight that the young man couldn't look away for long seconds.

———

Two days later, Patterson's fingers were back to normal. In that time, he stayed mostly in his motel room trying to figure out what to do next. At the bar the other night, Anna Mae had asked if he was going to go to his third life—the married-with-children life.

"I don't know. If so, not for a while. The trip to lizardland was enough for the time being."

"So you're going to stay here in this one?"

"For now, yes. I'm gonna get back in my new car, start driving west again, and think all of it through. After what just happened, *this* here and now is fine for me."

She nodded. "I wonder . . . "

"Wonder what?"

"I was wondering if what you say is true, why *do* we go back after we die? What's the purpose of returning to our past lives after death, if the experience is like you say?" She stopped to gather her thoughts. "What's there to gain, especially if we revert to being lizards—or whatever—in our minds as well? If I went back to being a dinosaur but kept my human mind, *then* it makes sense—I'd learn something about dinosaur life I might be able to process and use in my next one. But if I just go back to having a gecko brain or something . . . It makes no sense to me."

He thought about her words in the motel room while looking out the window. Sometimes he took photos of his strange fingers in different poses and positions. When they began to transform back to being human, he was not especially surprised or grateful. Patterson now knew and pretty much accepted the fact he lived in a changed world where essentially anything could happen and was possible.

"Pinecone 3."

It came out of nowhere. One evening he just said it on the spur of the moment. At twilight he was lying on the bed, one arm behind his head and the other stretched out in front of him so he could look again at his now fading horrible fingers. He'd been thinking about what to get for dinner. He'd been thinking about what Anna Mae said about reincarnation.

But what he'd been thinking about most was his second self with the Mohawk haircut and *his* hugely successful career as a standup comedian. That subject painfully poked Patterson's thoughts like a big thorn in his foot. He kept going back to the phone call he'd overheard Mohawk having where he spoke about all the wonderful offers he was receiving now that he was doing so well. And the brilliant routine he did at the comedy club, ending with the story about Christian weightlifters that brought down the house. Then there was the love shown him by the gay couple in the parking lot afterward . . .

Years before while in college, he had taken a course in world literature. While discussing Goethe's *Faust*, the professor posed what she called "The Ice Cream Question":

People like ice cream. You're offered a bowl of the greatest ice cream ever made, out of this world, never to be equaled, *the* absolute best. The only condition is you will never be able to have it again. As a result, you'll compare any afterward to this wonderful bowl, and naturally none of them will ever taste as good. But if you choose to *reject* it, you'll often have what you *believe* is wonderful ice cream only because you've not eaten the ultimate.

Which do you choose—a single taste of heaven, or a lifetime full of okays? As examples, the professor mentioned the many rock stars who peaked with one or two hits in their early twenties but then disappeared forever into obscurity. Or the sports stars who played only a few years before getting hurt or before they simply lost the magical *something* that had made them so good. They ended up selling used motorcycles in South Dakota.

If Mohawk had survived, Patterson was almost certain he would have chosen to live the other man's life instead of his own. How glorious to be revered and rewarded for something you love doing! What could be better?

But Mohawk ended up dead, and then in a fucking past-life prehistoric *creature*. Yet for a while, 2 lived the life Patterson had always dreamed of. So yes, he'd choose to eat the great ice cream once because then at least in *this* life he'd be king, like Dr. Faustus after selling his soul to the devil for twelve years of unimaginable power and wealth.

Another thought came to him for the first time: Maybe Graham 3's life would be great, too, only in a wholly different way. Despite what he had once felt, maybe a domestic life centered on children and a loving wife *would* suit him in a way he had never experienced and lead to a whole new perspective. He still loved Ruth Murphy. There was no question about it. He just hadn't wanted the life she did, which is what destroyed them. But now their relationship was over, what worried Patterson was that Ruth and their bond would become the ghosts in the story of the rest of his life, haunting all his houses and future relationships—walking with loud dragging Frankenstein footsteps through too many of his days and dreams.

Pinecone 3.

He could always come back here in an instant if he didn't like it there.

Pinecone 3.

So what if Pinecone 2 had been a disaster that led to scary Giant Romeo Mrvic and the life of a gecko? Maybe Pinecone 3 would be just the opposite, and . . .

He sat up, glared at the wall in front of him and, as if to challenge the gods, touched his tattoo and said loudly, *"Pinecone 3."*

———

"No."

It took some moments, more than a few, to grab hold of the new reality around him and bring it into clear focus. It was not easy to take in all at once. After the word "No" was said in a very familiar voice, the next thing he heard was the soft sound of water lapping on rocks. Wherever he was, it was night, and warm. In front of him were many bobbing boats moored at a dock. Yellow lights dappled and danced on dark water, quiet music, the distant *putt putt* of an engine, the murmur of people talking nearby.

He was sitting at a white plastic table with a burning candle set in a coffee saucer in the middle of it. The small flame flickered as a delicious fragrant breeze took it for a quick dance. There were two drink glasses and a half-filled bowl of nuts on the table.

"Did you hear me, Graham?"

Turning to the left, he saw Ruth Murphy sitting next to him. She was staring across the table at Graham 3, who was staring down at his lap. She looked spectacular in a sleeveless white summer dress that contrasted dramatically with a tan he could make out even in the dim evening light. And her hair . . . he had never seen Ruth's hair so wild, unkempt, and free. It made her face look like it was in full bloom.

Graham 3 said quietly, without raising his eyes, "*Hear* you? Yes, you said no."

She paused, waiting for him to continue. When he didn't, she asked in a peeved voice, "That's *it*? That's all you have to say about this—you *heard* me say no?"

The world surrounding Graham was still sinking in, beautiful, sensuous, and seductive as it was. They were somewhere summery, close by a yellow-lit harbor. The enticing smell of grilling meat mixed with the tang of the sea and the delicate sweetness of mimosa swirling around them. Patterson turned his head hard from side to side and saw they were sitting at a bar next to water, full tables surrounding them, although the noise of other conversations was low and muted, intimate except for the momentary cackle of a woman's ugly laugh.

What a contrast to how he had landed before in the world of Graham 2 starring Death, Giant Romeo Mrvic, Butch Harris, and then Graham the dinosaur lizard, or whatever the hell it was.

He rubbed his hands together. He absolutely had to find out where they were. There was a white matchbook with red lettering in an empty ashtray next to the candle. Leaning forward, he read

Stavros by the Sea
Mykonos

"*Mykonos!*" He couldn't believe it. Patterson had always wanted to visit Greece, and Mykonos was at the top of his list. Steve Bergman had gone there several times and raved about its beauty. Patterson did another scan from side to side while the realization sank in: He was actually on the island of Mykonos in Greece with Ruth right this minute—a dream come true.

"Graham? Are you really not going to say anything more? Don't you want to know *why* I said no?" A bitter combination of hurt and scold in the tone of her voice demanded his full attention instantly.

Graham 3 looked up from his lap. That seemed to placate her a little. She reached for his hand and held it between hers while she spoke. "I love you, you know I do. And I love that you brought us here. It's beautiful, and I've been so happy. Everything has been perfect, really. Thank you. And I knew as soon as you said we were coming here that you were going to ask." She paused in case he wanted to say something before she went on. He apparently didn't.

"I *want* to spend the rest of my life together with you, but not without children, Graham. Or at least, not without trying to have them. I've wanted kids my whole life. Call me old fashioned, or whatever, but I want to try to have a family. I want to stand on a beach like the one we were on today holding our baby's hand, showing them the sea for the first time. Can you imagine what that must feel like in your soul? Introducing your own child to the *world*? I want to go shopping at Christmas in toy stores for some doll or truck or crazy action figure they've been begging for from Santa for months . . . " She shook her head as if to tell herself to stop rambling and get to the point. "I want all of it, Graham, and I really don't think it's asking too much. I love being here with you, and I'm so . . . touched you proposed tonight. I've always wanted that, too. But I don't want to marry . . . I *can't* marry someone who doesn't want children in their life, too. Maybe I'll never get pregnant, and maybe saying no to you will be the biggest mistake of my life, but I have to be willing to take the risk. Please say you understand."

"I do. I understand completely."

Silence fell between them like a five-hundred-pound velvet curtain. Patterson's brain and psyche had finally caught up to the weight and import of the moment. Now he had full comprehension and focus on where he was, and what was going on.

Apparently, just before Graham "arrived" in this life, Graham 3 had proposed to Ruth Murphy, but she said no. Throughout their relationship she'd always said she wanted children, but he did not. He wasn't against having them, *per se*; he just wasn't for it, either. He knew what kind of lasting commitment it entailed. The supposed delights of having kids and that way of life was as appealing to Patterson as a trip to some undeveloped country where the blue mountains were lovely and the beaches pristine, but the food was iffy, mosquitoes bit you with potentially frightening diseases, and the toilets didn't always flush.

He looked at Ruth and saw she was crying. She smiled sadly at Graham 3, then looked away, embarrassed. This great woman. How on earth had he ever allowed this great woman to get away?

Once, when they were first going out, she'd sent him this hand-written letter in the mail:

> *I want to be sitting somewhere with you. Somewhere as the sun yellows down to orange, and night leaks blue, then purple into the sky, like ink dribbled slowly into a glass of water. Far above us, the glint of a plane draws a white contrail as vivid as school chalk across the evening canvas.*

We're in Greece, somewhere by the sea. It's hot—summer. Or maybe a late fall day somewhere up north. Crisp, when sunsets come and go quickly so you have to pay full attention or you'll miss them. Two Adirondack chairs side by side, forest green, or no color at all because they've lived out in the hard weather for years.

You are telling me a story I've never heard before about your childhood. Your voice is quiet and intimate, and so alive and peppery with humor. Your hand is on my arm. I am grinning. I'm grinning because it is you talking, and your story is good and I know soon we will rise together and have a wonderful meal where the food and talk will be just as good. Afterward, perhaps we will return to these chairs by the sea, or a forest, or a desert, or by nothing important at all to listen to the night, as dense and black as the inside of a closed drawer by then.

And you will say.

And I will say.

That is all I want on this foggy winter evening.

And now here they actually *were* "in Greece somewhere by the sea," but Ruth was crying and saying she was going to leave him. Graham 1 wanted to reach across the table and throttle Graham 3. In effect, to throttle himself in another skin and say, Don't do it! Don't let her get away *again*, for God's sake.

"I can't." Graham 3 mumbled while looking down again. It was clear he couldn't meet Ruth's gaze.

"You can't *what*, Graham?" Her voice was stern, ready to pounce.

"I can't let you go. I just can't, Ruth. I'll do anything. Just don't go."

Grahan looked back and forth from one to the other, gauging their reactions. Ruth was fully confused now, at a loss for how to react. Obviously, what he had just said took her by complete surprise. Graham 3 stared out at the water, still avoiding her eyes.

Her voice considerably softer, Ruth said, "But I don't want to force you into anything, Graham, certainly not something as important as having children. I want you to want them as much as I do."

Graham 3 lifted his head. Tears glistened in his eyes; he tried unsuccessfully to blink them away. "And I want you to love my jokes and routines, but I know you don't, not really. That doesn't stop you from being my biggest fan and supporter."

She started to protest. He shook his head to stop her. "Don't say anything—it's not necessary. I know you love me and would do anything for me. You come to my shows and see the rooms are half empty, jokes fall flat, and too many people talk right through the whole act. But you're always there and clap the hardest, no matter what. Breaks my heart. I love your loyalty.

"It's not that I don't want children, Ruth—I just don't *know* if I do. Know what I mean? I'm not crazy about them like you are. But I *am* crazy about you and want you to have everything you've dreamed of. So I'm in if you'll have me. I swear to God—if kids do come, I'll work my ass off to be the best father I can be."

Watching him she crossed her arms, but then immediately uncrossed them. Her mouth was tight, her eyes gave away nothing. Both versions of Graham Patterson stared at her and had no idea what she would say next. It could very well be no again, she still didn't want him.

Ruth stood up. Graham 3 started to stand, too, but she stopped him with a curt shake of the head. "I'm going to take a walk. I need to be by myself for a while, okay? All of this is making my heart pound, and my head is all over the place. So I'll be back in a little while. Do you want to stay here or meet back at the hotel?"

Both men wanted to say something, *anything*, to make her stop and . . . just stay. Graham 1 already knew what it was like in his heart and life to lose Ruth Murphy. Graham 3 was suddenly faced with the very real possibility that this might be the end of their relationship no matter what he said or promised.

They watched her walk away. It took a moment for Graham 1 to remember he was invisible here and could follow Ruth without her knowing it. But should he? Wasn't it an invasion of her privacy, whether she knew he was following her or not?

Damned right he should follow! This was supposed to be the life where they got married and raised a family together. So why all *this* now? The hesitation on her part was not only unexpected, it was frightening. His thoughts were all "What ifs?" as he got up from his seat and went after her. What if she said a final no? What if he had been tricked, and this third life possibility was not anything like what he'd been told but might end up being something just as grim or unimaginable as Graham the prehistoric lizard, back in life number two?

What if what if what if kept time with his steps as he hurried to catch up with her.

For a moment, her white linen dress from behind looked like a cloud moving down the narrow, cobbled sidewalk. Catching up to her, Patterson grinned, thinking of Ruth as a moving cloud. All of a sudden, he remembered she had worn that same dress on their trip to Mauritius. He had followed her then, too, through the street markets of Port Louis. How happy both of them were on the trip, enthralled by the never-ending, exotic razzle-dazzle of the romantic, distant island.

The tortoise. Now he remembered that Ruth was wearing the turtle brooch on her dress tonight. It was a silly little wooden turtle figure he had bought for her from a street vendor on the last day of their vacation. But she said it was one of her treasures because wearing it always reminded her of the trip and the special night at the ambassador's villa.

Patterson's pal Steve Bergman knew the French ambassador to Mauritius at the time. The man was legally blind, but Bergman had been able to save some of his sight through a very risky but ultimately successful eye operation. Steve arranged for them to have dinner with the ambassador and his family when they were down there.

It was truly a special evening in many ways. But the incident Ruth loved most and spoke of often afterward happened at the very beginning. The ambassador sent his car to pick them up at their hotel and bring them to the residence. Riding up the driveway to the villa, they saw something that made both Ruth and Patterson come to attention: a little girl in a frilly dress the color of pink cotton candy, no more than four or five, sitting serenely on top of the most gigantic tortoise either of them had ever seen. It moved in a slow stately crawl across the perfectly kept front lawn. They later found out its name was Louis (pronounced "*Lou-ee*") and was well over a hundred years old. The little princess in pink obviously felt right at home on its back. A servant came out of the house with a handful of what looked like lettuce and gave it to her as she and Louis went by. Wherever they were going, Louis' passenger was apparently in charge of feeding her taxi.

Interestingly, the girl's name was Louise. Apparently, Louis and Louise were inseparable. She was the granddaughter of the ambassador and deigned to join them for dinner that night. She sat at the table with great dignity, just like a princess, rarely saying a word but paying what looked like full attention to whomever was speaking. When she had finished her helping of the perfect crème brûlée dessert, she politely asked to be excused so as to rejoin Louis on his evening ramble around the lawn.

A few days later, when Patterson gave Ruth the turtle brooch, he prefaced it by saying, "Now you have your own Louis." Afterward, it always touched him to see how often she wore it.

Following her now through the night streets of Mykonos and then onto the small beach at the end of town, his mind was full of Louis the tortoise, the brooch, and their trip to Mauritius. They had spoken at length about the trip earlier in the evening, reminiscing about that magical evening and what a good time they had.

Distracted by his thoughts, it took the invisible Patterson a few seconds to realize she'd suddenly stopped a few feet in front of him. Staring at something nearby, she put both hands to her cheeks and made a loud sound somewhere between a gasp and a laugh. She touched the brooch on her chest with both hands.

Patterson caught up and turned to see what she was looking at that caused her to react so dramatically. It was lucky she could neither see nor hear him because, when he saw what it was, he said a loud, "Oh jeez!"

Down the beach was a young boy, an old man, and a very large leatherback turtle between them. The two people appeared to be trying to lead the turtle back toward the water.

After some time, Ruth said in a small, delighted voice, "It's Louis, and he's *here*." Patterson could not see her close her eyes tightly and tense her mouth, almost as if trying to tightly seal the vision into her memory. Then she turned around and started back toward the cafe. He followed. Halfway there, she stopped again. This time, she walked to a nearby stone wall and, leaning against it, began to cry. Why? Had something else hurt or scared her? No one else was around. Helpless, he stood there, looking everywhere to see if he had missed anything that might have caused her to be upset.

She pushed off the wall and wiped her eyes on the back of her hand. When she spoke, it was to no one but herself, yet her voice was firm, convinced. "It's a sign. It *has* to be. I'm going to say yes because *that*—" she stuck out her arm and pointed back toward the turtle down the beach. "That has to be a sign. Why the hell else would it be here? Why now? We were just talking about it an hour ago. It *has* to be a sign.

"I'm going to tell him yes. I'm going to say yes and take my chances." She was talking to no one. She was talking to the world and to her future. She tried to smile but failed. Looking down the front of her dress, she put a hand over the turtle brooch. Closing her eyes, she said to no one but the invisible Graham Patterson 1 standing nearby, "I'm going to tell him yes."

Tin Eye

"Maid service." Three hard knocks on the door interrupted his reverie.

Patterson was sitting on the side of the bed staring at his hands in his lap. He had been doing it for a long time. Looking up now, he had no idea what time it was.

Last night after watching Ruth walk away, back to the seaside bar where she would tell Graham 3 yes, she would marry him, this Patterson said, "Pinecone 1," touched the tattoo on his arm, and in an instant was back in his motel room in the Illinois town where he had seen the successful Graham 2 perform and then get kidnapped.

"Yes, come in."

The door opened, and a thin woman with small eyes behind big silver-rimmed glasses and wheat-colored hair in careful cornrows walked in with a red bucket in one hand and a mop in the other. Hanging like a six-gun from her thick belt was a spray bottle of blue cleaner. "Good morning."

"Good morning." Patterson stood up and took his jacket off the back of a chair. "I'll get out of your way. Could you tell me if there's a good diner or someplace around here where I could get a decent breakfast? I've been eating at the place across the street, but the food's not so good."

She smirked and leaned the mop against her leg. She pointed north. "I know exactly what you mean about that dump—I wouldn't even drink their coffee. No, here's what you do—go two blocks down on the left to a diner called Fucci's. The food there's really good. You can go for any meal, and they'll treat you right."

"Great, thanks a lot. I can walk from here?"

"Absolutely. Build up your appetite." She smiled and stood aside to let him pass.

Outside, the sky was a striking splash of red, yellow, orange, and plum-purple clouds swirling dramatically around and through each other. Patterson remembered reading somewhere that vivid cloud colors were often due to sand in them blown from as far away as Morocco. Researchers had even found dust from Mongolia in clouds over Denver.

Walking to the diner, he went over and over in his mind whether it had been the right decision to return to this life last night from Greece. At the time, he had been so confused and overwhelmed by what had happened that he felt if he *didn't* get away from there he'd freak out. He couldn't process it all. It was just too much.

The turtle appearing on the beach was the perfect thing, maybe *too* perfect, to convince Ruth to say yes to 3's marriage proposal. Without it, without such a dramatic impossible sign at that exact moment, it was very likely she would have returned to the table and said no, she couldn't be with him.

After all the things recently happening to him, was there any reason why it happened that way? No magic, no secret summons or incantation on his part, but there it appeared at the perfect time. He and Ruth walked on the beach, and right in front of them—there it was. Deus ex machina, or just the most perfectly placed tortoise ever?

Fucci's was one of those nicely renovated 1950s All-American diners often found in college towns that served basic but well-prepared hearty food: lots of meat, daily special soups, good french fries, and mega-desserts that were a delicious nightmare for the arteries—hot fudge sundaes, banana splits, and fresh apple pie with a scoop or two of vanilla ice cream on the side. Patterson liked diners. He liked the food, the diverse clientele; he liked the usually friendly waitresses who weren't hesitant to tell you what was good or bad to eat on the menu that day. He'd once encountered a waitress who was easily one of the funniest people he had ever met in a small Missouri town called Galen.

When he walked into Fucci's, the diner was midmorning quiet and half empty. He had his choice of either a booth or a seat at the counter. He slid into a booth that could easily fit six people. Both the Naugahyde seat and Formica table were bright yellow, which perfectly fit the feel of the place. He wondered how many tons of cheeseburgers had been consumed at this table while people schemed and dreamed, flirted, lied, and promised while passing the salt and pulling ten thousand paper napkins out of the metal dispenser to wipe ketchup off their lips.

"Hi there. What can I get you? Wait a minute—I know you! I know who you are."

Patterson the comedian had never been "recognized" by a stranger in his life. How ironic it was happening now after he had retired from comedy. Nevertheless delighted, he straightened up and beamed. "Really?"

"Yes, of course! I've read all of your books almost. I love them. You're one of my favorite authors, and I read a *lot*. I just finished Dance Daddy Death last week. It kept me up for two nights."

Patterson tried to keep the happy on his face but could feel it slipping away, despite his best effort. What kind of writer would even think to give a book such a stupid title?

She said in a joyful fluster, "Oh, I just remembered—I have it here in the back. I was going to lend it to my girlfriend who loves your books, too. Would you sign it for me?"

"Sure—why not?" he mumbled with a lame smile. When she brought the book he'd look at the cover to find out the name of the idiot who wrote it and sign that name for her. Handing back the menu, he ordered bacon, a cheese omelet, and coffee.

After writing it on her pad, she continued to stand there beaming at him. "I can't *believe* it. I can't believe you're in my booth, just having bacon and eggs like the rest of us."

He sighed and decided to play along. In for a penny, in for a pound. "Well, you know, we writers have to eat, too. Got to have fuel to keep up the old word count."

Unable to stop herself, she impulsively reached over and shyly patted him twice on the shoulder. "This is *so cool*. I'll be right back."

And she was—minutes later, she returned and put a thick purple book with gold lettering on the table. Just by the look, it had to be five or six hundred pages long. The title and size were bad enough, but Patterson winced when he saw the cover image: On a white dinner plate was a large severed hand wearing a gold wedding ring. The final insult was the author's name: Gerber Pinkey. What kind of name was that—*Gerber*? He had to see what the guy looked like. He turned to the back inside jacket for the author's photo. All in all, Gerber *did* sort of resemble Patterson, but certainly not one hundred percent.

He took out a pen and opened the front of the book to the title page. "Tell me your name."

"Tina, but would you sign it to Tin Eye? That's my nickname."

Patterson looked up from the book and asked doubtfully, "*Tin Eye?* Really?"

She nodded. "It's a name my brother called me when we were kids. He's . . . handicapped and could never say Tina right. The name just kind of stuck."

He gave her a thumbs up and wrote in the book, This DANCE is for Tin Eye, the queen of Fucci's. He sneakily checked the cover again to see the way Gerber Pinkey spelled his ridiculous name before writing it under the dedication and then dating it. He handed the book back to Tina, who immediately opened it to read what he had written.

"Oh, that's terrific. Thanks so much, Mr. Pinkey. I really do love your work. This means so much to me."

"No problem. I just hope you keep liking what I write."

"Oh, I know I will. I'll go get your food."

Tin Eye—such a strange, interesting name. Patterson always carried a small notebook in his pocket to write down things he wanted to remember or spontaneous ideas that might float in for comedy material. He took it out now and wrote the name. When he was done, he left the pen and notebook off to the side of the table.

Tina came back with his food but seemed distracted. After a quick smile, she left without a word.

A little while later, two big, burly men entered the diner and sat down facing each other at the booth in front of his. Both wore green and white trucker baseball caps with HOLBERT HOMES written across the top. A different waitress came to their table, and both ordered the day's special.

The one facing Patterson leaned across the table and shook a finger at his friend. "Listen, trying to convince a stubborn woman of *anything* is like trying to tie water into a knot. Believe me, I should know because I've been married twice. And your sister was the worse of the two."

Grinning, Patterson slid the pen and notebook back over. He opened it and wrote "tying water in a knot" below "Tin Eye."

His breakfast was delicious, and eavesdropping on the men's conversation the whole time turned out to be an added delight. Both men had the kind of working man's insight and gravelly, unconscious wit he loved.

"Listen to me, Donny, memory has no heartbeat. You understand what I'm saying? It's dead stuff, a museum. You want to walk around in a museum for the rest of your life, or do you want to fucking *live*? Your memories of her and the good times you two had together are beautiful, absolutely, but you gotta move on from them and start living again. No offense, but you're getting to sound like a parrot now. Because you keep squawking the same things about her—*how could she? I thought she loved me*—"

Donnie cut him off. "*You're* one to talk—I ain't been divorced twice. I may be wearing my heart on my sleeve these days, but at least I never let my exes take it as part of the alimony, along with everything else."

His partner held up a fork and waved it at him. "Touché."

The waitress came with their food. Curious to see what the day's special was at Fucci's, Patterson leaned forward to get a good look at their plates. Chipped beef on toast—his favorite meal when he was a little boy. His mother made it for lunch every Saturday. Their tradition—just before noon he would prop up a portable metal tray in front of the television set and his mother would bring in the chipped beef on toast just as his favorite cartoons were about to start. The only requirement was he had to drink a large glass of milk, which he hated, along with the meal. But that was the deal he made with her. One of the funnier bits in his latest comedy routine had been a long riff on the food kids like when they're young.

"You know what they call this meal in the Army? Shit on a shingle."

"I don't care—it's good shit. Pass the salt. And tell me about the accident, Donnie."

"Well, you know, we were coming down off the site last night. Jennifer was driving the truck because I was just fucking wiped out. Ever since C.J. busted his hand and we had to go double shift . . . *Anyway*, about halfway through the trees on Hastings Avenue, our headlights flash across a crash. This car's smashed straight up against a tree. Really a wreck, not just some little oopsy fender bender. Goddamn—it looked bad. We could see a few people standing by it, so we slowed down to have a look and see if anyone was hurt or if they maybe needed help."

"Did they?"

"Hell no! This was the crazy part of it. We pull over and get out of the truck. We see it's three teenage girls, and two of them are just standing there looking at their fucking phones like nothing's happened. And you know what? I swear to God, one of them was watching a music clip! It was really loud. I recognized the song. What are these kids these days, brain dead?

"So we ask if they're okay, and they're all like yeah, sure, what's the big deal—we crashed. But get this—guess what kind of car it was? A '64 Impala SS, and even though it was dark, it looked beautiful—like it had been perfectly restored."

"Probably Daddy's car. Ooooh, somebody's going to be pissed."

"Same thing I was thinking, but the girls were cool as Uma in *Kill Bill*. I'm telling you, one of them was looking at a fucking *music video* on her phone. So Jennifer naturally asks if any of these geniuses had called the cops. The three of them look at each other like the question was hilarious.

"That's when I got pissed off. I told Jen let's just get out of here. So we left. They're probably still out there looking at their phones."

"Did they thank you for stopping?"

"Are you kidding? They barely looked at us."

The man facing Donnie glanced over his friend's shoulder and saw Patterson looking back. He must have assumed Patterson had heard the whole story because he shook his head and said to him, "Fucking kids."

Patterson didn't pretend he hadn't heard and shook his head too in commiseration. Donnie half turned to see who it was behind him his friend was addressing. He and Patterson exchanged glances, then he turned back around and continued eating.

The story stuck, and later that day back in his room Patterson wrote down the gist of it in his notebook. He could picture the scene so vividly: The beautiful car wrecked against a tree, three girls looking at their glowing phones in the dark, truck headlights lighting just one part of the eerie scene.

Years later, when they were hanging his famous car crash photo "Borrowed World" at the Venice Biennale, Patterson thought again of that day at Fucci's diner. He thought about how surprised Donnie would be to learn his story told to a pal over a lunch of chipped beef on toast ended up being the inspiration for a photo seen around the world.

In interviews, Patterson was very open and honest about where he got the inspiration for the picture. One snarky Russian journalist asked, "So basically one of your most famous works wasn't your idea at all—you stole it from someone else? Did you give him some of the money you have made from this picture?"

Patterson didn't take the bait because the statement had been made before in one form or other, both to his face and in print. It didn't faze him at all. This time he grinned and very calmly said, "The difference between your job and mine is simply this—yours is to ask questions and then record what I say for your readers. You can edit or cut some of it, you can shade it by describing me as a phony or a pretentious asshole, but the heart of your article is to record my words verbatim. You're a human tape recorder. If you're a good journalist, you'll do that and not let your biases get in the way, no matter what you think of me personally.

"On the other hand, my work is *based* on my biases. I get to pick and choose material from my life. Then I mix it up and maybe include some of it in my finished work. The job of a photographer or any artist is to sift through his life experience and decide what parts of it he wants to add or keep in the work.

"I have no idea if my photograph is in any way similar to what Donnie saw that night. I don't care, to be honest. As soon as I heard the story it became mine, and I could do whatever I wanted with it. Since I'm a photographer, I created the scene as I envisioned it and made it into an image people seem to respond to. Is it then a collaboration between the storyteller and me? In part yes, sort of. But the artist, as opposed to the journalist, has no obligation to be honest or factual. The audience likes my individual vision, not my ability to replicate exactly what happened. People always ask where I get the ideas for my work. Ideas come from everywhere, every day. The more important thing is what you *do* with them once they arrive."

———

A few weeks later in Los Angeles, Patterson was shopping for vegetables at Farmers Market in Los Angeles.

"Don't you agree?"

Surprised by the low, smoky female voice very close behind him, Patterson turned around. "Excuse me?" A moment before, he had been trying to choose between avocadoes at a vegetable stand.

"Don't you think most men look dumb in cowboy hats?"

Who was this woman? He'd never seen her before. Why was she asking him? Quite tall, nice looking, mid-forties, maybe, long blond-streaked brown hair pulled back in a girlish ponytail, calm grayish-blue eyes under dark, dramatic eyebrows and a perfect nose. Her wide mouth offered a small smile, a waiting-for-an-answer smile.

Patterson looked at his hand and saw he was holding a fat avocado without realizing he had picked it up while she spoke. "Cowboy hats? I never thought about it. Baseball caps worn backward when you're over forty—now *they* look stupid, yes, but I never thought about cowboy hats in general. You're probably right, though. *Most* people look dumb in big hats, women and men." He put the avocado back down carefully in its place on the vegetable display. "Sombreros especially. It's impossible for almost anyone to look cool in a sombrero."

That earned a bigger smile from her. She pointed to the hat store next to the vegetable stand where he had been browsing. "I was just looking in the window there and saw how many cowboy hats are for sale. Is this an American thing? I'm not from here."

He'd already guessed that. She had a foreign accent that he couldn't place. She was also standing too close to him in the inviolate private space reserved only for close friends and intimates. Patterson crossed his arms and leaned back to create a little more distance between them. "Well, Americans *do* like big things—Big Macs, Big Gulps, Big Wheels . . . Where are you from?"

"Greece." She offered to shake his hand. "I am Antheia Lambrinos."

Patterson took her hand gently. "Graham Patterson."

"I know. I know who you are."

Instead of being thrilled, he immediately thought, Here we go again. It was like he was right back in Fucci's diner and being mistaken for Gerber Pinkey.

"You *do*? Have we met before?"

Eyes closed, she shook her head hard, like an adamant little girl. Her ponytail swayed from side to side. "I saw you perform at Cynthia's in Montreal."

"You *did*?" Cynthia's Comedy Club in Montreal was one of his last gigs before the dismal last show in Providence.

"Yes. Half of it was very funny."

Patterson laughed out loud. His reaction was instantaneous because her line was so perfect. As soon as she said it, he couldn't help but, even though it was praise with a punch in the nose. But this Antheia Lambrinos had summed up his career as a comic in six words better than he ever could have in six hundred. He was *Mr. Half-Funny*. That said it all.

"Did I say something humorous?"

He sighed, but it wasn't an altogether sad one. "Yes, you said something *fully* funny. Not that it matters, but I'm not doing standup comedy anymore."

She looked at him and closed one eye. "Why not?"

"Because you said it exactly—I'm only half funny."

"But it was a *good* half funny! I laughed a lot."

"Well, thank you, but . . . " He didn't know what else to say. After pausing a moment, he shook his head, throwing away the rest of a dishonest sentence on the tip of his tongue.

Witnessing Graham 2 wow the crowd in the small Illinois club flashed across his mind now. Watching a different version of himself make all the right moves, say just the right things timed so damned word-perfectly . . . He knew he could never have reached that level. Never. It was him performing, yes, sort of, but a Graham Patterson with a Mohawk haircut on some kind of wondrously creative psychic steroid that made everything he said golden, hilarious, and complete. Even the way he'd handled the heckler with just two lines—"I rode in on the back of your IQ. Luckily for both of us, it was a short ride." Snappy, with just the perfect dusting of nasty to flush the wise guy away without another peep.

Besides the requisite luck, talent, and personal drive, there was a secret to great public success in any field. You either inherently knew or through life experience figured out the secret along the way and then moved toward glory. Everyone else sat in the audience wondering, How the hell do they *do* that? The brilliant comedian or the star athlete, a titan of business, the award-winning actor, the incomparable teacher or surgeon, a word magician novelist . . . all of them took their correct secret answer with them when they leave the stage.

"I wouldn't mind."

"Excuse me?"

"I wouldn't mind a cup of coffee. Would you like to have one with me?"

"Coffee? Uh, sure. That would be nice." Patterson was not used to company. He had arrived in Los Angeles the week before and rented a room at a comfortable family-run motel he knew in Westwood near the UCLA campus. His only companion on the drive across country had been the radio, but even that got on his nerves after a while—both the music and the talk shows—so he switched it off, preferring to ride in silence for hours at a time.

After his experience on Mykonos, he had no desire to return to the life of Graham 3 to see how the relationship with Ruth had progressed. He assumed it went well, but just the memory of seeing the giant tortoise, *there* in Greece, at just that moment, still gave him the creeps. He was convinced more than ever he had summoned it, and that certainty canceled out everything else.

When he was a boy, a favorite cartoon was the one where Mickey Mouse played the part of the sorcerer's apprentice. The sorcerer goes out and leaves his magic wand on a table with strict instructions to the apprentice *not* to touch it under any circumstance.

Naturally, as soon as the door closes, Mickey picks up the wand and, waving it around, starts giving the world around him orders. For a while, good things happen. The broom sweeps the floor by itself, the bucket jumps into the sink to be filled with water. But too soon the broom goes crazy and maniacally sweeps everything in sight, water overflows in the sink and can't be turned off . . . Havoc follows everywhere, until at the last minute the sorcerer returns. With one wave of the wand, he brings everything back to normal.

Moral of the story? Don't mess with things you have no idea of how to control.

Patterson was certain he had somehow made the turtle appear in Mykonos—a good thing, because the magic convinced Ruth to say yes to 3's marriage proposal. But he was also paranoid enough to know you do not play with fire when you have no idea of how to control it. As far as he was concerned, you don't even get near it. In Graham 3's world, Patterson was capable of performing wonders, yes. But as the

Japanese proverb says, there's always a reverse side to the reverse side. After experiencing the nightmare of Graham 2's afterlife, he wanted to avoid the reverse sides of anything as long as he could.

So as he drove across Death Valley toward Los Angeles at four in the morning to avoid the heat of the day, he had made up his mind to stay in this life, at least for now, and see where it took him. If things turned bad, he could always pinecone over to Graham 3's world to see what marital bliss looked like. Or, if for some mad reason he wanted to jump into oblivion altogether, he could even go back to the world of prehistoric Patterson the gecko. He was sure life there was short and brutal, but with a brain half the size of a peanut, how was he to know until the moment he was gobbled up by something even more horrible?

Antheia walked fast. She wore a pair of pumpkin-colored high-top sneakers beneath slim jeans and a white t-shirt that looked sculpted to her figure. She taught English at an international school in Greece and was in the States to visit friends, she told him. She came every year. She'd been in Montreal at the comedy club that night with her friend Elgin Hall.

"Elgin Hall the actor?"

"Yes. We have been friends for many years. Before he became famous, he was the drama teacher in my school."

"In *Greece*?"

She stopped and frowned at Patterson. "Yes, in Greece. But you make it sound like another planet."

He shook his head. "It's not that. It's just you never think of what a famous person did or *was* before they became famous. Elgin Hall is, well, Elgin Hall—" He waved a hand across the sky as if putting that name up in giant lights.

Antheia shrugged. "He farts a lot. He has a bad stomach, and so he farts. See—Elgin is a human, too, like you and me."

Patterson smiled and nodded. "I could sell the fact to a celebrity secrets website. It would make a great headline: *Elgin Hall, heartthrob to millions, has bad gas.*"

She shook her head. "Not so bad. 'Popcorn farts,' he calls them. He also likes to cook, but it is terrible. Never let Elgin cook you a meal."

"What were the two of you doing in Montreal?"

"He is filming a television show there. When he learned I was coming to America, he invited me to come up there and stay with him for a few days. It was nice—we had fun. Here—this place looks nice." Without checking to see if Patterson agreed, she walked into a small café on the edge of the huge market.

Just before they sat down on opposite sides of the table, she leaned in very close to him again and sniffed. "What kind of cologne do you use?"

Taken aback both by her gesture and the question, he shook his head. "I don't know. I don't have a favorite."

"And I bet you don't wear one enough. You should—this is a mistake for men. The world is full of bad things—bad people, bad food, bad smells, bad situations. The man who walks through life smelling beautiful always has an advantage. Women are expected to smell clean and wonderful, but the man who does has already unbuttoned the top two buttons of her shirt without ever having to touch her. Let's sit here. Then we can look out the window."

He pulled two menus from a holder and handed one to her. "You should write a book of rules for men. Rule number one—no cowboy hats. Number two—always wear cologne." A thought suddenly came to him. "You said Elgin was with you the night you saw me at Cynthia's?"

Looking at the menu, she nodded.

"Did he say anything about my performance?"

Without looking up from the menu, she said, "You made him smile, but didn't make him laugh."

"Oh."

"But I told you, I laughed at a lot of what you said."

Patterson hid behind the menu.

She reached across the table and pushed it down with two fingers so she could see his face. "If you aren't going to be a comedian anymore, what are you going to do?"

"Good question. To be honest, I don't really know. That's why I came to California—it's better to be lost in a warm climate." He smirked and tried to raise the menu again, but she wouldn't let him.

"Are you married?"

He frowned. "No. Why?"

"Because you don't look married. I was right."

He was offended. When he spoke, the tone of his voice said so. "What does a man who's not married look like? Is there an invisible mark on our forehead, like the sign of Cain?" He touched his with his thumb. "Is it another one for your book of rules?"

"You look glamsy."

That stopped him. "*Glamsy*? What does that mean?"

She put her menu back in the slot. "Blueberry pancakes. I will have them." Slapping both hands flat down on the table, she smiled and said, "It is a wonderful word, but nobody knows or uses it. I love strange obscure English words no one ever uses but are perfect for describing certain things.

"Glamsy means how the sky looks before a big storm—dark and turbulent over here, while at the same time you have brilliant sunlight cutting through the clouds over there—like in some kind of bad Biblical movie when God talks to the hero. And all of the time the sky is moving and changing, *roiling*—another great word—the clouds are roiling and charging across the whole sky. You know everything is going to explode any minute. I love it when a day is like this. So *powerful.*" She stopped and sighed, enchanted by the words and mental picture they painted.

Patterson wasn't impressed. "And how am I, Mr. Unmarried, *glamsy?*"

"Oh, it's not a bad thing. I am glamsy, too. Most unmarried people are. Once you know how to look for it you see it a lot—either on people's faces, in the way they behave, or you sense it about them."

He shifted in his seat. "You're not married?"

"I was, but my husband is dead."

"I'm sorry."

She nodded. "What are you going to eat?"

Patterson realized he was hungry. "You're having blueberry pancakes? I will, too. You still haven't told me what a glamsy person looks like."

"Mercurial. Untethered. Unsure. *Interesting.* The sky on your face is changing all the time."

The waitress came and took their orders.

When she was gone, Patterson said, "People who are mercurial and unsure don't sound interesting. They sound neurotic."

Antheia nodded eagerly. "They are—*we* are. But how many interesting people do you know who *aren't* neurotic? I can't think of any. Everybody I know who is interesting is at least a little bit fucked up in one way or another; they've been bent this way or that by life. It gives them an out of the ordinary way of looking at things. It's what makes them glamsy. Clear sky people are pretty dull."

She paused to reconsider and then put up her left thumb, as if counting. "Except my husband. *He* was an interesting man, and very unfucked up. But I think he worked out all of his neuroses rock climbing. That was his passion and that's how he died. He fell while climbing a cliff called Ghost Kitchen on Kalymnos. This is an island in Greece. We have a house there."

"Wow."

"Wow *what*?"

"That's a dramatic way to die."

"It is. He was young, too—thirty-nine. His great dream was to climb El Capitan at Yosemite National Park. That's where I was last week. I wanted to go there for him. I took a stone from our garden in Kalymnos and put it at the base there. It was a kind of little way of giving Alexander his wish.

"Do you want to hear something very ironic about my husband? Three days before he died, he was climbing at another place on the island called Big Shadow. Metal bolts are drilled into the rock face so climbers can clip their carabiners and ropes into them and be safely caught if for some reason they slip and fall. Big Shadow is the name of the cliff, right? Well, the bolts Alexander clipped into that day were very old. Now, I know they've had problems with them before. That day, one pulled out of the rock while he was making a move very high up. His rope came loose, and he dropped many feet straight down. Luckily the other bolts held, and his fall was broken. So Big Shadow almost killed him. I always am thinking maybe he should have taken that shadow as a warning."

Luckily for Patterson the food arrived then, and they began eating. He didn't know what to say about her stories. While she spoke, he kept wondering if her husband could have been like him and been given three lives to choose from—but happened to choose the wrong one, and it killed him before he was forty.

"And what about you?"

"What *about* me?"

"How did Mr. Graham Patterson get here—shopping at Farmers Market in L.A.?"

The comic in him wanted to say something witty or funny, or some brilliantly appropriate *bon mot* barb, but he could think of nothing except the sad truth. "The life I wanted didn't want me, so I'm looking for one that does. My brother lives out here, and if worse comes to worse I can go to work for him. But I really would prefer not to, even though he's a very good guy."

About to put a big forkful into her mouth, she stopped. "Is he glamsy too, or a clear sky guy?"

"Clear sky—all the way, but in the best way."

"Are you a good photographer?" She tipped her chin toward the camera he had placed on the seat next to him.

"I just started taking pictures. I've always wanted to, but now I've got all the time in the world to do it. Thought I might as well take up a new hobby."

"Have you taken many pictures?"

"Yeah, quite a few."

"Can I see them?"

"Sure." He picked up the camera, switched it on, and pointed to a button on the back. "Just press this one and you can scroll through them on the screen." He handed her the camera. She put her fork down so she could use both hands.

He had taken a lot of pictures on the leisurely drive cross-country. From in the car through the open window or out of it, he photographed whatever caught his eye or imagination. At night wherever he was staying, he studied the camera manual and later a thick paperback book on photography he picked up at a college bookstore in St. Paul.

"*This* one. This shot is very good, Graham." Antheia turned the camera around so he could see the photo she was talking about. It was the one of Anna Mae Collins' mother's hand as she was serving the tomato soup.

"It *is?*" His voice was all surprise.

"And this one."

To his even greater astonishment, she had chosen a photo he'd taken early one August evening of an abandoned motel sign somewhere between Reno and Ely, Nevada.

Patterson particularly liked ghostly abandoned commercial places—the failed, faded brown or pink motels, "*Home of the Tripleburger*" diners. A smashed-windshield, wheelless, thirty-year-old Dodge pickup truck the only permanent occupant left in the deserted, cracked pavement parking lot in front. Or gas stations that died decades ago in the middle of absolute nowhere, left to rot, rust, and fade away to nothing in their own sweet time. The back roads of the West were peppered with these forlorn relics.

"Why those two pictures? What do you like about them?" He tried to modulate his voice so it sounded professional and not needy, although he was more than eager for a big fat compliment at that stage, even if it came from this stranger.

She put down the camera, picked up her fork and stabbed a piece of pancake. "In Europe I love to travel by train, especially what they call the ICE trains—Intercity Express. They are these super sleek, futuristic ones that go like rockets from big city to big city. So comfortable, they have every amenity you can imagine, and as I said, they are *very* fast. Zoom—the whole ride is a blur. In Italy and France, they go over two hundred miles an hour. Looking out the window, you barely get a chance to focus on what you're seeing before it's gone."

Patterson sat back. He liked listening to her. She had a good voice, and the touch of foreign accent added a nice individuality to it. He wanted to hear what she had to say about his photography, but she could be talking about anything, and it was nice to hear. At the same time, he wondered if he felt that way because of her company, or just because he had been alone so much of the time recently.

"What?"

He blinked. "What's the matter?"

"You're smiling—did I say something funny?"

"No, I was just enjoying listening to you. That's all—nothing else."

She narrowed her eyes suspiciously but also half smiled. "I'm watching you—so be careful."

"Yes, ma'am. So what about these trains? I thought we were talking about my pictures."

She bit off a piece of bacon. "We are—be patient. So there are these ICE trains, and they are lovely to ride. At the same time, you're traveling so fast you barely have a chance to appreciate what's passing outside. You can be riding for five hours and of course you're going to see interesting things out there, but in seconds they're gone. Sometimes it almost makes you wonder, did I really see it? I *think* I did.

"To me, life is too much like riding an ICE train. Every day, or almost every day, we are absolutely zooming through it and give ourselves no chance to—"

"Smell the roses?" Patterson cut her off with the cliché.

"No, I don't like this phrase—it's as stale as old bread. Look at this picture—" She picked up his camera and scrolled through the shots to find the one of the abandoned motel sign again. "When I saw this one, it physically stopped me. My ICE train—life absolutely stopped.

It stopped me and said, 'Pay attention! Look carefully at this unimportant thing. Do not just click to the next. There's something in this image that matters to you.'"

Patterson shrugged. "What? It's just an old sign."

She scrunched up her shoulder and squeezed her eyes shut. "*No*, that's not true, and you know it. You chose to photograph the sign three times from different angles. There was obviously something about it that hooked you, too. And this is the magic of good photography, or any art: What hooked you the photographer into taking it may not be the same thing that hooks me the observer, but both of our very different lives say yes to the image.

"Elgin told me a great story. He was invited to this very important arts festival in Finland. They had him on a panel discussing what is either art or 'great art.'" Her voice dropped into a bass note when she said the last two words, as if "great art" needed a dramatic male radio announcer voice to speak them.

"One of the people on the panel was an avant-garde filmmaker who'd just made an exhibition of video art. He had a film of a dancing ballerina projected on large television screens. In something like ten different galleries around the world, the film was being shown at exactly the same time every day for a month. No matter where you were—Paris, Helsinki, Mumbai, or wherever—what you were watching was what everyone else around the world was watching simultaneously—a ballerina dancing."

"That's it? That's *all*?"

She nodded. "Yes. I said the same thing when he told me. But wait—it's not the point of the story. After this poseur talked about how his show was bringing the world and humanity closer through technology and didn't need any language to communicate its universal point, blah blah—you know, typical intellectual bullshit—he talked on and on, boring everybody there about how great and original his work was. But finally it was Elgin's turn to speak, and this is the part I love. He said because of his experience both as a teacher and an actor, to him there is only one criterion for what makes great art or even just worthy art in general: either 'Wow!' or 'So what?'"

With his mouth full, Patterson barely managed to say, "*What?*"

She held up a hand for him to wait. "If you and I walked into a gallery where that ballerina video was playing, both of us would have the same reaction—'So what?' Right? But just now when I saw your photo of the road sign, *something* in me, some important part went '*Wow!*' immediately, without thinking.

"Elgin said the same thing to the guy on the panel: If he went into a gallery and saw the ballerina dancing on TV, he'd go, 'So? What's the point?' But when he was a boy, the first time he saw Dali's melting clocks painting ,he actually said out loud *Wow!* I'm sure it's happened to you with your favorite photographers—"

Patterson interrupted. "Vivian Maier. Wee Gee. Lee Miller. Walker Evans. Duane Michals. Robert Capa, so many more. It's why I love photography. When it's great, I say wow a lot."

"And you've also said—or at least *thought*—'so what?' about many uninteresting photos, right?"

"Yup." The pancakes were delicious. Lowering his head, he went back to eating while mulling over what she'd just said. It made a lot of sense.

Antheia began to surf through his photos again. "I wanted to ask you something. What's *this* picture?" She turned the camera around to the picture he'd taken of his reptile hand just after returning from the death and reincarnation of Graham 2, the Lizard King.

Patterson mumbled something through his pancake, hopefully indistinguishable.

She shook her head. "What? I didn't understand."

"I said you wouldn't believe me if I told you."

"Try me. No, but wait—I want to show you something first." She slid to the edge of her seat until she was almost out of the booth. Untying the sneaker on her left foot, she took it off. Patterson thought this was odd.

When her foot was bare, he saw what was on top of it—*the tattoo.* The breakfast tattoo, as Anna Mae called it. The bee inside the frog inside the hawk inside the lion. Exactly like his. *Exactly.*

He dropped his fork. It hit the plate with a loud clatter. People in the next booth looked over at them.

"No *fucking* way!" he muttered while staring at her foot with his mouth open.

She wiggled her toes and nodded. "It's true. This is why I came up to you in the market—I saw the one on your arm. I also saw you perform in Montreal, it's true, but never would have approached you today if I hadn't seen your tattoo." She pointed to it. He was wearing a smoke-colored t-shirt that exposed most of his arms. "It's the second time I've seen it on someone. When we were in Rome a few years ago, there was a teenager sitting on the Spanish Steps with it, but I didn't say anything. I guess I was too rattled—is this the right word, *rattled?*"

Patterson slid down the booth to the end to get a better look at her foot. It was the same tattoo, no doubt about it. Same size as his, same beautiful intricacy, the same everything. "Where did you have it done?"

"In London, when I was there with my husband."

"London?"

"Yes. That's not where you got yours?"

He was almost as amazed by this information as he was by her tattoo. "No, I got mine in North Carolina. The woman who did it said she learned it from a master in Japan."

Antheia nodded. "My tattoo woman learned it there, too."

Both were silent a moment, these coincidences sinking slowly in. Then they spoke at the same time.

"Did she—"

"She told me—"

Patterson stopped and gestured for Antheia to continue. He'd ask his question in a minute.

"My woman said she was one of the only ones in the world who knew it and how to make it. It's why I was so surprised to see it on the kid in Rome, and now you."

Awed by all of this, Patterson shook his head. "My tattoo artist said the same thing to me. Did you happen to get her name?"

Antheia shrugged. "No. I remember she was American and spoke with an accent. But I don't remember her telling me her name."

It *had* to be Anna Mae. She said she had either studied or worked in London, he couldn't remember for sure. But what were the chances *this* meeting could happen: A woman from Greece visits London and chooses to get the rarest, most magical tattoo in the world from one of the only people who knows how to do it. Years later while visiting Los Angeles, she sees her tattoo on a man in a market and it turns out his was done by the same artist, but this time in *North Carolina?!?*

Convinced, he said, "It had to be the same woman who did both of us. This is absolutely incredible. My tattoo artist name was Anna Mae Collins. Does that mean anything to you?"

"No."

Enough talk about the amazing coincidences. Patterson had to ask her the big question. "Have you done it yet?"

"Done what?" She bent over and pulled the sneaker back on.

He made an exasperated face. "Gone to your other lives. Seen what could be."

She looked . . . puzzled. "No, I like my life. I am content with it. The only time I was ever tempted to try another was right after my husband died. The only thing I wanted in the world then was to stop hurting and missing him. I thought it might be the best way to do it. I assumed he'd still be there in at least one of my other lives."

"So why didn't you?"

"Because sometimes you've got to be lost to find yourself again. I sank down to the bottom of my soul after he died and went through some black times. One especially horrible day, I stood at the base of the mountain where he died and screamed at it. I could have lifted a hot air balloon with the heat from my anger against that mountain and life. A part of what saved me in those days was knowing I could always go to one of those other lives if the pain got to be too much.

"But eventually I realized two things, Graham. The first was I really *liked* my life and had no desire to change it, even though my man was gone from it now. I liked where I was, the job I had been doing, my plans, hopes . . . all of it.

"The second and most important thing had been staring me in the face the whole time, but the blackness of my sadness blinded me to it: The greatest gift Alexander ever gave me was the strength to know in my heart I could go on without him. All the time we knew each other he treated me not only like his best friend and partner, but his absolute equal. Before we met, I didn't have much self-confidence. But his love and respect, year after year, made me one hundred times more independent and stronger. Strong enough to still love a life we had created and built together, even though he was not there anymore to share it with me."

Patterson asked quietly "How long ago did he die?"

"Two years in March. Love died for me March seventh."

For the moment there was nothing else to say, so they finished eating in silence. Patterson kept looking at her while putting all the information she had given him into as good and sharp of focus as he could at that moment.

When she was done and had wiped her lips with a paper napkin, she said, "I'd like you to tell me about what you saw when you went to your other lives. But before you do, would you take my picture?"

"Really? Why?"

With her pinky, she pointed to his camera. "Because you have no people in there. Not one. Do you realize that? You have a personless camera."

"What? *Really?*" Taken aback, he looked at the camera on the table between them as if it had suddenly become a mysterious object. Then he looked at *her* as if she'd asked him to solve a difficult physics problem. The fact hit him hard. He didn't exactly know why, but it was disturbing. He'd been taking pictures for weeks, but of no human beings.

She shook her head. "Not one, from what I saw. The closest you come is the one of the hand serving soup, but it's just a hand. I think you should have at least one whole person in there, don't you? Add some humanity?"

Tying Water in a Knot

Two days later they went to the beach together. It was Antheia's idea, but they had to go to a special one far down the coast in western Malibu because of the dog. Antheia was staying at Elgin's house in Brentwood. Although the actor was supposed to join them that day, he had to back out at the last minute. But he asked her to take his miniature bull terrier, Fellini, along with them so the young dog could have a good long run around in the sand and surf. She called Patterson to ask if it was okay. He said sure, and a couple of hours later they were tooling along Pacific Coast Highway with the top down on the Mustang, the two of them wearing sunglasses. Antheia had on a new Montecristi Panama hat Elgin had given her, and the sweet dog was standing at attention on her lap, taking it all in. All they needed was a Beach Boys song playing on the radio, and the image of a perfect L.A. couple out for a drive would have been complete.

With a snort, Patterson thought, How California we must look today, but how California we *aren't*—a Greek widow and a failed East Coast comedian with a borrowed dog in a red convertible with New York license plates.

"What did you do when you saw the turtle that night, Graham?"

"Shit my pants."

"Really?"

"No, not really, but my brain shit *its* pants, that's for sure."

"And this turtle was real? You touched it?"

"I assume. Both the old man and the boy were touching it."

He had told her everything. He did not know this woman at all, but in the course of their first day together he told her all that had happened to him since getting the breakfast tattoo. And why not? If anyone could accept the mad turn his life had taken since the morning his car broke down in North Carolina, it would be someone who also had the tattoo and knew its significance.

When he was finished talking, she said, "We are like astronauts. Both of us trained to fly to the moon. You actually chose to do it, but I stayed back on earth. I don't know if it means you're brave and I'm a coward, or I'm lucky and you're to be pitied."

Patterson told her about his college professor's "ice cream question." Pouncing, Antheia said, "I would *never* choose the magical ice cream! I don't want to regret anything. To mope through life wishing I had this or that—my God, it is the strongest poison. I had the best partner I could ever imagine, but now he's gone. That's enough regret to fill my heart forever. I don't need any more, small or large. Keep your magic ice cream away from me so I don't have to think about it for even a second. I don't care how good it is.

"The best thing in the world, the most anyone can hope for, is to wake up in the morning liking where you are, what you do, and, if you're very lucky, who you're with. Ask or expect more and you're a greedy fool. Right now, I still have two of them, once I had all three. Two is enough for me. I still think I am very lucky. My Alexander used to say all the time when we talked about these things, 'Be quiet. Be grateful.'"

Patterson tried to speak without sounding resentful. "But by that measure, I'm a greedy fool for trying out my other lives?"

She didn't hesitate. "In one way, yes. But we have very different lives and goals, Graham, so who knows which of us will be right. Maybe I'll just end up a bitter old bird in black widow's clothes sitting by myself, chewing bread with my last three good teeth by the sea."

"Do you think you'll ever get married again?"

She rubbed her hands together as if they were cold. "I have no idea. But I made a promise to myself never to sleep with anyone again unless I love them. Not lust for them, *love* them. I know it sounds like a teenager's promise, but I hope I keep it."

"Would you like to have children?"

"With the right man, yes. But because I teach, I see how difficult it is to raise kids successfully. If you really care about them it's constant hard work, and there's no guarantee you'll succeed, no matter how hard you try. I've seen too many family fights, misunderstandings, and even tragedies with my students to believe anymore that love conquers all. It doesn't. Many parents love their children but make little effort to understand them."

"You could say that about a lot of adult relationships, too."

"True." Antheia laughed and patted Patterson on the shoulder. "Very good, and very true. Ah, the beach—here we are."

He pulled the car into a large parking lot. It was early afternoon in the middle of the week, so the lot was mostly empty.

Stretching his arms over his head, he said, "I feel sort of guilty being out here, like I'm playing hooky from work. Or my life."

She clipped a leash onto the dog's collar. "What's hooky?"

They climbed slowly down a sun-bleached set of steep, worn wooden steps to the beach, Antheia's hand on Patterson's shoulder to steady her. There were several dogs out there running around anywhere and everywhere, barking at the waves or plunging fearlessly in and out of the water. Joy was in everything they did, no matter what it was. Way down the beach, a man was throwing a bright orange Frisbee for a raggedy mutt. The dog sped after it and leapt up to catch it on the fly every time.

In the other direction, Patterson saw a large Weimaraner standing at the water's edge, its beautiful gray body still, but the short tail wagging furiously. He pointed to the dog and said, "We had a Weimaraner like that when I was a kid, really a nice dog. His name was Pinecone." They moved down toward the water, Fellini pulling hard on the leash. He was in paradise. He wanted to be free to enjoy it.

"Elgin said I can let him off the line and he'll be good. Said he'll come if we call him. Do you think I should?"

Patterson slapped his legs and said, "Fellini!" The thick little dog whipped its head around from staring at the water and came right over to Patterson as if he had been given an order.

"Sure, look at that. Let him go—he'll be good."

To both of their surprise, as soon as the bull terrier was taken off the leash, instead of bolting off, he fell into slow step beside them as they continued ambling down toward the water.

"Look at him—I thought he'd run off as soon as I let him go."

Patterson couldn't resist saying, "He's like you with your tattoo—given the choice to explore, he's happier staying where he is."

Antheia stopped walking and made a face but couldn't help smiling. "Ha ha, very funny. You must be a comedian."

"Ex-comedian," he said, watching the Weimaraner. "My father had a hundred-dollar hat. This was back in the day when that was a lot of money. I used to do a routine about it. A hundred-dollar hat."

"Why are you telling me this?" Antheia took a deep, delicious breath of ocean air.

"Because of the big guy over there in the hat—it reminded me of my dad. He loved our dog Pinecone and loved really nice clothes. Tailor-made suits, Italian shoes—"

"And a hundred-dollar hat?" A gust of wind swept over them. Antheia grabbed her hat and held it on her head.

"Exactly."

She asked softly, "Did you get along with your father? Did you like him?"

"Mixed. I loved him half the time and didn't the other half."

"Why didn't?"

Patterson liked the way her English was sometimes a little off. "He could be a bully. He *was* a bully, and didn't need to be."

They were walking toward the gray dog. It still stood looking out at the water. Fellini trotted over and said hello. The big one looked down at the smaller one indifferently. It wore a bright leather collar the color of an egg yolk.

Patterson tilted his head a little to one side, like he was trying hard to hear a distant sound. "Strange."

"What's strange?"

"It's wearing a yellow collar. So did Pinecone. My Dad loved yellow things, so he had one made especially." He couldn't resist walking up to the dog and offering it the back of his hand to smell. He made no eye contact with it because his father had taught him dogs take that as a direct challenge if you do it when you first meet them. The Weimaraner sniffed the hand and gave it a gentle lick.

"He's the color of tin, Graham. Don't you think? Everything about him. Even his eyes are tin."

Patterson remembered the diner in Illinois and the waitress there who asked him to sign her book. Tin Eye.

"*Pinecone?*" He said the name half as a question, half as fact. It flew to the front of his mind and memory and then his mouth like a bat out of a cave.

The big dog kept staring at him.

This Weimaraner—Pinecone—a foot in front of him with its familiar yellow collar, Antheia saying eyes of tin, his father and the hundred-dollar hat, other disparate memories of how his old man had treated him, the Tin Eye waitress, things he'd already witnessed in his other two possible lives . . . All of it together suddenly rushed at Patterson at once, slamming into and over him with the force of an angry, forty-foot-high storm wave. It dragged him down deep into a frightening mental swirl he had never experienced before, his mind tumbling all over the place until he felt he was losing it. His life, this one—not Graham 2 or 3—*this* life's past and present engulfed him, and it felt like he was about to drown.

Most of the time, we decide which part of our life we want to dwell in or visit—the present moment, some past one, or what we hope will be next. But right then, Graham Patterson had no control over any of them or where he even wanted his mind to *be*. It was terrifying.

It stopped as suddenly as it had come.

But he was no longer standing on a California beach with Antheia Lambrinos. Instead, he was in a school classroom, and it was instantly very familiar.

Patterson was sitting at the back of a long room—a study hall with thirty desks in three rows of ten. His seat gave him a full view of everything and everyone in there. And he *knew* them. He had not seen these people for over a quarter century but knew most of them on sight. Cindy Gudger, Mary Alice DeNardo, and Janine Brindle (as gorgeous as he remembered her). Alan Creedy, Johnny Orlando, Gary Voss, and three or four others whose faces he recognized but whose names he couldn't remember. Giant Romeo Mrvic and Butch Harris sat on either side of Janine and were talking to her.

By the tight hunch of her shoulders and the way she kept her head down, it was clear she didn't like what they were saying. "Would you please just leave me *alone*? You're both *disgusting*." Romeo looked over at Butch and stuck out his tongue in delight at having gotten a reaction from the beautiful girl.

"Gentlemen, I have already asked you to be quiet and leave Miss Brindle alone. The next time, you will both go to the principal's office." Mr. Whitlock, Patterson's tenth grade math teacher, stood at the front of the room in his always impeccable blue blazer with gold buttons, a white shirt, and repp tie. He was the only teacher in school who dressed beautifully every day. That great style along with his thick Southern accent made him a figure of both derision by the bad boys ("I bet he's a fag") and speculation by everyone else. Years after graduating, Patterson heard from someone that the teacher had died.

But right now, it was twenty-five years ago at Crane's View High School, and all of the dead were alive and here—Whitlock, Romeo, Butch, and Patterson's other teenage peers. He was definitely back in his high school days.

"Would you like to take your photos now, Mr. Patterson?" Mr. Whitlock looked directly at him, pretended to bring a camera up to his eye and take a picture.

"Yeah, take a picture of me and Janine." Romeo tried putting his hand on Janine's shoulder. She immediately brushed it away and whined, "Ewww, don't touch me, creep."

Looking down, Patterson realized he still had his camera hanging around his neck. He'd brought it along that day to take pictures at the beach.

"Uh yeah, sure." He stood slowly, still getting his bearings, unsure of what to do next. How did Whitlock know his name?

Across the room, Butch Harris saved the moment for him. The tough guy stood and, in an impressive display of athleticism, leapt straight onto the top of Janine Brindle's desk. Balancing there, he pulled off his t-shirt, pounded his chest like Tarzan, and struck the classic strongman/Popeye pose—both arms up in the air, elbows bent, biceps bulging. "Take *my* picture, man!"

"*Yeah, baby!*" Romeo howled approval and punched a meaty arm in the air.

"Get off that desk!" Whitlock hollered while pointing an accusing finger at Butch. Not moving, the teen looked at the teacher, leered, and shook his head no.

Patterson raised the camera and took three quick shots of the scene—*click click click*. Turning, he photographed reactions of the other kids to the unfolding chaos in the room. Janine sprang up from her desk and scurried to the front of the room and the protection of the teacher. Head down low, Mary Alice DeNardo gathered her many books quickly and stuffed them into her schoolbag. She sat on the edge of her seat, ready to run. For a moment, she turned and looked at Patterson, face pained and scared, as if he might somehow be able to help. *Click.* In total contrast, Gary Voss was leaning back in his chair, legs stretched out in front, arms crossed and a big smile on his face, obviously enjoying the show. *Click.*

Of all the pictures Patterson took at the school that day, the one of Butch standing on the desk was the most memorable, but for a wholly unexpected reason. Harris up there, shirt off, posing like a cross between Popeye and one of the famous Italian Fascist sculptures from the 1930s surrounding the Olympic Stadium in Rome. A blur off to one side of the picture was Janine fleeing to the front of the room. But the most interesting part was the look on Romeo Mrvic's face and his body language. Patterson had no idea how he had done it, but Romeo's face was in perfect focus. The photograph captured all the joy there, the almost ecstatic happiness of the gigantic teen as he gazed lovingly up at his friend above him. Mrvic's arm was reaching out toward Harris, and the combination of the adoring look on his face and the way his arm was stretched straight out toward his friend made the whole scene look almost like a religious sculpture or painting. *The Adoration of Saint Butch.* The photograph was an impossible combination of the comic, the compelling, and the mysterious. If you didn't know who the players were and what was really going on when it happened, you might look at it and at the very least ask yourself, "What the hell is happening here?"

Mr. Whitlock was furious. He went over to the desk, and without hesitating, pulled one of Harris's legs out from under him. The kid came crashing down, luckily without breaking anything. Grabbing him up by the scruff of the neck, Whitlock marched shirtless Butch out of the room and presumably to the principal's office. Patterson then remembered the teacher had been in the Marines and sometimes told stories in class about what it was like to be in combat to illustrate a point he was making about math.

Romeo Mrvic remained in his seat with an enormous shit-eating grin on his face, as if what had just happened was all his doing and not his friend's. He caught Patterson's eye and pointed languidly to the door. "Did you see it? That's my *man.*"

Patterson nodded and made his way out of the room.

Out in the hall his nose kicked in. The smells there were immediately familiar. But why? Patterson wondered. Why do we instantly remember the smell of school hallways and classrooms if we happen to revisit them again twenty years later? Why do our brains retain these trivial details; what *use* are they? Why don't *we* get to choose what memories we keep alive—smells, sights, sounds—rather than our shadowy, inscrutable minds which often work in such puzzling ways. We remember the face of our third-grade teacher but not the face or the name of the first person we kissed. Why?

If for whatever reason Patterson was really back in his hometown during his school years, he did not want to waste whatever time he had here at Crane's View High checking out old classmates and smells.

Of course, he knew the way out of the building. He had taken it thousands of times before. In minutes, he was standing out in front, looking up and down Windsor Avenue running in front of the school, trying to decide where he wanted to go first.

Across the street and down to the right was the Mayflower Diner, everyone's after-school hangout. In the other direction, a few blocks away, was his long-ago best friend Paul Turton's house. What had happened to Paul over the years? Would his mother be home now if Patterson went and knocked on the door? Beautiful Mrs. Ruth Turton from Sedalia, Kansas. Patterson had a crush on her for years.

Home. He'd walk to his house via downtown Crane's View. It was a couple of miles from the school, but he wanted to see and remember everything about the town where he grew up. He had no idea what he'd do once he got to his boyhood home, but he was hoping an idea would come to him along the way.

The Shell gas station where he used to buy his sodas after school, Lumsden Chevrolet dealership, Stiller's Hardware. He passed them all, smiling and trailing memories like vapor trails behind him. A block later, he couldn't resist going into Suchin's stationery store. Opening the door, again the smells inside were so instantly familiar—old paper, the sweetness of fifty different brands of candy for sale, dust, sweat. Crabby Mr. Suchin behind the counter with the stub of an unlit cigar in a corner of his mouth, exactly as Patterson remembered the man from half a lifetime ago. His daughter Mona Suchin sat next to Patterson in Whitlock's geometry class and was always huffing on an asthma inhaler. Where was she now?

"Can I help you?"

Grinning and shaking his head, Patterson remembered Mr. Suchin didn't like people hanging around in his store for too long without buying anything. You had maybe five minutes before browsing time was up.

Patterson picked out a Hershey bar and a box of Good & Plenty licorice. He placed them on the counter. "Also a *New York Times*, please."

"Behind you."

Patterson turned and saw a stack of the newspapers on a table. He took one, then panicked for a few seconds, wondering if he had any money to pay for these things. Digging into his pocket, he felt the reassuring touch of paper bills. Taking them out, he peeled off a five and slid it over the counter. For another second or two, he realized his jig might be up if for some crazy reason Suchin looked closely at the bill and saw the date on it far in the future. But the storeowner barely glanced at the bill, put it in the cash drawer, and handed over the change.

"Are you from around here?"

About to leave, Patterson stopped at the door. "Excuse me?"

"You look sort of familiar, but I don't remember from where."

Patterson was pleased to be recognized, sort of, but was careful in his reply. "I used to live here when I was a kid. You have a good memory."

"So they tell me." The look on Suchin's face said as far as he was concerned, that was the end of their conversation. Patterson took the hint, gave a weak wave, and walked out.

On the sidewalk again, he shook his head in wonder at the impossibility of what had just gone on.

"*There* you are! We've been looking for you." Down the street walking toward him were Antheia and Fellini, clipped back on his leash.

Patterson gaped at them in disbelief. He put his hand on top of his head and stared incredulously as the two got closer. Antheia was smiling and looked utterly at ease here in Crane's View, New York, twenty years ago with a dog that wouldn't be born for two decades.

"How did you get here? "

She shrugged. "I have no idea. We were on the beach, and then we were here."

"How did you know where to find me?"

"I didn't. We've been walking around town since we got here trying to figure out where we are and why. But maybe I figured it out a few minutes ago, Graham. We're like the turtle in Greece. I think somehow or other, *you* brought us here from California."

Patterson wasn't having it. "But this is different—this is how this town was when I was growing up. It's something like twenty-five years ago here, Antheia!"

She took the news calmly. "I thought something was off. All the cars are old, and the women have *Charlie's Angels* haircuts. The prices in the stores are so cheap, too."

"You seem completely cool with this. How can you be so cool? *I'm* freaked out, and this is my hometown."

"Because the same sort of thing happened before to me with my husband. I'll tell you about it, but first I want something sweet to eat. Is there someplace nearby where I can get a donut or some cookies?"

The photograph Patterson took of Antheia eating a jelly donut with jealous Fellini glaring at her in the background was shot in front of Mitzi's Bakery in Crane's View in the mid 1980s. When he later made a print of the picture, he wrote PINECONE on the back, and it was one of the photos Ruth Murphy gave the biographer James Arthur years later. The photo of Romeo Mrvic reaching out to Butch Harris with the words GIANT ROMEO written on the back was also in that envelope.

———

They sat on a bus stop bench halfway between the center of town and Patterson's old house. After Mitzi's Bakery they stopped at Turco's butcher shop and bought a fat bone for Fellini, which he contentedly gnawed on while they sat on the bench and talked.

"Why didn't you tell me this before, Antheia?"

"Because I wasn't ready yet. I don't like to talk about Alexander too much. It always makes me sad."

"But this isn't only about him, it's about you and me, too."

"I know."

"So tell me exactly what happened." Patterson took a jelly donut, his first out of the bag they'd bought at the bakery. Antheia was working on her third.

"It was Alexander who thought it would be sweet if we both got the same tattoo when we were in London on that trip. I thought it was a beautiful idea and was excited to do it. I loved him so much. It was his idea, but he wanted me to choose which design. I chose—what did you call it, the breakfast tattoo?"

Patterson nodded.

"We were staying in London for a week, so we made time every afternoon to go to the tattoo parlor until they were both finished. On the last day, the woman who did them invited us to go for a cup of coffee. We thought she was just being nice and friendly. But when we got to the place, she told us the story of what the tattoo meant and what it could do. Alexander didn't believe her, so right there in the Costa Coffee he went to one of his other lives."

Patterson shook his head and said ruefully, "I did the same thing—and found out I was a gecko."

Antheia had the jelly donut up close to her mouth, about to bite it, but hearing this, she burst out laughing. The white powdered sugar on top blew all over the place. She couldn't stop laughing. Even Patterson started smiling at the ridiculousness of it all.

"Go on," he said.

Shaking her head and grinning, she lowered the donut to her lap and brushed the back of her other hand across her mouth. "Alexander's experience was very different from yours. No lizard life for him. He was one of the gym teachers at the school where I work. That's how we met. He had been there several years before me. He was a very athletic man, very fit and active. He loved his job, and loved teaching kids.

"But he had this uncle, a very successful businessman, who was opening up a chain of fitness studios all across Greece. He wanted Alexander to run the biggest one in Athens. The opportunity was amazing, and the salary was much more than he was making as a teacher. It was a very tempting offer for him for a number of reasons. We talked it over for a long time before he finally said no. Because he loved our life as it was, right *where* it was.

"When he slipped over to experience his other life that day in the café, it turned out to be what our life would have been like if he had taken the job in Athens. We would have still been together."

Patterson held up a finger to interrupt. "Wait a minute—I want to know something. When he went over to that other life, did he disappear from the café? Did he suddenly vanish or fade away?"

Antheia shook her head. "No. He was right there with us the whole time."

"When he was in both lives simultaneously, you saw *no* difference while it was happening?"

"None. The tattoo woman told me only she could tell when he was in both and not just this one. I guess it is part of the ability of the people who can make the tattoo."

"Okay, go on. What happened to him when he went over?"

"The first time?"

"Wait—you're saying he went over *more* than once to the same life?"

"Yes. The second time, he took me with him."

Patterson slid forward on the bench. His voice notched up in intensity. "But how did he *do* that? Do you remember? Because I sure as hell don't know how I brought you here now."

Antheia paused, thinking how to say it right. "I believe it happens when you lose control. Alexander did, too. He said when you're doing this life-slipping thing back and forth, there are moments when everything about it is too much, you know? Crushing. You feel like you're going mad from too much input. Whirling you around inside your own tornado, the chaos sometimes takes things with you into whatever life you're living at the moment—especially anyone who also has the tattoo, like me. Because we're on some kind of same wavelength. *That* part doesn't surprise me at all.

"The summer after we got back from London, Alexander returned to this other life for a second time. He was so confused and conflicted by what he experienced there that it just overwhelmed him. At some point his confusion was so great, it pulled *me* into his tornado with him.

"I think the same thing just happened to you. The difference is you're living in your real life. This time right now, your past, is just part of it. We all live in our past sometimes. Our memories become our present. Any life is a past, present, and future, not just a series of right nows. For whatever reason on the beach, all of it came together at once for you, and here we are." She spoke in a very serene, untroubled voice, as if satisfied with both her explanation and where they were.

In a kind of silent intermission, both of them watched as Fellini worked on his bone. A bus came by and slowed to a stop, and a woman got off. When Patterson recognized her, his back straightened, and his left hand tightened into a fist. The woman looked at Fellini and frowned.

"That dog looks like a pig! How could you live with it? I hear they're very dangerous."

Patterson said sweetly. "You don't have to worry—he only bites nice people."

"*What did you say?*" The woman was tall and steely—not used to anyone talking back to her. She had a two-hundred-and-fifty-pound husband and two sons who played varsity football, and all of them were cowed by her.

"I said he only bites nice people. You don't qualify, Alayne."

That stopped her. Who was this man? How did he know her name? Patterson knew she couldn't remember ever seeing him before and certainly not the woman sitting next to him. Her face tightened, and her eyes got beady. She was ready for battle with whoever he was. She relished confrontations.

"How do you know my name? Do I know you?"

Sneering, Patterson seemed to ignore the question. He took a bite of jelly donut and stared cold bullets right back at her, his look saying only *Fuck off.* Which was the worst thing you could do to this woman. She was used to people either cowering or running for cover when she turned her anger's high beams on them.

After swallowing, he said calmly, "Yes, I know you, Mrs. Newsome. I know all about you. The vicious gossip no one here in town likes, infamous in your small, nasty way. You mistake fear for respect, but no one really respects you.

"I know about the lies and rumors you've spread about the Patterson family, Mr. Whitlock at the school, and, worst of all, Cody Martino. You've actually had the gall to say terrible things about a kid who's severely handicapped." He turned to Antheia. "What kind of person says bad things about a handicapped child? How much lower can you go?"

"I *never* said anything about poor Cody." But her face said she did.

Patterson had to hold himself back from blowtorching her. "*Bullshit*! You told—" He almost said "my mother" but switched at the last second. "—your *son,* Charlie, the Martinos should either 'stick her in a home for retards' or at least tape ski gloves on her hands so she didn't play with herself all the time. Your words exactly, Mrs. Newsome. Verbatim."

Antheia whistled long and low in disgust while looking at this woman as if she stank. *"Malakas."*

"What did you say?" Alayne Newsome demanded.

Mrs. Newsome was dumbfounded. Who *was* this man, and how did he know these things about her? More importantly, she wondered, what *else* did he know? What about her affair? Or the fact that half an hour ago she had been at the Hostways motel three towns over with her lover, Byron? Had this stranger been waiting here at the bus stop to confront her? It couldn't be possible. She'd always been so careful since it began, that glorious afternoon two months ago in the back of his dry-cleaning shop amid metal hangers, plastic wrap, and chemical smells.

She knew people in town disliked her. So what? Until today it didn't matter, because generally, she didn't give a damn about other people's opinions. But she also knew she had enemies, always watching and waiting for ways to catch and ruin her. She'd said a lot of bad things about people here over the years, some of it true, some made up out of spite or envy.

Her paranoia growing rapidly, she turned and walked quickly away from this mysterious couple and their ugly dog. She looked back over her shoulder twice to make sure they weren't following her. If they had been, she would have started running.

Patterson and Antheia watched her go. Fellini tried to climb up on Antheia's lap, but she pushed him back down. Turning to Patterson, she asked, "What was *that* all about?"

Instead of answering, he locked his fingers behind his head and beamed like he'd just won a prize. "That felt so damned good. *So damned good!* I can't tell you how happy I am right now." He pointed down the street toward the woman. "Alayne Newsome is—*was*— one of the worst people I've ever known. Mean as a badger, a cruel, dishonest gossip, she never had a nice thing to say about anybody, including her poor family. As you heard, she even made fun of this little neighborhood girl whose brain was cooked to cinder by meningitis. Just a horrible human being, believe me. Seeing the look of dismay on her face and even some twitches of fear made my fifteen-year-old heart happy. She once said my mother kept a dirty house and it smelled in there. I never forgot that."

He pulled out his camera. "Hold on a minute—I need to take a picture of her in full retreat before she disappears. She lived two doors down from us and was always pestering or complaining to my poor mother." He swung the camera up and snapped off a bunch of pictures of ant-sized Mrs. Newsome, way far down the sidewalk, scurrying toward the safety of her unhappy home.

He set the camera aside. "Tell me about what happened when your husband took you into his second life."

"It was beautiful. We had a wonderful apartment, much bigger and airier than the one we had been living in. It was near one of Athens' open-air markets, so I was able to shop there every day and cook the freshest things. I love to cook. Alexander liked his new job very much. It gave him opportunities he had never had before. But the best part, of course, was I was pregnant there. It was all joyous."

Patterson winced on hearing she was pregnant in this other life, remembering her husband was dead. He didn't know if it was right to ask but decided to anyway. "Did you . . . did you want to have children?"

"Oh, very much! We had always planned to—" Her voice fell away.

"Listen, I'm sorry for asking. I didn't mean to . . . It must have been very hard for you afterward . . . "

"*Afterward*? You mean after Alexander died? Yes and no. The yes part is obvious, but the no part—" She looked down at Fellini and slowly stroked his head a while before answering. "Because he died, I never got a chance to know what it would have been like to have children with my man. But for that short time we were together in his second life, I did. Or at least, I got to know what it was like to be pregnant with him. I loved it, especially because it *was* his.

"Remember your 'ice cream question'? This was a little like that. For a magical time, I experienced what it was like to carry my Alexander's child inside me. It is one of the greatest memories.

"One day I was shopping at our outdoor market. Suddenly a thought came to me so strongly I almost stumbled from the force of it. I touched my stomach and said out loud, *I will never be alone again.* It was the most satisfying, *spiritual* feeling, Graham. I will never forget it. I had our baby inside me, and I knew as long as I did, I would never be alone again, no matter what else happened.

"So in that case, I *did* taste the best ice cream in the world for a while. At least, the best for me. My ice cream dream. It's part of the reason why I was so angry when he died, because I'll never be able to have this joy again with Alexander. If I *do* meet and fall in love with another man, I'm hoping those beautiful memories won't spoil any new relationship . . . " She shook her head, made a face, and began petting the dog again. "I'm lying—I am totally afraid it *will* affect my feelings toward someone new. But I hope not."

Another bus passed by, this time without stopping. It was old, made lots of noise, and blatted out a thick gray-black murk of exhaust smoke. Fellini sneezed.

"I don't know how to ask this right or diplomatically, Antheia, so I'm just going to ask straight out. If you don't want to answer I totally understand, but I've got to ask: If things were so great in that other life, and it sure sounds like both of you had exactly what you wanted, why didn't you two stay there?"

She answered immediately. "Because it wasn't *our* life, Graham. It wasn't the real life we'd already made together. It was one we would have made if we had chosen differently, but we didn't. It was B, and we'd already made A together. At the time, both of us were very happy living A. When Alexander was offered the job in Athens, we talked about it for weeks before deciding no.

"It was interesting to see how well B would have worked out, and lovely to know it for a while. But the whole experience was like living in someone else's beautiful house. The fact I would have gotten pregnant if we had moved to Athens is the only regret I have about not having done it. I didn't regret the choice when Alexander was alive because we were certain one day soon I'd get pregnant in *our* life, where we were both very content in the beautiful house we had built together." She stood up. "Let's go. You said your home is close?"

As they were walking, she asked Patterson what his special password was. He knew what she meant but hesitated to tell her. What if divulging it was taboo? What if you were supposed to keep it secret?

"Alexander's was *Magkas*. It means tramp in Greek. That was the name of—"

"His first dog?"

"Yes. Yours too? The name of your first dog?"

"Yes. It's Pinecone."

She thought a moment. "In Greek, pinecone is *koukounaries*."

"Koukou *what?*"

"Koukounaries. There is your Greek lesson for the day—magkas and koukounaries. Tramp and pinecone. When people learn a new language, they often learn the dirty words first. But not you."

He thought a moment and then said, "Magkas Koukounaries sounds like the name of some Greek shipping magnate: Stavros Niarchos. Magkas Koukounaries."

"Yes, it sort of does."

A few minutes later, Patterson slowed to a stop and frowned. "Something's wrong." He looked left and right several times as if searching.

"What? What's wrong?"

"The Gioe house. It's not here." He pointed to a modern house of glass and steel just down the street. "That place—it's where the Gioe house used to be. Their's was a kind of beat-up saltbox, as I remember it—not that modern thing."

"What are you talking about, Graham?"

"The Gioes were our neighbors. Their son Tony and I used to walk to school together. Their house was right there, but it's gone now. The glass one is there instead. What happened to their house? I don't understand this." He walked quickly until he was facing the unfamiliar building across the street. He shook his head but said nothing. He started walking again, Antheia and Fellini following. A few doors down he stopped in front of another house. He let out his breath in a loud rush, as if he had been holding it for some time. As if afraid of what he would find when he got to this spot.

"This is our place, my house, where I grew up. But I don't understand it. Why is everything in town just as it was when I was a kid, except for the Gioes' house? It's gone."

"Graham, you said something before that's been bothering me, but I didn't want to talk about it yet. Maybe it has to do with this."

"What was it?"

"Remember you were describing what happened before, when you were in the classroom? How the teacher knew your name and asked if you wanted to start taking pictures? How did he know who you were now, as an adult? And how did he know you wanted to take pictures there?"

"I don't know. I was too shocked by where I was and what had just happened to pay attention to anything specific at that point. But you're right. How *did* he know who I was? I had him as a math teacher when I was fifteen, sure, but that was over twenty-five years ago. I doubt I look the same now as I did back then."

Fellini was pulling on the leash. Antheia bent over and pushed his butt down. "And even if you did look the same, he would have freaked out seeing one of his students was suddenly a forty-year-old man and not fifteen from one day to the next. No, I believe something else was going on, Graham."

"Like what?"

They heard a door close. A woman came out of Patterson's old house. He didn't recognize her. Walking toward the street, she took a bundle of keys out of her purse and used them to open the driver's side door of an orange Chevrolet station wagon parked in front of the house. She glanced at Patterson and Antheia while opening it.

Patterson called out to her. "Excuse me?"

"Yes?"

"Are the Pattersons home?"

She looked surprise to hear the name. "The *Pattersons*? Wow, no, they haven't lived here for a long time. We bought the house from them two years ago. As I remember, I think they moved to Dobbs Ferry, but I'm not sure."

"And the Gioes?"

"Who?" She looked at her car, obviously wanting to be gone.

"The Gioes—they live at 185 across the street—where that modern house with all the glass is now?"

"I don't know anyone named Gioe. The family at 185 is named Jennings. Our children play together. Sorry I can't be of more help." After throwing up both hands and shrugging helplessly, she got into her car. She started it and pulled out onto the street. Something was wrong with the muffler, and the Chevrolet was loud driving away.

"Hastings."

Antheia turned to him "What?"

"Hastings—it's a town. My parents moved there from here, not to Dobbs Ferry. I need to do something. You can stay here—I'll be right back." Without waiting for her to reply, he crossed the street and walked to the modern house where the Gioes used to be. He rang the doorbell. A few moments, later a woman answered. She stood inside the house while they spoke.

On the sidewalk, Fellini started pulling on the leash again. Antheia took the bone out of her bag and gave it to him. Across the street, the woman in the doorway laughed at something Patterson said and brushed a lock of hair off her face. What was going on? Why did he want to talk to her?

The two shook hands, she went back inside, and he returned, the expression on his face a mystery.

"What's going on, Graham?"

Picking up the dog's bone, he handed it to her and took the leash. "Let's go. I'll tell you as we walk."

But he said nothing for a long time. Antheia was all right with his silence because she was mulling things over, too.

He spoke quietly, measuring his words. "We moved from here when I was sixteen. My parents sent me away to private school that year because I was messing up. They were afraid I'd end up working on a garbage truck or something. I did my last two years at this very traditional prep school in Connecticut, which I hated, and it hated me. The worst time of my life. I failed out of there twice before they let me crawl back in and graduate.

"Years later, someone told me a few months after we moved out, the Gioes' house burned down and they left town, too, because Mr. Gioe got a new job in Oregon." He stopped to look at Antheia and hiked a thumb back over his shoulder toward where they'd just been. "I *knew* their house was gone, but I'd forgotten. It happened twenty-six years ago. All of this was part of my life, but who remembers everything? My father used to say memory is like an attic where old dusty boxes full of useless, forgotten crap are stored.

"And you know what else? What I've seen so far here? It's all from my past, but some of it I never knew or saw because my family had already moved away from here. The kids I recognized at school today stayed, and so did horrible Mrs. Newsome. The Gioes' house burned down, and another family moved into our place. All of it happened while I was away at private school.

"What happens on the other side of any door after we close it? Life still goes on over there, we're just not around to witness it. This was my town when I was a kid, but what we've been seeing today is the town after I left.

"I also think Mr. Whitlock knew who I was back at the school because somehow, some way, I'm experiencing my *whole* life—past, present, and future. I can even see what happened here in my old hometown after my family left. It's all part of *this* life, Graham 1, the one I'm living right now. But all mixed together, like a tossed salad.

"You and the dog are from my present, but the town and everyone here is my past. To top it off, somehow or other taking pictures is going to be part of my future. That's what I think. Does it make any kind of sense to you?" He looked at Antheia imploringly.

She shrugged. "Why not? It's as good an explanation as any. After my experience with Alexander in Athens, I believe anything is possible."

"You don't think I'm nuts?"

"Everything is nuts about this situation, Graham. Our tattoo is a magic lamp. It makes impossible things happen, whether we like them or not. We've seen it again and again—in my life, Alexander's, and now yours."

"How did your husband bring you both back from the life in Athens to the one you'd been living?"

"He said his dog's name, and the number one."

"Nothing else?" Patterson couldn't believe it was so simple.

"No. But by doing it, he used the second of his four return visits to our life. "

"I can return us to my normal life by saying my word and the number one. Because my life does not include moving in and out of the past and future, like now. No, this here is a mishmash version of my life. If you're right, we can escape it with the words." He rubbed his hands together to get some heat back in them. His confusion had turned them icy cold. "Neither of us want to stay here. But if you don't mind, there are a few more things I'd like to see before I try to get us back."

———

"Where are we going?" She was growing a little impatient. They'd been walking a long time.

"Did you have a serious boyfriend when you were in school?"

"Yes, of course. Vasilis. Vasilis Katsavou. He was a very tall boy, tall and sweet—a basketball player. Why do you ask?"

"Because we're going to my old girlfriend's house."

Antheia perked up. "Really? How romantic. What was her name?"

"Carson Schreiner."

"Were you two in furious love?"

Patterson smiled. "I guess as furious as teenagers can be."

"Were you her first? Was she yours?"

Even after all these years, he still felt shy answering that question, as if saying yes would somehow retroactively smear Carson's high school reputation. He said hesitantly, "I was. She wasn't."

"She wasn't what?"

"My first." He purposely looked straight ahead, fully aware Antheia was watching for his reaction.

"Were you kind to her?"

Taken aback by the question, Patterson hesitated. "I hope so. As I remember, I tried to be." He felt a small flutter of apprehension in his heart, thinking back a quarter century to the night in Carson's basement playroom where the big event happened. *Had* he been kind? He remembered wearing English Leather cologne and new Bass Weejun loafers he'd bought specifically for this occasion. Shoes he could slip off and on quickly. He remembered planning his outfit for that night down to the smallest detail . . .

Antheia said, "Vasilis was my first, too." She grinned and shook her head, remembering. "I wouldn't let him use a condom the first time we did it because I wanted to know what it really felt like to have sex without a rubber chaperone on his *poulaki.*"

"His *what?*"

"Poulaki. His . . . what do you call it in English . . . his *dick.* Poulaki in Greek means little bird. I think the whole thing scared him, though, poor boy. But I really liked it—right from the beginning, I've always been crazy for sex."

Patterson didn't know what to say to that one, but luckily Carson Schreiner's house was in sight by then. He pointed to it and stepped up his pace. Antheia and Fellini hurried to follow.

"What are you going to do when we get there?"

"Ring the bell and hope someone is home."

"And then what? What are you going to say, Graham?"

"I don't know yet. First I want to see who opens the door."

Patterson rang the bell and took two big steps back so as to give whoever answered space to check him out.

The door was opened by a pleasant looking middle-aged woman with beautiful strawberry blond hair that came to her shoulders. Her freckled face blossomed into a huge smile when she recognized him. Delighted, she put her hands on her cheeks. "Oh Graham, you *came*! I'm so glad. I thought it was a crazy shot in the dark, writing to you out of the blue like that after all these years. I didn't even think you'd get my letter. But my God, here you are. You came!"

Patterson and Antheia glanced at each other, stunned.

"Come in, come in—please. You don't know how happy it makes me to see you." Suddenly embarrassed, she put a hand over her mouth and took a step toward Antheia. "Oh, I'm so sorry for being rude. I'm Carson."

"Hello. I am Antheia."

"Please come in, both of you." She bent over Fellini and stroked his head once. "You, too. I know someone who's going to be very happy to see you." Turning, she entered the house.

Patterson clapped once and said, "Here we go. This should be interesting." Antheia and Fellini followed him in.

Moments after Carson closed the door, a giant Weimaraner came bounding full speed down the long front hall toward them. It looked so much like Pinecone that his first reaction was to touch a nearby wall to steady himself against the sight of this déjà vu dog in his old girlfriend's house. Ignoring the humans, it went right up to the much smaller bull terrier and said hello, tail wagging furiously. Fellini, the cooler of the two, didn't move while being checked out except for his tail, which flew back and forth like a windshield wiper on high speed.

Carson touched Patterson on his elbow. "Doesn't he remind you of someone you used to know?"

Patterson looked at her blankly.

"I fell in love with Pinecone the first time I met him at your house and have had Weimaraners ever since. Curly here is the fourth."

"*Curly*? You named a short-haired dog Curly?"

"No, my son did. Curly is the chubby one in The Three Stooges with the bald head who makes the crazy noises. This guy makes noises, too. Come on in." She walked down the hallway, followed by the small parade of humans and canines.

The living room was nothing like Patterson remembered. He'd spent a lot of time in there as a teenager. Back then, it was a cozily packed jumble of a well-worn comfortable sofa, too many mismatched chairs, and a giant faded Oriental carpet covering most of the floor. Carson's mother was an untalented, albeit enthusiastic, sculptor and ceramicist. Where there wasn't furniture, her works of various sizes and shapes were scattered here and there throughout the room. She had two rambunctious sons who were always wrestling or horsing around with each other and, in the process, continually breaking their mother's artwork—which didn't seem to faze her at all. "It's only clay, boys. Let's just take care not to break the important things."

The Schreiner living room he entered now was completely different from the one he had once known so well. The wooden floor was bare and polished to a gloss. In the middle of the room were clustered a sleek black leather couch, a low coffee table made from weathered railroad ties and steel beams, and two black matching Barcelona chairs facing it. The walls were white and bare. At first glance, Patterson thought it was beautiful but anonymous. There was not a trace of coziness or warmth. He thought it looked like a successful architect's waiting room.

Amused by Patterson's expression, his old girlfriend watched him looking around and said, "It's a little different in here than when we were kids, eh?"

"Carson, is it really you?"

She nodded slowly and sighed. "It's me, Graham, one hundred percent. Do I look so different? I'm almost afraid to ask. It's been what, twenty years since we saw each other? More! You look pretty much the same. I could still pick you out of a police lineup." She grinned and patted the cushion next to her. "Come, sit down. I have so much to tell you."

Patterson sat on the couch. Antheia took one of the chairs, while Fellini stood guard next to her keeping an eye on Curly, who stood a few respectful feet away, tail still wagging at warp speed.

"Do you want the long version or the short?"

Patterson said, "Start with the short."

"I graduated from high school here, went away to my second-choice college in Boston, where I met my husband Steve. Got pregnant junior year and was married right before my son was born. After college, Steve was accepted into business school in Philadelphia. We lived there three years. I got pregnant again with my daughter. While working on his degree, Steve partnered with a medical student and a computer whiz. Together they invented a computer app used in pharmacies everywhere today. It immediately took off like a rocket and made them a ton of money very fast. But our marriage died when dear husband met someone he liked more than me. He left us for her, but the divorce cost him a bundle."

She was about to continue when a teenage girl who looked spookily like the young Carson Schreiner Patterson dated decades before entered the room carrying a large paperback book. Without saying a word she went to the couch, sat down next to him and put the book in his lap. She did not look at him.

The feeling in the room suddenly grew tense. The balance of moments ago was thrown off, both by her appearance and her strange silent action. Both Patterson and Antheia looked at Carson to see if she would say something about it. Curly walked over and gently rested his big silvery brown head on the girl's knee. She put a hand on top of it but did not pet him. He seemed content with her touch and didn't move.

Antheia stared at the girl. From years of teaching and observing kids that age, right away she guessed what was probably wrong. She also knew it was not her place to say anything about it unless the mother chose to.

Long seconds passed with nobody moving. Eventually the girl reached over and tapped on the book three times with the bottom of her closed fist, as if knocking on a door. Patterson glanced at Carson, whose face watching was a smash of love, sadness, and anguish in one.

She spoke gently. "This is my daughter Roxanne. We call her Roxy. She wants you to look at the book with her."

Patterson turned to the silent girl to see if this was true. She remained expressionless, but when he didn't move, she reached over and rapped on the book again, this time making a high, harsh sound in her throat.

He looked at the cover for the first time and was surprised to see it was a book he also owned: The Family of Man: The greatest photographic exhibition of all time—503 pictures from sixty-eight countries—created by Edward Steichen and Carl Sandburg for The Museum of Modern Art.

"It's Roxy's book, Graham. She loves photographs. They're her favorite thing in the world. She loves looking at them together with people. Would you do it with her for just a few minutes? You don't have to say anything, she'll let you know when to turn the page. It would make her very happy. Then I'll explain."

"Sure, of course." Patterson slowly opened the book. The girl slid closer to him and bent way over so her face was almost directly above the page. While they looked at the pictures together, she never lifted or turned her head. She was so close he could smell her clean hair.

Fellini, bored, plunked down on the floor with a loud grunt.

Antheia, sitting patiently in her chair, realized Carson was looking at her, intrigued, most likely trying to figure out the connection between her and Patterson. She caught the other's eye and said, "We're just friends. Nothing more."

Embarrassed, Carson sat back on the couch and opened her mouth to speak.

Antheia waved her off. "It's fine. I understand." Tipping her chin in the direction of Patterson and the girl, she asked quietly, "What level is she?"

Carson looked surprised.

Antheia said, "I teach kids her age. I've had students like Roxy."

Understanding, Carson nodded and said without hesitation, "Two."

Patterson looked up from the book. "Level of what?"

"Autism."

To the women's surprise, he didn't appear fazed or turn to the girl to look at her after having learned this new information.

"Does she speak?"

"Not really. She lets us know what she wants in a variety of ways, but it's almost entirely nonverbal. She'll tap the book when she wants you to turn the page. About half the time she makes it pretty clear what she wants and doesn't want."

"What happens when you don't understand?"

Carson smirked. "Then things get a little wild around here. It's one of the reasons why I have Curly—dogs calm her when she gets frazzled. Understanding her sometimes is like tying water in a knot."

Patterson frowned. He'd heard that singular phrase somewhere before and it had stuck. How unusual for Carson to say the same thing.

"And your son? How does he deal with this?"

"He's away at college. He's always been good with her. He's a very caring person."

Roxy tapped the book with two fingers and Patterson turned the page. She tapped it again very quickly.

"She doesn't like that picture, Graham."

"So I noticed." He smiled and turned to the famous photograph "Migrant Mother" by Dorothea Lange. Pointing to it with his thumb, he said to Roxy, "This one is really famous. I like it. But you know what I like best about this book? It's got over five hundred pictures in it and is probably the most famous photography book around. But half of the pictures are by amateurs."

"*Is that true?*" Carson was amazed, particularly after having looked at the renowned photos in the book dozens of times over the years with her daughter.

"Yup. To me it's one of the really interesting things that sets photography apart from other art forms—you don't have to be famous or even talented to make a great picture. In some cases, never having touched a camera before, people have created masterpieces. You just have to be at the right place at the right time and have a good eye—and a lot of luck, obviously."

"Is that why you got into it?"

"Into what?"

"Photography. You *are* kind of famous for it, Mr. Patterson."

He stared long at her, then at Antheia, whose smile turned quickly into a quick laugh.

"I *am*?"

"Uh, yes, Graham. You don't have to be modest about it here—you're among friends." Carson made a funny face at him, a face she used to make when they were teens. Seeing it now instantly flashed him back to those days.

"It's why I got in touch with you and am so grateful you came. I mean, of course I'm glad to see you *anyway* after all these years, but the fact you came because of my letter . . . " She stopped and looked away. There were tears on her cheeks when she turned to him again. "I can't express how much it means to me, and I'm sure Roxy, too, if she could tell you."

Patterson didn't know what to say because he didn't know what the hell she was talking about. When he snuck a glance at Antheia for help, she gave him only a little shrug that said don't ask me.

"I want to show you something. I'll be back in a minute." Carson stood and left the room. Roxy patted the book. Patterson turned the page like a robot.

"I guess you're famous in the future, Graham. That's exciting."

He shook his head in despair. "For *what*? My whole life is now officially gravity-less."

"Be calm. Just ask her *why* you're famous and go from there."

"Go *where*, Antheia? Right now, my life, this number one Patterson life, is happening in all three time zones—past, present, and future. How am I supposed to deal with it and not go nuts? Maybe I already *am* nuts, and all this is just-—"

Roxy tapped the book and made a sound. He assumed she wanted him to look and stop talking to Antheia.

Carson came back carrying a picture frame. They couldn't see what was in it because it was turned toward her body. She stopped and said, "As soon as the settlement money came in from my divorce I bought this signed print, Graham. It was crazy expensive, but I had to have it. When my parents died and left me the house, I decided to move back in with the kids to get away from everything that had to do with my old life with Steve. I wanted this picture to be the first new thing inside our new home for so many good reasons." She went over to Patterson and turned the frame around. It was the photograph he had taken of Anna Mae Collins's mother's scarred hand serving him her tomato soup.

"Holy shit! Can I see that?" He closed Roxy's book and put it in his lap. Carson handed him the frame and stepped back. He took it in unsteady hands and stared in wonder at the photograph he had so casually taken that night in North Carolina what felt like a long time ago. The image had obviously been enhanced by a pro who knew exactly what to highlight and what to fade into the background. It was as if a photo he took had been given to a gifted makeup artist who transformed it from the mundane into a movie star.

Antheia got up from her chair and walked around behind the couch so she could see what he held. "Wow! It's beautiful. So sad and beautiful at the same time."

The print was not large—maybe ten inches by fourteen. The frame was brushed aluminum and looked very expensive. The matte around the photo was a dark gray, which perfectly complemented the vivid reds and white in the photo.

Carson said, "I must tell you a story about it. The day Steve announced he was leaving, we were in a restaurant in New York having lunch. It was his crass idea of the perfect setting for letting me down gently. When he was finished sticking his dagger into my heart, without saying a word I stood right up and left the fancy-shmancy place. I was so angry I could have blasted right through a steel wall.

"I don't know how long I walked, but I ended up in Chelsea staring in the front window of the Mary Miller Gallery." She paused and looked at Patterson as if he should say something or show recognition at the name. He didn't, because he had no idea what she was talking about.

"This photo was on display, along with two others of yours. But this was the one I immediately loved. The ravaged hand offering a bowl of the most basic but delicious soup . . . It reminded me of a favorite line from a novel I once read: 'I'll cook you soup and hold your hand.'

"I know everyone interprets things differently, but to me the picture has always said no matter how damaged or ruined our life gets, there's always things in it somewhere to save us if we are just open to them, whether it's a person, a crazy hope, or even something as basic and nourishing as a bowl of tomato soup. Seeing it right after the ghastly lunch with Steve saved me—it really did, Graham. I had no idea who the photographer was who took it, but I knew I had to find out.

"Since it was such a bizarre day I went straight into the gallery, which is not something I normally do, and talked to the owner about it. Imagine my shock when she told me *you* were the photographer and were quite famous. She was sort of aghast I'd never heard of the renowned Graham Patterson, my old boyfriend!

"I couldn't believe it. The wise guy who used to tell jokes all the time and made me feel like a million bucks." She pointed at him and said enthusiastically to Antheia, "He was a *great* boyfriend."

Patterson kept looking at the picture, shaking his head in both wonder and disbelief. He knew he had taken it—he remembered the moment he raised the camera and focused the lens on Uschi Collins' scarred hand serving the soup. But the original shot was still on the first memory card he slid into his camera the day he bought it. A few days ago, back in his real life he'd replaced the card with a new one, but he'd never downloaded or printed any of the photographs on the first.

"You should have heard the gallery owner swoon on about you, Graham. She said you're not only a great artist but also a master at manipulating, framing, and visually elevating whatever your subject happens to be. I love that she used the word elevate. It's exactly what I feel when I look at this picture in particular." She sat down next to him and touched his hand. "It's why I contacted you, although I really never believed you'd respond, much less actually *come* here after all these years. It's wonderful Graham, so generous of you to do it."

Clueless and uncomfortable because he had absolutely no idea what Carson was talking about, he didn't want to make things worse by asking.

Luckily, Antheia saved him. "Graham didn't say why we were coming here today, just that I would like it. Could you tell me now?" She walked back around the couch and sat again in the chair facing them.

Roxy reached over and ran her left hand back and forth several times across the photograph, humming loudly while doing it. Carson looked at Patterson to see if he minded. He made a smile he hoped said it was not a problem.

"As you can see, my daughter loves photographs. Looking at them together is one of the only things I can do with her where I feel we're in any sort of contact and really communicating on some level.

"Since discovering Graham's work, I've been searching for it everywhere. I'm completely smitten. Even if I didn't know you, I'd be a fan. It fits into my soul. You capture such a beautiful range of feelings. From one picture to the next, I never know how I'm going to react when I see them for the first time. It's definitely part of the kick for me with your work—the never-knowingness.

"This picture—'The Queen of Tomato Soup'—makes me glad and grateful to be alive, but the next one I see could very well make me cringe and want to hide my eyes. One of my other favorites is 'Mr. Breakfast' because it's so haunting, sad, and beautiful all at the same time."

"*Mr. Breakfast*? He has a picture with that name?" Antheia looked at Patterson who'd lowered his head and was slowly rubbing his forehead with the flat heel of his hand. Roxy liked the gesture and started doing it too.

"Yes, I think it's one of his best. I wanted to buy a print of it, too, but I guess it's a very limited edition, and copies cost a fortune. I'm waiting for the book to come out and hoping a print of it will be in there."

"Book?"

"Yes, Graham's book—I read Taschen is going to publish it?" Carson glanced at Patterson for confirmation. He looked back at her blankly. "Anyway, after I bought this print, I got the crazy idea to write you and send it in care of the gallery. And it obviously worked, because here you are!

"In my letter I asked if he would photograph Roxy," she explained to Antheia. "It would be something I'd treasure for the rest of my life, and I know she'd love it, too. I'll pay whatever you charge for a portrait—"

"Carson—"

"No, really—I can pay. As I said, my divorce settlement set us up. I've also invested well and—"

Without thinking, Patterson said, "I would never charge you for taking a picture. You were my girlfriend, for God's sake." He grinned for the first time in minutes, relieved to hear this was all she wanted from him. No big deal—he'd take a bunch of pictures of the girl and let her mom choose which one she liked best.

Carson leaned over and hugged him. She hadn't expected any of this, yet here he was in her living room saying yes so easily to a dream she'd held ever since seeing and falling in love with his photograph the first time in the gallery window.

She didn't reveal to him, and didn't think she ever would, why it really meant so much to have a picture of her still-healthy child taken by a great artist who, by happy coincidence, was an old friend. Now that Graham said yes, it was unnecessary and unfair to burden him with talk about the Huntington's disease and what it was already beginning to do to her poor daughter.

Two hours later, Patterson had photographed a surprisingly cooperative Roxy all over the house. Finally, they moved with the dogs to the backyard. By then, Curly and Fellini were great pals and scampered around after each other all over the place. Roxy stood in the middle of the yard watching them.

Being in that yard again after so many years brought back a ton of memories for Patterson. "I remember how your father loved to grill over there near the shed. The biggest steaks I ever saw. And your mother with a glass of iced tea in her hand."

"Always fortified, of course." Carson raised her eyebrows.

"What do you mean?"

"Graham, you didn't *know*? Mom's iced tea was always laced with a big wallop of rum. She called it fortified tea."

He took in the info, and somehow it made the memory sweeter. "Maybe so, but fortified or not, I remember she was really fun to be around."

"You're only saying that because she laughed at your jokes."

"Probably." Holding the camera up in front of his face, he tracked Roxy on the screen as she slowly crossed the large yard following the racing dogs.

It had begun to drizzle. The three adults stood under the eaves of the back porch, watching the lively action in the yard. The great shot came a few minutes later.

Arms crossed over her chest, Antheia said while watching Roxy, "There is a Greek word to perfectly describe this moment for me— *xarmolipi*. Basically, it means joyful sadness. A contradiction in terms, I know, but it says exactly how I feel looking at your daughter out there with the dogs. It's wonderful but breaks my heart at the same time, knowing what I do about her."

Carson touched her lips, then took the hand away, as if part of her wanted to respond to Antheia but another part wanted her to keep quiet. Instead she said, "There's a *lot* of xarmolipi going on in this house these days, believe me."

The dogs played their game of whirling, racing, leaping tag. Roxy started chasing after them, arms waving, laughing a halting, strangled laugh. The rain came down in a misty curtain. The air smelled of cut grass, wet earth, and wood.

Carson knew there was no way she could get her child to stop and come out of the rain, especially when she was so wound up and joyful in her singular way. Roxy did not like to be touched or inter-rupted when she was deeply involved in anything. You never knew if she understood when you tried to give her instructions or an order. She very much existed in her own mysterious world, which only oc-casionally intersected—and even more rarely fit together like a puzzle piece—with her mother's. Better to leave her alone now and not risk a scene or one of the awful, uncontrollable tantrums that so often left Carson feeling exhausted, hopeless, and bleakly depressed. Let the girl have her rain dance with the dogs. She could dry off later when their guests had gone.

The women talked about special needs children and teaching. Patterson stepped out into the yard, shooting picture after picture of the girl and the dogs from every angle. Roxy fluttered around like a bird taking a bath in a puddle. There was so much motion, energy, and happiness in the interplay between the three of them. He felt if he could capture *that,* then surely somewhere in all of the shots he took there would be a bit of magic in at least a few.

Carson said he was (going to be) a famous photographer. How could that be? He'd had the camera only a few months. And sure, he'd taken a lot of pictures with it, but so what? He hadn't even printed any of them yet. Seeing and hearing the story of the framed, reworked shot of Uschi Collins serving tomato soup was an amaz-ing, thrilling surprise. But looking at it felt like an out of body experience for Patterson: *I* took that picture? It's so powerful—did I really?

The phrase "tying water in a knot" kept knocking around in his thoughts as he photographed the girl playing with the dogs. He didn't know why it stayed with him, but he had a feeling it was significant, or applicable in some way to the events of today and what he had seen and learned.

The idea came to him in a flash. As the three romped around a few feet away from him, Patterson bellowed, "*Roxy!*" and—click click click—fired off a fast burst of shots that caught them all in the air whipping their heads around, staring with wide-eyed surprise at him, all with what looked like huge grins on their faces. Roxy's arms were raised up next to her ears, fingers outstretched and pointing toward the dogs. She looked exactly like a magician or witch casting a spell on the animals. The misty rain added a kind of shimmering curtain between the camera and the three jumpers.

Click click click . . .

Up on the porch, Carson groaned, "*Oh no!*" as soon as Patterson shouted the name. Without hesitating, she hurried onto the lawn and over to Roxy, who stood stock still now, hands in tight fists pressed to her sides, eyes closed, mouth open as wide as it would go.

"What happened? What's the matter?" Patterson shook his head, alarmed and confused.

Carson got up close to Roxy, face to face, but didn't touch her. She spoke in a very quiet voice he could barely hear. "She hates loud noises. They set her off, especially loud human voices. Even someone shouting down the block can do it sometimes."

Patterson winced, helpless in his guilt. "Oh God, I'm so sorry."

Not taking her eyes off the girl, Carson shook her head to say it was not his fault—he couldn't have known.

"Is there anything I can do? I'm so sorry. I can't—"

"It's all right, Graham. But you'd better go now. Stuff like this can make her do crazy things. I never know how she's going to react or how long it will take before she's okay again. I need to be alone with her."

"*Shit!* I'm so sorry."

Eyes still closed, Roxy started rocking her head from side to side like a pendulum while repeating the word in a very strange, deep voice. "*Shiiiiiiiiiiiiiiiit . . .* " It was the first time she had said an actual word since they'd arrived.

"Can you find your way out? I need to stay here with her now."

"Sure. Of course. Carson—"

"It's okay, Graham. It's happened many times before. Listen, it's so good you came. Thank you. I'm proud to have lived on the outskirts of your life for a little while."

Distraught, he looked away. "I'll send you pictures." Feeling stupid and totally responsible for this mess, he held up the camera with both hands and kind of shook it as proof there was treasure inside.

She tried to smile but failed. "Please do." Patterson's old girlfriend patted his arm and turned back to her daughter. He called Fellini over and walked toward the house.

Antheia only heard part of what was said but could tell none of it was good. Climbing the three steps to the porch, he brushed by her on the way to the front door and grumbled, "Let's go."

"Graham?"

"Come on, where's his leash? I'll explain outside."

Big Gray Hat

Looking at the dismal food on the tray in front of her, old Ruth Murphy grimaced and sighed. Hot mud, leaden chicken nuggets, and creamed corn for dinner. Again. Hot mud was her name for the tepid black bean soup served at her retirement home. Granted, some of the food there *was* tasty. The bread was good, fresh baked, usually, and most of the desserts, which tended to be over-sweet. But that was okay because Ruth liked sweet, savory, or spicy foods. Anything that made her tongue jump and think. Sadly, the people who ran this place seemed to go on the assumption old people lost most of their tastebuds along with their teeth (and everything else) on the way to their wheelchairs, oxygen masks, and finally the Great Beyond.

She knew they were right. But for God's sake, who needed to be reminded of this bleak fact three times a day in the form of bland, flavorless, *soft* food? Oh, for the crunchy first bite of just-fried chicken, the lavish lemony tang of Béarnaise sauce, or the heft and five strong flavors smooshed gloriously together in a hot pastrami sandwich on rye bread with coleslaw and Russian dressing, a Polish dill pickle that *snapped* when you bit into it, and a cream soda to wash it all down! She should have asked James Arthur to bring her some kind of wicked-for-every-inch-of-the-body fast food when he came to visit earlier. I'll answer any questions if you bring me a Big Mac with large fries and a chocolate milkshake. Not that she could have eaten much of it. But a few bites and sips would surely have lifted her spirits.

Why had she lied to the interviewer? He seemed like a nice man, and his enthusiasm for any stories or tidbits about her history with Graham was touching. So why *had* she lied to him and said she could see four of Graham's invisible photographs when, of course, she couldn't? No one could, or no one *had* who'd looked at them before. After tricking him into thinking he was the only one who had ever seen Pinecone, she gave Arthur the photographs to take with him, hoping she'd live long enough for this young man to return one day and describe the other four to her. Because anyone who could do that would also be able to tell her what had really happened to the love of her life after he left her life, so many years before.

Long ago, when she'd received the photos in the mail from Graham, part of his letter accompanying them briefly explained what was on each of the—to her—blank sheets of paper. When the biographer described "Pinecone" to her earlier today, she was impressed by his enthusiastic response and comments about it. Maybe, finally, here was the person who would be able to find out what had really happened to Graham after he went away, disappearing first into fame and later into complete mystery.

She had lied about that to the biographer as well—telling him she had wanted no contact with Patterson after they broke up. Of course she had. But he never returned, and whatever she later learned about him she got from newspapers and magazine articles, like the rest of the world. Now and then, in the beginning, he sent a postcard, but they said nothing he wouldn't have written to anyone. She hated those postcards. She longed to receive them.

Ruth had no idea whether they would have spent their whole lives together if things had worked out differently between them. Back then she wanted children, but Patterson didn't. He wanted to be a famous comedian, but she was intuitive and savvy enough to know from watching him perform so many times that he didn't have the special human alchemy needed to make it happen.

Years after they broke up, she married a perfectly nice man who had some of the same qualities as Graham but none of the special ones that had sealed Patterson permanently into her heart. But her sweet husband wanted children too, and that more than anything convinced her to settle down with him. They had a son, Kevin, who despite all the love and care both of them gave him grew up to be a thoroughly unpleasant, selfish man who didn't even attend his father's funeral. Ruth assumed he wouldn't attend hers, either, when the time came, but by now she was so inured to Kevin's shitty behavior that the thought didn't hurt as much as it could have.

Her husband had been successful in business and left enough money for her to live comfortably for years. She moved into the retirement home after ruefully admitting to herself her memory was developing holes in it like cheesecloth. She had this terrible, frightening image of some bad day in the future standing in the middle of a sidewalk somewhere in nothing but her bathrobe, not having the slightest idea where she was or how she got there. Because her old brain had finally turned on her and become the enemy. No, better to swallow her pride and give up some independence (most of which she didn't use anymore) for a safe, warm place where they knew how to deal with an old woman's growing list of daily woes.

On top of her dresser across the room, lined up carefully next to each other like soldiers at inspection, were three objects she looked at every day, sometimes several times a day if she was feeling particularly low or lost. Each reminded her in a different way there *had* been shining moments in her now-moribund life, whole days, weeks, even, when she'd been so grateful to be alive and exactly where she was that the only words in her soul's vocabulary at those moments were yes and thank you.

One of those objects was the turtle pin Graham had given her while on their magical trip to Mauritius. It was also one of the reasons why she'd moved into the assisted living home. One grim day months before, she had looked at the turtle in her small pink jewelry box and for a few eternity-long, lost-in-space seconds could not remember where the pin came from or why she owned it. When her mind fog cleared, realizing she had not been able to recognize one of her most cherished possessions, Ruth knew she needed help before things got worse for her.

Next to the pin on the dresser was a tiny brown leather Doc Martens shoe in pristine condition, although it was decades old. The day she learned she was pregnant, Ruth's husband was on a business trip to London. She called him there and shared the happy news. Standing on the street in front of a Doc Martens store when they spoke, he immediately went in and bought the smallest pair of shoes in the place, even though he knew it would be years before his child could wear them. He later told her he was so excited by the news that he had to buy *something* immediately as a souvenir to mark the great occasion. Their son Kevin was about two before the shoes fit, but the

even-then petulant little boy said they *hurrrrt* and were too heavy.
Under loud protest, he wore them only a few times. But she kept one
over the years to remind her of the glorious moment Dr. Zlabinger
said to her, "You're going to be a mother." Life is not often generous
with making our big wishes or dreams come true, she knew. This had
always been one of hers, and to this day she was grateful . . . despite
the fact her son grew up to be a skunk.

The third object on her dresser was the photograph. A deep-
pocketed collector of original "Patterson" photos would have paid
a fortune for the small snapshot if they knew of its existence, but
no one did now other than her. Maybe the next time she saw James
Arthur, she'd give it to him and explain its significance.

Ruth had given the famous "Patterson" his first camera. Not his
first first, because he'd had one when he was young, but back then taking pictures didn't interest him. The one she gave the adult Patterson
was his first "big boy camera," as she called it. Only it wasn't really a
big boy camera at all.

One summer Sunday when they were together, they went to a big
outdoor flea market in Brooklyn. Graham had talked on and off for
a long time about sometime taking up photography as a hobby. Ruth
kept urging him to do it, but time went by, and all he did was mumble
and sigh about maybe buying a camera in the future. Which, knowing
him, meant probably never.

At the market that day, he went off to buy them a couple of kiel-
basa for lunch because he knew how much she loved the spicy sausage.
Ruth wandered around until she stopped at a table full of "who would
buy *thats*?" But in one corner was something which made her smile.
An idea popped into her head, and she reached for it: a Kodak Brownie
Hawkeye camera in what looked like perfect condition, sitting in its
original box along with two unused rolls of 620 film. Ruth had owned

the same model camera as a girl and loved it. She remembered holding it two handed up against her stomach to steady it, looking through the viewfinder on top for the image she wanted to capture, and pressing down hard on the square gray shutter button. A loud *click*, then the slow winding of the big round knob on the side of the camera a few turns to advance the film to the next exposure. She'd drop the finished roll of film off at the town drugstore to be developed. At least a week later—sometimes longer—the finished snapshots would be ready to be picked up.

This Brownie camera cost $27.78. When she asked the seller (who was wearing an enormous Mexican sombrero) why such an unusually precise price, he said he liked to be creative with his pricing. He also said if she bought the camera, she could have the film for free. Without trying to haggle the price down, she handed him $30 and, rejecting the change, said she was just being creative, too. The seller tipped his big hat to her and said, "Welcome to the club."

"What've you got there?" Graham held an open yellow box with two Cokes and two giant sausages inside hot dog rolls when Ruth walked up to him a few minutes later. She was also holding a yellow box with the camera and two yellow rolls of film inside it.

"Your new hobby, Patterson."

"Is that a *Brownie* camera? For real?" His face lit up. "God, I haven't seen one of those in years. I had one as a kid."

"Me too, but you've got *no* excuse now, Graham. You have to start taking pictures. The guy who sold it to me said it works perfectly."

They walked to a corner section of the market where picnic tables had been set up.

He asked hesitantly, "Did you pay a fortune for it?"

Frowning, she blew out her cheeks and shook her head slowly. "You don't want to know. The things we do for the people we love. . . ."

He grimaced. "Really? It's so nice of you--—"

"$27.78."

Patterson wasn't expecting that. About to sip his Coke, he snorted a laugh into it instead. Some spilled out onto his hand and the table. Smiling, Ruth wiped it up with a paper napkin.

"A Brownie camera. What a fabulous gift, Ruth." He picked it up and, admiringly, turned the camera this way and that.

"But you have to use it, Graham. You can't just put it on your shelf and smile when you remember today. It's a tool, not a souvenir."

"Yes, sir." He put up his right hand as if swearing an oath. "I promise to use it. In fact, let's start now."

After they'd eaten, he opened the back of the camera and fit the film into a slot, threading it in. "I hope this film isn't a hundred years old."

Ruth craned her neck over to watch what he was doing. "Maybe if it is, you'll get some really cool effects."

Patterson stopped what he was doing, put the camera down, and looked at her. "You're always positive about things. It's such a rare, lovely quality in a person. I wish so much I had it. How do you do it? You're never thirsty because your glass is always half full."

Considering what he said, Ruth stuck a finger in the small swab of hot mustard left on her paper plate and licked it off. "People want life to be their friend. Some even expect or believe they *deserve* it. But I think of life only as a companion, and an unpredictable one at that. If it were my friend, life would be hurting or disappointing me all the time. But if it's only a companion, we're just traveling the same road together. I'm happy when it's in a good or generous mood, but I don't expect anything from it.

"Most of the time we have the ability to make ourselves content, or at least comfortable. We shouldn't need to depend on others or outside sources to supply it or to get us there." She smiled and rubbed her hands together. "What are you going to take for your first picture?"

"*You.* Where's your big gray hat? Put it on—you're going to be my very first shot. It's only appropriate."

Delighted, Ruth dug around in her straw bag and pulled out the crushable gray Borsalino hat with the great wide brim Graham had given her on her last birthday. She loved the style and swagger of the hat. It fit a certain secret peacocky part of her personality perfectly. Graham was the first man she'd ever been with who saw that quality in her. And he said he loved it.

He was there when she put the hat on for the first time. Clapping his hands together, he said, "*Incantevole! Favoloso!*" Taken aback, she asked what the words meant. He told her they meant ravishing and fabulous—in Italian. Impressed, Ruth asked if he spoke Italian. He admitted he didn't and had only learned the words so he could say them when she wore it. Italian words for a smashing Italian hat was only fitting.

Patterson gave great presents. He always knew the sort of things she liked but would never have thought to buy for herself. They met because of one of his gifts.

Both of them loved to write by hand. Both owned vintage fountain pens they had bargained for at flea markets. The day they met, they were in a pen and stationery store trying out different inks for their pens. Ruth was particularly taken with a deep grayish blue by a Japanese company she'd never heard of before. But it was expensive— just too much for a bottle of ink—so, tempting as it was, she couldn't bring herself to buy it. She thanked the clearly disgruntled salesman and wandered off to browse the rest of the store.

A few minutes later, the nice-looking man she'd noticed earlier out of the corner of her eye at the other end of the sales counter came up to her and offered a small chartreuse bag with the name of the store printed in beautiful black calligraphic letters on the side. Smiling slightly but very much on guard, Ruth shook her head that she didn't understand what was going on.

The man said, "It's the best ink. Really, you have to try it. I use one of theirs called *Yama-Budo* and almost nothing else. What the salesman *didn't* tell you is it also comes in small travel-sized bottles, too. I know it's kind of obnoxious, but after you left I asked him what color you were testing." He pointed to the bag with his free hand. "So you can try a little now. If you like it, buy more later."

He offered the bag again, and she took it hesitantly. "Why—"

He put up both hands to stop her. Smiling, his voice was friendly and warm. "It's a bribe. No, an invitation. No, it *is* a bribe, sort of . . . Anyway, whatever it is, please take it. I'm a comedian and I have a gig tomorrow night at a place called The Mickey Mouth Club—"

She nodded, impressed. "I know it. I saw Jerry Seinfeld there a few years ago."

Patterson sort of cringed and rubbed his chin nervously. "Yeah, well, I'm not Jerry, but I *am* there tomorrow night. I'd love you to come if you're not doing anything. Or if you're doing everything, I'd still like you to come."

"What's your name?"

He paused, surprised at her directness. "My name? Graham Patterson."

She'd never heard of him. "Are you funny?"

He crossed his arms and immediately uncrossed them. "I'm a comic. I try to be."

"That's no guarantee." She slipped the ink into her purse, which he took for a good sign. "Don't you agree one of the most insulting things you can say to someone is they have no sense of humor? I think it's as devastating as saying they're lousy in bed."

"Kind of a one-two combination, eh?"

She frowned "What do you mean?"

Patterson brought both hands up to his chest and made them into fists like a boxer. Throwing a punch, he said, "You have no sense of humor." He punched the other arm in an uppercut. "*And* you're lousy in bed. BONG K.O.!"

—

To Ruth's surprise and delight, in his performance at the Mickey Mouth Club the next night, Graham did a really sharp and witty riff on telling someone they have no sense of humor and how that was much worse than telling them they were lousy in bed.

"Think about it for a minute—if you *are* bad in bed, you can definitely *improve.* You can read books, or take online courses from experts on how to be a better lover, go to a sex therapist, and if you've got real guts, you can actually *ask* your lover what they like. But how do you create a sense of humor? How do you teach a person to know what's funny?"

He knew where she was sitting in the club because he'd reserved a table for her in case she came. In the pen store, he'd even asked what her favorite drink was. As soon as she was seated that night at the Mickey Mouth Club, a waitress brought her a Dark 'n' Stormy. Ruth was both impressed and touched.

Normally when performing, Patterson wore a sweater and jeans. But that night he had on his best sports jacket and a brand-new

Oxford shirt he'd bought for the occasion. After finishing his set, he straightened the snappy outfit and made his way over to Ruth's table. Nervous, he gestured to the empty chair across from hers, silently asking if he could sit down.

She looked up at him and, suppressing a grin, said, "I'm flattered."

"I'm Graham. Nice to meet you, Flattered," he said, completely deadpan.

Her smile broke free. She drew a vertical line in the air with her finger as if to say one point for you.

"Have a seat, Graham, and tell us where you get your inspiration for these stunning insights."

He slid the chair out and, sitting down, said, "Genius finds inspiration everywhere, Flattered—even in pen stores."

They got along. They got along beautifully. From that first night at the comedy club onward, they connected in ways neither of them had experienced before with others. We all hope the love of our life will appear with the rumble and crash of a thunderclap, turning our leaden, ho-hum, black-and-white days into Wizard of Oz Technicolor in an instant. But thunderstorms pass quickly, and as the Japanese proverb says, "an easily heated thing is easily cooled."

Ruth's best friend Samar, a no-nonsense woman if ever there was one, asked what she liked most about this new major man in her life. "But in one sentence, dear, and the shorter the better. Don't mush on about him."

Ruth answered immediately. "The way he pays attention to me. When we're together, I'm always the one-hundred-percent center of his attention. Do you know how refreshing that is? A circus could parade through the room, and he wouldn't give it a glance. When he's with you, you're *it*—the only thing he wants to see, hear, or talk to.

I love that. Most men I've been with were so easily distracted by just about anything—a pretty girl, a cool car, even a big dog. It was really humiliating sometimes. But not Graham. When we're together, he's all mine."

Impressed, her friend started to speak, but Ruth interrupted.

"He also sees things."

Samar closed one eye and pursed her lips. "Uh oh—now I'm worried. What does he see, little green men?"

"No, smartass, he's just super observant. He notices things I never would, but when he points them out, it makes things so much richer and more interesting."

"For example?"

Ruth crossed her arms and smiled. She was delighted to tell this story. "For example, the other day we were walking down a street where there was a big traffic jam. Cars and trucks were backed up bumper to bumper. Nothing was moving an inch. All the people inside the cars looked angry or frustrated. God knows how long they'd been sitting there before we arrived.

"Anyway, we passed a city bus while I was talking. Graham put a hand on my arm to stop. I thought for a moment he was being rude and telling me to be quiet. But he said, 'Check out the driver.' We were standing right next to the bus. I looked up and saw the guy was holding something to his nose and smiling. It was a sprig of lilac. It was the most marvelous, tiny thing, Samar. In the middle of everybody furious and fuming because of a traffic jam, the driver was like a Zen monk appreciating the only beautiful thing in an unhappy moment. It was great. I wouldn't have seen it if Graham hadn't brought it to my attention. He does it all the time, which makes me feel a little blind to my own life, but at the same time also more attentive, too. When stuff like that is right in front but you don't notice because you're too caught up in being pissed off or distracted by dumb things."

Years later, when Ruth read yet another article about the mysterious disappearance of famous photographer Graham Patterson, she learned for the first time that the name of his company was Big Gray Hat. It made her weep because written in Graham's nice script on the back of that decades-old first Kodak Brownie camera photograph of her in her hat at the Brooklyn flea market was the inscription: "A Big Gray Hat Production by Flattered and Patterson." The photograph lived in a driftwood frame Graham bought for her in a store on Block Island when they went there for a weekend.

For a few years after he left, there were the postcards he sent her. Sometimes they were a very large format, other times normal. What he wrote on the backs didn't often relate to whatever the picture was on the front. Ruth had the feeling he wrote most of them while alone and having an imaginary conversation with her in his mind.

A large card with a color photo of Mount Lassen, postmarked Susanville, California, read:

> Did I ever tell you I love watching women put on hand lotion? I'm sitting at a roadside diner in the middle of nowhere watching the woman in the next booth do it. They apply it so thoroughly but with a kind of careless ease. They're usually occupied with something else while doing it—talking to you, watching television, or reading a book. It's one of those small but graceful talents you women have—like putting up or arranging your hair—that you're unaware of. If you bring it to a woman's attention, they look at you quizzically and maybe say "Why do you think it's beautiful?" And truth be told, it's hard to explain why it is, but it is.

A photo of a Lucky Sevens slot machine, postmarked Elko, Nevada:

> In the country of Georgia, there is a brandy named Chacha.
> In the country of Ghana there's the word "pelinti," which means to move very hot food around in your mouth.
> In Arabic, the word "gurfa" means the amount of water you can scoop up with one hand.
> "Make visible what, without you, might perhaps never have been seen."
>
> —Robert Bresson

And one card she hated came postmarked from an island in Greece she'd never heard of:

> In some ways as I grow older, it feels like I'm slowly curling in on myself like a piece of burned paper. Turning into a gray ash trace of the man I once was or wanted to be. I don't mean it in a self-pitying way, just as fact.

When they were together, she and Graham often talked about one day going to Greece together. After the lovely trip to Mauritius, she had been sure they would.

She'd not looked at the postcards in years. Long periods passed where she forgot all about them. But one day not long after her husband died, while feeling lost, lonely, and nostalgic, she went searching in her closet for the red and black shoebox containing them. It was gone. Distraught, she spent an hour looking everywhere, to no avail. Had her husband taken them? It was hard to believe. He'd known about the postcards from Graham all along but said he had no objection to her keeping them. Besides, there was nothing naughty or secret written on any of them to have hurt him or made him jealous. Several times she'd said he was welcome to read them, but he demurred.

Never once did she suspect her *son* had stolen the shoebox after Ruth told him about it when describing her long ago romance with the famous photographer—"the only celebrity I ever knew."

In college, at the time he took the box, Kevin planned to sell the postcards as soon as his mother died, or if he really needed money— whichever came first. He knew she'd probably leave the collection to him anyway when she kicked off, but you never knew. He wanted to make sure he had them all in hand, just in case she changed her mind for some reason and did something stupid like donate them to a museum or a library. The way she talked about her relationship with Patterson the famous photographer, Kevin knew his mother would never sell the postcards, but he sure as hell would.

Out of mild curiosity he once looked through a book of Patterson's photographs, but he thought they were no big whoop. He put it back on the shelf in less than a minute. Why was the man famous? Anyone could take pictures of old diner signs and car crashes. What was so special about them?

Kevin Murphy was one of those people who were vaguely suspicious and envious of those who can do things they couldn't—like fix a car, cook, or take memorable photographs. As a result, he justified his inability or lack of talent to do those things by thinking I could do it too if I wanted, but why should I? Any dummy can learn to fix a car, make Brunswick stew, or take a picture of a group of blind kids in Western wear and cowboy hats at the Calgary Stampede rodeo. That was one of the lesser known photos in Patterson's book. But unbeknownst to the world, that picture happened to be very important for another reason.

The last time Graham wrote to Ruth, he sent a long letter years later, the longest he had ever written to her, explaining everything that had happened to him since they broke up. At the time he wrote it, his heart had suddenly begun doing mysterious, worrying things. Sometimes it beat so fast he thought it would either give out or explode. Sometimes he suddenly staggered and felt so faint he was certain he was about to pass out.

Although he hated going to doctors, Patterson became so concerned that he had a full medical exam, including a treadmill stress test, EKG, cardiac MRI, complex bloodwork, and others—grim reminders of his inevitable mortality. But to his relief and happy surprise, they concluded, for now, he was fine. Whatever symptoms he'd been experiencing were most likely some form of panic attack connected to his high-pressure lifestyle.

He wasn't convinced. Just in case, he wanted Ruth to know everything what had been going on since they last saw each other. The fateful tattoo, what it meant, and how it had changed everything for him. Anna Mae Collins, the access to his three possible lives, the experiences he'd had going to them, the final choice he would one day have to make, the works.

He finally got around to writing the letter on a legal pad of yellow lined paper in a motel room on the night he took the photo of the blind kids at the rodeo. It took hours to compose because he kept adding and revising. At times it felt like he was writing his last will, leaving the details of his new life and how he got there to someone he trusted and still loved.

The next morning, the letter went in the nice messenger bag he'd recently bought in London. He asked at the motel desk if there was a place nearby that served a good breakfast. Patterson did this whenever he was on the road now. It was amazing how many good ideas he'd gotten for his photography from eavesdropping on others' breakfast conversations at the various places where he'd eaten. His plan that morning was to have a big meal and then find a post office where he could mail the letter.

The motel clerk suggested a café named Billy Cooks, which apparently had "super delicious" steel-cut oatmeal. That happened to be a favorite of Patterson's. Conveniently, the café was also only a few blocks from a post office.

When he walked into the place, it was about a third full of customers. A waitress told him to sit anywhere and she'd be right over to take his order. He didn't look at the menu. When she came, he asked with a smile if their oatmeal was as good as he'd heard it was. She grinned and said, "You'll want to marry it."

"Then I do. I'll have oatmeal and coffee, please."

After she was gone, he took the biography of Robert Capa he was reading out of his bag and became quickly immersed in the story. He didn't look up again until a few minutes later when someone close by asked, "Is it okay if I sit here, Mr. Patterson?"

One of the blind kids from the rodeo yesterday stood facing him on the other side of the table. An Asian girl about fifteen, he remembered her in particular because of her glamorous jet-black hair cascading straight down her back from beneath a beige cowboy hat. Like she and all the kids had been the day before, she was dressed in what appeared to be new jeans, a loose-fitting pale blue chambray work shirt, and the big hat, which made her small head look even smaller. For an instant he remembered the line Antheia had said the day they met, about how no one looking good in a cowboy hat.

The blind girl held a collapsible white cane in her left hand. Before Patterson could answer, she was already folding it up and then touching the table to get her bearings, sitting down. Taking off the hat, she put it next to her on the seat, along with the cane.

He slowly closed the book and slid it back in his bag. He wanted to know how she knew who he was. How she knew he was here in this place at this moment. And if she really was blind, how did she even get here? Did she get here by herself or did someone bring her? If so, was that person someone he should know about? He wanted to ask a lot of questions, but all he did was clench his jaw, fold his hands on the table, and wait for the girl to say something.

Her eyes were large but unanchored. Their gaze floated freely back and forth, up and down. They didn't stop moving or rest on anything. It was like the eyes were watching a fly buzz around inside a jar.

"You can't send that letter, Mr. Patterson." Her voice was calm and respectful.

He said nothing, but a shock of *danger, beware!* adrenaline went off like fireworks up through his body.

"You cannot *ever* talk to anyone about what's happened to you—unless they also still have the tattoo, like your friend Antheia Lambrinos. Could I have it, please?"

"What, my letter?"

"Yes." She turned her hand over on the table and wiggled her fingers in the classic "gimme" sign.

Later, when he thought about it, Patterson realized it was her gesture which set him off. It was those fingers, the way she did it, that obnoxious, demanding *wiggle*. The way she wiggled them, as if expecting him to do exactly what she ordered right now, this minute. Like wiggling your fingers at a child to hand over a forbidden piece of candy they were trying to sneak in just before dinner. It annoyed him. He didn't like being told what to do.

So he asked a question rather than handing over the letter. His letter. *His* property, and no one else's. "Am I allowed to ask why?"

Spookily, her eyes stopped and appeared to rest on his face a moment before going back to the here-there-everywhere movement.

The waitress came with the oatmeal and coffee. She placed them in front of Patterson. Straightening up, she took in the girl and the white cane next to her on the seat. "Can I get you something?" she asked gently.

The girl smiled and very politely said no, thank you. Before leaving, the waitress glanced back and forth between the teen and Patterson, trying to figure out the connection between them.

"There are a number of reasons why you shouldn't send it. But I'll give the one most relevant to you—or at least I *think* it is, if you still care at all about Ruth Murphy.

"When she reads your letter, and if she believes what it says, she'll know, even all these years later, you *consciously* chose to reject the opportunity of ever having a family with her, even though you were given a second chance to say yes to a life together."

The girl paused to let that bomb hit. As soon as it did, Patterson closed his eyes and took a very deep slow breath. She was right. He took the letter out of his pocket and handed it to the girl.

"Imagine it. Today you're only the famous photographer, a man who she knows now through those postcards you sent a long time ago, and whatever she reads or hears about you. But now, out of the blue, this long letter from you suddenly arrives. Do you know anything about what's happened to her? What her life might be like right now, and how your letter might affect *it*? Did you even think about those things before you wrote it? No. You wrote a letter that will *for sure*, among other things, open old wounds and hurt her again, just as badly as you hurt her before."

Patterson sat back in the chair and rubbed a hand slowly back and forth across his forehead. "I never thought about it," he said sadly.

The girl let a heavy, uncomfortable silence sit between them a while, the better for the realization and guilt to spread in him and burrow deep. Eventually, she said, "Can I show you something?"

He looked at her confused. She was blind—how could she show him anything?

He nodded, "Yes, sure."

"Take out your cell phone and go to the photos app. There's a film there. Play it."

She didn't stick around for his reaction. As soon as she heard the thin sound coming from his telephone's small speakers, the girl put on her cowboy hat, stood, reached for her cane, straightened it, and walked out of the restaurant without another word to the man.

Soon after the clip finished on his phone Patterson heard, "Would you like some more coffee?"

The waitress had stood on the other side of the room watching the give and take between this odd couple. She saw the man take out his phone and the expression on his face change completely when he saw whatever was on it. He ignored the girl when she got up and left without saying anything more to him. A little while later, the waitress saw him put the phone down on the table and stare blankly into space, as if in shock.

What was going on? She picked up a coffee pot from the Bunn-O-Matic machine and went over to his table. A quick, sneaky glance at his phone on the table showed the screen was on its home screen.

He looked up at her. "I'm sorry—what did you say?"

"I asked if you'd like some more coffee." She looked and saw his cup was almost full.

"Uh no, no thank you."

"Are you okay, sir? You look a little peaked."

Patterson smiled. "*Peaked*? That's a nice word. I haven't heard it used that way in years. Yes, I'm fine, just trying to sort things out in my mind." He paused, gathering his thoughts, and said, "Sometimes our memory of the past takes no prisoners, you know? It can be a real bear."

The waitress was tempted to ask who the blind girl was but knew that was going too far with this stranger. The man's eyes slipped from her face back down to the phone on the table. She took it as a sign to leave.

After she walked away, Patterson picked up the phone and pressed replay on the clip. He didn't know if it would work, but he needed to see the film again, and probably again after that.

By now, Patterson was used to surreal things like this happening in his life, but of course, in another way, he would never grow used to them. Anna Mae Collins had not told him one essential detail that night years before at the comedy club when she explained the tattoo's significance and what it could do.

Whichever life of his three he chose to inhabit before making his final choice, Patterson would periodically be exposed to *all* of that life, past, present, and future—sometimes all at once—and how his choices would affect others. The first time it happened was the time with Antheia just after arriving in California, when they were transported from the beach in Santa Monica back to Crane's View, New York, twenty-five years earlier. In that one day, he encountered both the kids he'd gone to school with and the adult Carson Schreiner, along with her teenage daughter.

Also, and perhaps most importantly, Patterson witnessed in different ways how his behavior influenced and shaped others' lives even after he was long gone from them. In life, we pass through so many

doors and close them behind us, sometimes with an angry slam, sometimes just a gentle click. Moving on, we rarely think about most of the
people we left behind and what they did or how they lived after we
left. But they *do* carry on, too.

It can be enlightening or at least very surprising, in both good
and bad ways, to learn how much of an effect we had on them and
the direction their lives took afterward. The French word *sillage* means
the scent of perfume lingering behind in a room after the wearer has
left. Although we may be completely unaware of it, in numerous ways
our presence in others' lives sometimes leaves behind significant sillage
long after we are gone.

Their last supper was pizza, Ruth often remembered. The sentence would have been funny if it weren't true. The last meal Graham
and Ruth ever shared was pizza from their favorite Italian restaurant,
Evviva. It was supposed to be a quiet night together doing two of their
favorite things—eating takeout pizza and watching The Palm Beach
Story, a film both of them loved. Introducing her to the movies of
Preston Sturges was one of the many things Ruth was always grateful
to Graham for. She watched them over and over for the rest of her
life. In return, she taught him to cook his four favorite meals perfectly
instead of carelessly batching something grim onto a plate to eat while
watching whatever was on TV.

He was observant, funny, and generous. She was devoted, thor-
ough, and optimistic. He taught her to see with bigger eyes. She
taught him the joy of doing many things carefully and well. What
they planted in each other's gardens had not been grown there before,
and much of it flourished for a while.

After the pizza and movie were finished, Ruth cleared the coffee
table in front of them and handed him an envelope.

He took it and shrugged. "What's this?"

"Open it." She managed a sad smile, but knowing her different smiles so well, he knew this was not a good sign.

He looked at the blue envelope in his hand and straightened his back, as if girding himself for something unpleasant. One last glance at Ruth, then he tore the paper and took out what looked like a large ticket. Reading what was written on it, his mouth fell open. "Is this real? Is it *true*?"

She nodded. "Absolutely."

"I'm having lunch with Mark Pascal?"

"You are."

Pascal was Graham's favorite comedian. He was hugely successful. Films, one-man specials on television, sold-out performances at Lincoln Center . . .

"How did you *do* it, Ruth?"

"Samar has a friend who has a friend. You know how these things work. To be honest, it wasn't that hard to arrange. I thought you would enjoy talking shop with one of the big boys."

He shook his head in wonder and admiration. "Of course I would! But where did you get the idea—"

"It's my going away present to you, Graham."

His heart sank, but he knew it. As soon as he saw what was in the envelope, he instinctively knew this wonderful gesture was Ruth's thoughtful, generous way of saying goodbye.

In contrast, he felt stupid, helpless, and could think of nothing right to say. Thank you? For what, just this latest amazing gift? Or thank you for a relationship that was so good for so long but had been torn slowly and fatally down the middle by their different feelings about children and a family?

"I'm going to go now, Graham. But first, I want to say one last thing. I hope you'll take it the right way, and at least think about after

I'm gone. I love you, but I'm afraid you're going to end up being one of those who go through life wanting things or people they can't have, for whatever reason. So they become bitter and, ironically, choosy about what they *can* have, or the possibilities that *are* open to them."

"Are you saying—"

Ruth held up a hand to stop him. They looked at each other, and in that moment, years of closeness and understanding passed between them. He knew exactly what she was saying about his career as a comedian and possibly future partners. It hurt because she knew him so well. He also knew her words came only from love and concern for him, nowhere else. She was leaving and giving up any stake she had in the rest of his life. Until that moment, neither of them realized how important the last words you ever say to a person could be.

Ruth stood, kissed her open hand, and turned it toward Patterson a few feet away. He rose slowly but did not go to her. What could he say or do at that point? He watched helplessly as she crossed the room, took her coat off a hook, and, after one last, sad glance at him, opened the door and left.

But this is not what Patterson saw on his cell phone after the blind girl in the cowboy hat told him to check it. What he saw now was what Ruth Murphy did *after* leaving his apartment the last night they spent together.

The clip began with Ruth coming out of his apartment and closing the door behind her. He recognized immediately where she was and what she was wearing from that fateful night. Watching now, so many years later, his throat tightened, and unconsciously he began breathing in short, shallow breaths.

Ruth walked quickly down the hall to the elevator. Waiting there, she kept glancing back toward Patterson's apartment. Was she expecting something to happen? Perhaps for him to open the door and come get her? Or at least open it and ask her to return so they could talk over her decision? The expression on her face was impossible to read. She'd just left behind a years-long relationship, important for both of them, but neither her face nor body language gave any indication of how she felt about it.

Staring at the small phone screen, Patterson was once again mesmerized to witness not only a past event of his life, but at the same time how the occasion had gone on to effect those who'd been there with him and moved on.

The elevator doors opened, she stepped in, and they closed again. A moment later the view changed to inside the elevator car and a close-up on Ruth's face. Still nothing clear to see there, nothing to indicate whether she was sad, glad, angry, relieved . . . nothing but impassive. The same blank expression most of us have while riding in an elevator.

But then she did something shocking: Opening her mouth as wide as it would go and closing her eyes, she made a silent scream that lasted a very long time. The silence of it was much worse than if she had screamed at the top of her lungs.

The car stopped, the doors opened to the lobby, and Ruth stepped out. After a few steps she stopped and put a hand on her chest. Only for a moment, and she was off again, through the front door and out onto the street.

She quickly walked a few blocks, then stopped in front of a bar named The Gecko Lounge. There was nothing special about the outside of the place. Patterson had never seen it before. They'd definitely never gone there together. Standing still, Ruth nodded to herself as if agreeing with some kind of inner dialogue. A moment later, she went in.

"Ruth! Hey, there you are. So nice to see you again. Where have you been?"

"Hi, Astrid." Ruth lifted her hand in a small wave.

The bartender was a very attractive blond in her forties. She looked genuinely happy to see her customer. "It's been way too long."

Ruth walked over to the bar and got up on one of the stools. "I know. Bad me."

"What would you like, the usual?" Astrid started to turn, but Ruth stopped her.

"No, tonight I need something stronger. I'll have a Sea Breeze."

"A *Sea Breeze*, you? Wow! I don't think I've ever seen you drink vodka."

"I'm having it to honor someone. Or a dead relationship, I guess. Or—" She chuckled and shook her head. "Whatever. Tonight, I'm going to have the first and last Sea Breeze of my life."

The bartender was confused. She looked at Ruth with affection and genuine concern. "You want to talk about it? Half my job is listening."

Ruth waved the question away. "Maybe in a month or two, but right now, no. Thank you for asking, though. But listen, do you still have the Omar Souleyman CD Samar gave you?"

Astrid nodded. "Sure. We all like it. You know we usually play it on Saturday nights to get things going around here."

"Would you put it on now? Play 'Warni Warni.'"

"Okay. What's up?"

Ruth slipped off her stool. "I want to dance, and I need something crazy and great."

"Then 'Warni Warni' it is." Astrid moved to find the CD and put it on the player. There was a small dance floor off to the side of the bar. Ruth went over and waited for the music to come on.

Patterson watched in a state of small wonderment. In all of their time together, Ruth had never mentioned anything about The Gecko

Lounge, Astrid the bartender, or Omar Souleyman music, whatever the hell kind that was. Obviously this place was a regular hangout for her and her best friend, Samar. Even the bartender was enough of an intimate for Ruth to confide in her. Why had she never told him about any of this?

He realized once again that no matter how intimate you are with someone, in most instances you can only know a piece of their life's map. The rest is either out of reach or in shadow, sometimes hidden on purpose. It might even be right there in front of us, but then we turn away because we don't want to acknowledge or accept it as part of who they are. Sometimes the reason we never get to fully know someone loved, to the very heart of their matter, is because we don't *want* to know what lives in their shadows.

The music blasted on loud: electric, furiously fast Arabic music with what sounded like a drum-and-bass backing. Ruth started turning slowly in circles, eyes closed and arms straight above her head. As the music pounded, she turned faster.

There were few people in the bar, but they were all looking at her now. Another woman stood, and after futilely trying to persuade her boyfriend to get up too, she joined Ruth in the dance. Her partner sat at the table and began clapping along to the music. Others did, too. The two women turned faster and faster, lovely dervishes.

The camera went in close on Ruth's smiling face. For a moment it looked to Patterson as if she were genuinely happy—but it was not so. They had been together too long, and he knew her facial expressions too well, not to be able to distinguish the false smiles from the real.

As she turned, she began to cry. Still smiling, her eyes welled with tears. They slid down her cheeks and were reflected by the bright lights over the dance floor. She smiled and spun and wept.

This was what happened to Ruth Murphy that grim night years ago immediately after she left Patterson for good and walked out his door into the rest of her life. The picture on the small screen of his phone faded to black a few seconds later while still staying close on her face, turning and crying, turning and crying.

Lowering the phone to the table, Patterson just stared at it for a while, reviewing what he had seen and learned. The shock of being transported back to that night so long ago, her silent scream after leaving his apartment, this Gecko bar she frequented that he knew nothing about but was obviously important to her for some unknown reason. Her heartbreaking dance there, which was of course the final blow. Any one of those facts would have punched him in the heart. Altogether, they scorched black a part of his soul and left him reeling for a long time.

These days, Patterson was exactly where he wanted to be in his pixilated, unpredictable life. He couldn't imagine things being better. He was almost magazine-cover famous now in certain circles, his photographs published and displayed all over the world. To his amusement and his agent's fury, they were reproduced thousands of times without credit on the internet. Original Patterson prints sold for crazy prices. He was in the rare, delicious position of being wanted everywhere. Or at least, his work was.

At the time Ruth broke up with him, he never would have imagined his life turning out this way. Back then—which now seemed a century ago but was only thirteen years—he was a semi-successful comedian whose girlfriend and best friend both knew he would never make it big at the rate he was going with the uninspired material he created and insisted on using.

He was fifty-five now. Naturally, there had been women since that time, and two serious relationships. One for three years with a gallery owner who eventually told him, like Ruth did, that she wanted more—marriage, a spouse to grow old with. Unfortunately, they had the conversation soon after returning from a trip to Greece together to Antheia Lambrinos' house, where he realized he got along better on a day-to-day basis with Antheia than he did his partner.

Unlike Ruth, the gallery owner did not leave the relationship gracefully. There were lawyers and a palimony lawsuit thrown out of court, physical threats, and a loud, ugly night when police were called to his loft to remove her after she stormed over, high on amphetamines and rage at him for disappointing her and her vision of a future together.

Years before, Patterson believed one day it would be natural and fulfilling to have a family. But at this age and the way his life had turned out, he was happier alone or semi-alone, even if an intriguing woman appeared on the horizon. The gallery owner accused him more than once of loving nothing but his work. There was truth to that. He could spend all day and night taking and working on photographs. Not so with any of the women he had been involved with.

One of the unexpected drawbacks of prominence was people either wanted things from him all the time or they wanted to be near him, too near. That's why in recent years he spent more and more time on the road, zigzagging around the country taking pictures, staying for days at a time in modest motels while he checked out the countryside, always with a camera in hand.

Outside the small desert town of Hallet, Nevada, he stopped in the empty parking lot of a long-abandoned roadside diner named Mr. Breakfast. At the base of the empty neon sign out front announcing the place was a box of large, rusting metal letters, obviously used in the past to spell announcements on the sign.

Borrowing an extension ladder from the motel where he was staying a few miles away, Patterson drove his SUV back to the diner. Climbing the ladder with a few of the letters at a time under his arm, he hung the sentence

SOLITUDE CAN BE A MOODY COMPANION

on the empty sign, a line from one of the letters Ruth had recently written to him about how sad it was to be alone.

He shot over fifty photos of the sign from various angles using different lenses and filters until he took one he liked. He then spent several hours shooting pictures of and around the outside of the restaurant. After making sure no one was near, he forced open a back door to the kitchen and went inside. Surprisingly, nothing in there merited even one photo. It was the outside of the building, the chipping paint and broken windows, sloppy graffiti on the walls, the faded sign in front and the stark desert setting that interested him.

Patterson returned the next day because it was raining, and he wanted to see how the wet desert light affected both the restaurant and the billboard with Ruth's message still on it. He was sitting in his SUV with the door open, eating a candy bar, when a gleaming canary-yellow Dodge Ram pickup truck pulled into the lot and stopped a few feet away from him. An old man wearing a red and white UNLV baseball cap waved and opened the door. When he got out and stood up, he could not have been much more than five feet tall. Climbing out of his big yellow truck was a bit of a task for him.

"Afternoon. Seen you here yesterday, too. Whatcha doing?" he asked pleasantly.

"Taking pictures."

"Really? Taking pictures of *what*? This place's been closed years already. What's here to shoot?"

Patterson got out and brushed his hands off on his jeans. "That's what makes it interesting. I like taking pictures of dead old buildings. They have character. If you're lucky, sometimes you bump into an interesting ghost or two." He winked to show he was joking.

Unimpressed, the old man was looking at the words on the sign and pointed to it. "Who the hell wrote that?"

"I did." Patterson's smile grew.

The old guy sounded angry now "You *did*? Why?"

"So I could take a picture of it."

"I don't even know what it *means*, do you? Are you sure you're American?"

Surprised by the question, Patterson said nothing.

The man shook his head and decided to change tack. "Do you know who once worked here, at this very place, washing dishes?"

"No, who?"

"Minnie Yeggy."

"*Who*?" Blank-faced, Patterson shook his head.

"Minnie Yeggy, the serial killer! The Highway Hacker. They even did a documentary show on her on TV. Don't you watch TV?"

Patterson scratched his cheek. "No, not much."

This seemed to piss the old man off as much as the fact this stranger hadn't recognized the name Minnie Yeggy. Pointing a stiff, accusing finger at the building, he said, "Well, just to inform you, Mr. No TV, the Highway Hacker worked washing dishes in that restaurant for quite a while—without anyone knowing who she was, obviously. I'd bet a hundred dollars I ate off a plate she washed with her own murdering hands. The thought still gives me the fucking chills. Now they got her up in Ely Prison, just waiting to put her down like a dog."

Then he paused before saying, "You're a photographer? Got any of your pictures you can show me?" The old man was still skeptical of a guy who'd never heard of the Highway Hacker, put weird sayings on a sign in front of an abandoned restaurant, and freely admitted to not watching television.

"Sure. Hold on a sec." Patterson reached back into his van for a folder of a few of his photos on the passenger's seat. Beneath it was another folder the same size. He hesitated momentarily but then brought that one out, too. "What's your name?"

The man straightened up, not sure he liked being asked such a forward question by this stranger. "Hillman. Hillman Moss. What's yours?"

"Graham Patterson."

Neither of them offered to shake. Patterson handed over the first folder and crossed his arms, curious to see how the old fart would react.

Moss reached into a shirt pocket and took out a pair of ancient glasses that were black once but had since lost almost all color. Even from a distance Patterson could see the lenses were thickly smudged. He felt like offering to clean them so the other wouldn't be looking at his pictures through grease clouds.

There were ten prints in the folder. Moss looked at them slowly, his expression saying nothing. After some time, he said in a neutral voice, "I like these two the best."

"Which ones?"

Moss turned the pictures over and read out the titles on the back. "'Borrowed World' and, uh, 'The Queen of Tomato Soup.' Again, I don't know what the hell your titles mean, but these pictures are fine. Those dumb kids looking at their phones with a car wreck behind them? And the burned hand serving soup . . . strong, strong images. You're very good."

"Thank you. Can I ask a favor? I'd like you to take a look at some other photos and tell me what you think. I've been experimenting with a new developing process and want to know how people like it."

"Let's see them."

Patterson exchanged the first folder for the second. Inside it were five photographs. There were always just those five. He had never added more.

Moss saw nothing on any of the five sheets of photo paper in the folder. He frowned at the first nothing, then flipped quickly through the other four, which were also blank to him. "Nothing. I don't see nothin' on anything here. Are you bullshitting me? Is this supposed to be a joke?"

Now the photographer had to be careful what he said, as was always the case when he showed that file to anyone. Inside were the only five pictures he had kept from the day he and Antheia traveled back to his boyhood hometown. Over the years he had shown the file to a number of people. Only two of them had actually seen the images captured that day: Antheia and Mark Curry. The only two other people he knew with the breakfast tattoo.

———

Soon after returning from exhibiting his work at the Venice Biennale, Patterson was contacted by one of Mark Curry's assistants. She wanted to know if he would consider doing a portrait of Mr. Curry, who was a huge fan of his work. Patterson said yes, details were worked out quickly, and a date was set.

He knew very little about the famous man other than the fact he had once gotten the breakfast tattoo and changed his life after visiting the alternatives. Newspapers said Curry was reclusive, combative, and litigious when it came to anyone questioning or doubting his many successful projects. He had married and divorced the same South African woman twice, was a serious art and photography collector, and of course, being one of the wizards of Silicon Valley, was revered and rich as Croesus.

A few weeks later the wizard came to Los Angeles for business, and they met at Patterson's Big Gray Hat studio in Santa Monica. When they were shaking hands, the photographer remembered what Anna Mae Collins had said long ago about Curry—earlier in his life he'd worked at a store called Lazy Larry's. Just the silly name of the place and the thought of this world-famous man stacking boxes or sweeping a stockroom floor tickled Patterson.

The photo session went well. Curry was amiable and quite talkative throughout. When they were finished, he sheepishly said he'd seen an In-N-Out Burger restaurant several doors down from the studio. Would it be possible to get a Double-Double burger and a vanilla shake? He hadn't eaten anything all day. Patterson asked one of his assistants to go pick up burgers and milkshakes for both men.

While waiting for the food, Patterson went to a drawer and took out the folder with the five Crane's View photos inside. He'd been dying to do it since the moment Curry walked in the door but had held back till then.

"I thought you'd like to see some brand-new ones I've done. These are just early proofs."

Curry lit up. "New work? Indeed! I'd love to see it." He took the folder and opened it with eager hands. All the photos were face down. On the back of the top one was written the word "Pinecone." It was the picture of Fellini the bull terrier looking enviously at Antheia Lambrinos eating an ice cream cone. Curry read the title, then turned it over to see. Instantly his smile grew until his teeth showed. "This is terrific, Graham! But *very* different from your other work, don't you think?" He looked at Patterson, his expression hesitant, expectant. At the moment he was not Mark Curry, tech giant, but just another fanboy in the presence of a master.

"Maybe you're right," Patterson said.

Curry went back to looking at the photos. "Giant Romeo" showed Butch Harris standing shirtless and triumphant on top of a school desk while his friend Romeo Mrvic gazed adoringly at him from down below. "Tying Water in a Knot" was Carson Schreiner's daughter Roxy up in the air, dancing with the dogs in her backyard. The other two photos—"Tin Eye" and "Older Caveman" were also from that day in Crane's View with Antheia. Unlike James Arthur, eventually studying four of the blank sheets of photographic paper Ruth Murphy showed him, Mark Curry could see all of the photos. The comments he made about each were spot on.

He asked if he could buy prints of them. Patterson looked at the folder a long time before saying he would think about it, but only after the pictures were exactly the way he wanted them. Curry hesitated before asking if Graham would ever consider selling him exclusive rights to all five of the photographs. He could name his price. Patterson asked if he meant no one else would ever see them.

Staring him straight in the eye, Curry immediately and firmly said, "Yes—just me, no one else. I'm greedy that way." Then he grinned slyly.

Patterson almost grinned too, thinking no one else ever *could* see them unless they had gotten the breakfast tattoo, so the point was moot. It was almost like the fairytale of "The Emperor's New

Clothes," but in reverse: In this case, the emperor *would* be dressed, while everyone else would be naked. Patterson said he would think about that offer, too.

Curry liked both answers. He was accustomed to people saying yes to him, especially when he dangled big checks or opportunities in front of them. He had always loved Patterson's photographs, but now he respected the man as well for not snapping at bait like so many others had.

Later, while they were eating, he looked a long time at Patterson's arm and said, "That's a really remarkable tattoo. The detail is so intricate and perfect. Is it new?"

Over the years, Patterson's tattoo had remained as distinct and vibrant as the day it was made. None of the colors faded; none of the lines were stretched or distorted by the fading elasticity of his aging skin. He knew the same thing was true of Antheia's tattoo. He guessed that as long as you never used up all of your visits to the other lives and made a final choice, staying in the original life in which you got the tattoo, it remained. But if, like Curry, you chose to live forever in one of those three lives, both tattoo and any memory of it disappeared as soon as you made the choice.

Patterson had purposely worn an short-sleeved shirt that day so the tattoo would be on full display to his famous guest. He wanted to see if there would be any reaction to it. Now he swallowed a mouthful of burger, took a sip of shake, and wiped his lips on the back of his left hand. "Are you a tattoo guy, Mark? Do you have any ink?"

Curry shook his head. "No. But I like looking at them on other people. Frankly, I never saw one I'd want on me forever. Yours is pretty damn cool though. The detail is amazing. Where'd you get it?"

"A small town in North Carolina, of all places. My car broke down, and I was stuck there for two days. While it was being repaired, I wandered around and came across a tattoo parlor called Hardy Fuse." He stopped and looked to see if the odd name got a response from the other man.

Nothing.

Curry tipped his chin toward the tattoo. "What does it mean? Does it have any kind of special significance? Is it some kind of a totem, like Inuit art?" Before Patterson had a chance to respond, Curry continued. "I read an interesting article in the newspaper the other day about tattoos. A man in Florida died. In his will, he asked that they tattoo a redwood forest across his torso before he was buried. Apparently it was a copy of a photograph of the only place he had ever been happy in his life. He said no matter what happens after death, he wanted to take that place with him. But his wife was Muslim, and tattoos are generally forbidden for them because it's considered mutilating the body, changing Allah's creation."

Patterson nodded. "Tattoos are *haram* for most Muslims. I learned that traveling in the Mideast."

Curry pointed at him as if he'd given the correct answer in class. "Haram, that's the word—forbidden. So anyway, some of the dead man's children wanted their father to have his wish, but others and the mother didn't. So the case went all the way to superior court."

"Who won?"

"The dead guy. In Florida, a decedent's will takes precedence over anything else. If the will states he wants his corpse tattooed, he gets it. Anyway, the article got me thinking. Tattoos are with us our whole life, but they're also there after we die, unless we're cremated. If I had to tattoo one image on my body for now and the hereafter, if there really is a hereafter, what would it be? I loved the idea of the man wanting a special forest on him to take along. Since reading about him, I've been thinking: What single image would I choose to take with me when I go?"

Patterson smiled. "And if there *is* an afterlife, will taking that image along have any effect on what happens to you or your spirit when you get there?" Part of him so strongly wanted to lean in and say with total confidence—Mark, there is *definitely* an afterlife, and I've been there.

Of course, he didn't, but then a jarring thought swooped in and took hold of his brain: What Curry described had already *happened* to Patterson, in a way. When in Greece with Ruth, the turtle had reappeared on the beach in Mykonos at just the right moment. Somehow, he really believed he had brought it with him from this life into that of Graham 3, like Curry's story of bringing a tattoo from life into death.

"Can I take a picture of your tattoo?"

Patterson was so absorbed in thinking about the Mykonos turtle that he didn't really hear the request.

"Excuse me, what did you say?"

Curry had already taken a cell phone out of his pocket. He pointed it at Patterson's arm. "I really like your tattoo and would like to take a picture of it, if you don't mind."

Patterson thought, Man, if you only knew . . . "Sure, go ahead."

Putting the phone close to the photographer's arm, Curry shot a quick burst of photos. "Great, thank you. Let me just check to see if I got a good one. I'm a terrible photographer, so I always have to look." He smiled and glanced down at the phone. Frowning, he moved his thumbs around on the screen, then frowned some more. "What the hell . . . ?"

Patterson couldn't see what was going on but instinctively knew it had to be something to do with the photos of his tattoo. He wasn't at all surprised. "What's the matter?"

"My phone—it just died. It went completely black and won't turn back on. I was scrolling for the pictures, and suddenly the screen went dead. Damn! And I didn't bring my other phone with me."

Commiserating, Patterson shook his head. "Tech is not always our friend. Give me your email address and I'll send you a picture. It's no problem."

"An original Patterson photo of the Patterson tattoo? Fantastic!"

An hour after Curry left, Patterson set up a small tripod on a desk and took some shots of his arm with a new point-and-shoot Leica camera he was trying out.

When examining them, on a quick first glance they seemed okay. But he always went over all of his work very carefully under a loupe, and these pictures were no exception. He transferred them to a large computer screen where he could see every detail of what were basically just snapshots. After spending a good deal of time staring at them, wonder and delight slowly began bubbling up inside him like carbonation. Finally, he laughed so loudly an assistant came into the room to see if everything was okay.

To her astonishment, the famous photographer did a little dance step before waving her over. As long as she had worked for him, the woman had never seen Mr. Patterson *dance*. Grinning, he told her to look very carefully at the photos of his tattoo on the monitor.

She had graduated from Cal Arts and only recently landed her dream job of working for *the* Patterson. So if the boss told her to look carefully at pictures of his tattoo, she would have spent all night looking, although she had no idea what for. Why was he taking pictures of *that*?

After some time, impatience got the best of him, and Patterson told her to look at the real tattoo on his arm. Did she see *any* difference between the photo and the real thing?

Worried she'd say the wrong thing, the young woman hesitantly said no, they looked the same.

"You're sure? You see absolutely no difference?" Glee rising, he tapped his tattooed arm.

"Nooooo . . . " She stretched the word out for at least three seconds, afraid she was talking herself into a trap, or failing a test, or . . .

Patterson clapped his hands as if giving something a round of applause. She stuck her own hands into the pockets of her jeans, as if to close herself off from whatever odd thing possessed him.

"Thank you, Marcy, that's all for now. You can go back to what you were doing."

She hurried from the room, relieved to get out of there.

With one hand over his mouth, Patterson stood staring at the computer screen. He could only conclude the tattoo itself, or whoever oversaw it, would not allow Curry's camera to photograph it at all. That's why the man's phone died. Patterson had the tattoo, so he *was* allowed. Nevertheless, *any* reproduced image would never be identical to the real thing. A photo or any kind of copy of the breakfast tattoo would always be slightly strategically off, wrong, at best a cunning counterfeit. And only those people with the real one would be able to recognize the differences.

His assistant had spent a long time studying both the photo and his real tat. She said they were the same. But Patterson saw many minute differences, although he could not believe his eyes at first. He had to keep checking from one to the other to be sure. Several curved lines here, three pointillist dots there, one frog eye just a little bit tilted . . . all over the photos were small but distinct differences.

He wondered if Marcy would have seen them even if he had pointed them out to her. He doubted it. Which meant the only places where the real tattoo could be seen was either on those who actually had it under their skin or in the books of tattooists who'd been entrusted to make it.

—

"Phew! That is one *large* fella. Is he with you?" Back in the pitted parking lot of Mr. Breakfast, Hillman Moss sounded impressed.

Immersed in the memory of the day with Mark Curry, Patterson didn't really register what was said. Blinking his mind clear, he turned and looked to where Moss was staring.

Giant Romeo Mrvic was walking toward them with a sly smirk on his face. Stretched tight over his huge frame was a black t-shirt with the word BLOODSTONE emblazoned on it in flaming, melting yellow and orange letters. Below the word was a large image of the main monster from the infamous Midnight horror films of the 1980s. Mrvic also wore new-looking blue jeans, wide enough to be the sail on a catamaran, and huge black-and-white Converse high-top sneakers with a lot of mileage on them.

"What's up, Patterson? Happy to see me?" Mrvic looked at the two men. Before either of them said anything, he clapped his hands toward Hillman Moss. The old man froze in place just as he was about to speak. He remained frozen the whole time Mrvic was there.

Patterson looked left and right to see if Romeo's scary pal Butch Harris was there, too, but he wasn't.

"Did you miss me, Graham?"

"Why are you here? *How* are you here—you're supposed to be dead. You *are* dead."

Romeo crossed his arms and nodded. "True, but today's the beginning of part two of your little life adventure here. They sent me over to give you some instructions and advice. You know, from a friendly face and all."

Patterson pointed at the little, unmoving Hillman Moss. "What's with him?"

"He's fine—just resting till we're finished talking. Don't want him interrupting. Are you hungry? I'm starved. I hear they serve a very good tuna melt in this place. What do you say we chat over lunch?"

Patterson didn't know what Romeo was talking about. His back was to the building. Only after the other gestured toward it did Patterson turn around to face it. "*Holy shit!*"

Amused, Romeo said, "I don't know if they serve that too, but we can ask."

Mr. Breakfast, closed and abandoned so many years before, was alive and open for business again—completely, one-hundred-percent back from the dead. Freshly painted, every windowpane unbroken and shiny clean. Through them, Patterson could see the place was packed. Snapping his head up, he looked for the battered, neglected sign advertising the place. The sign he'd been playing around with, putting words and phrases on to photograph. Now the sign looked brand new, painted, unrusted, no bullet holes or light bulbs broken on it like they had been ten minutes before.

"My little gift to you."

Still incredulous at what he was seeing, Patterson could barely tear his eyes away from the transformed sign to face Mrvic. "*What* gift?"

Romeo gestured toward the diner. "*This.* I thought you'd like to see what it looked like once upon a time. Come on, let's go eat."

Shocked but also fascinated by what was happening, Patterson followed his teenage nemesis across the parking lot and into a very much alive Mr. Breakfast.

The song playing on the sound system inside was instantly recognizable—he'd heard it over and over as a boy. Steve Perry singing "Foolish Heart." His high school girlfriend Carson Schreiner loved it. She turned up the volume on the car radio and sang along whenever the song came on. Walking behind Romeo to a booth, Patterson remembered Carson saying while in tenth grade she had once been cornered by Mrvic and Butch in the school hall and shown a Playboy magazine pinup photo of a naked woman they said looked like her. They wouldn't stop taunting her until Miss Hilty, the vice principal, came by and told them to knock it off and scram.

When they were seated now, Romeo took two orange menus out of a holder under the window and slid one across the table to Patterson. "Lunch is on me, so order whatever you want. I'm going with the tuna melt."

Patterson left the menu unopened. "I'm not hungry. Just tell me why you're here."

"Okey doke—after I order my sandwich." Romeo raised a hand, and a waitress came right over. "I'd like your tuna melt, a large order of French fries, and a Pepsi, please."

"And for you, sir?"

Patterson shook his head. "Just coffee, please."

After the waitress left, Mrvic said in a low voice, "She's got cancer but doesn't know it yet. She'll be dead in two years." He raised a hand and made a 180-degree arc with it. "Ask me about anyone in this room."

Patterson looked around. "Who are they? What *year* is this?"

"You'll see. They're people who used to come here. Regulars, long distance truckers, townspeople, tourists on their way west." Romeo pointed to a man sitting at the counter reading a newspaper. "His son is in prison for armed robbery. And speaking of prison, see the woman way over there in the corner, clearing the table? That's Minnie Yeggy."

Startled, Patterson strained to see her. "The serial killer?"

"The one and only. They had her doing all kinds of jobs when she worked here—washing dishes, busing tables, mopping up. Did good work, too, probably because she didn't want to raise any kind of suspicion.

"But let's talk about you, Graham. You haven't made your life choice yet. Why? It's been years since you got the tattoo, but still no choice."

Instantly on the defensive, Patterson put both hands against the edge of the table and pushed himself back in his seat. "Is it part of the deal? I have to definitely decide I want this life or one of the others?"

Romeo closed his eyes and nodded. "In fact, you do. Your friend Antheia's husband visited her last month and told her the same thing."

Patterson frowned. "Her *dead* husband?"

"Yup. Who better to tell her? She *has* decided, by the way. She chose *this* life. So the only difference when you see her again will be her memory of certain things that happened in her life and her tattoo will be gone. There *is* a time limit on this deal."

He let that sink in for a moment before continuing.

"Just before, when you were thinking about Mark Curry? Know how long it took him to decide?" Mrvic snapped his fingers. "Just like that. But you've never returned to either of your other possible lives after the lizard reincarnation and the one time in Greece with Ruth. I can understand why you don't want to go back to being some prehistoric reptile—" He paused and leered. "But what about Ruth? Aren't you at least curious what these years would have been like if you had lived together?"

Instead of answering, Patterson turned and looked out the window. The waitress came with their orders. Romeo looked at her ass and nodded in appreciation when she walked away.

For such a large, otherwise sloppy man, his eating style was surprisingly delicate and refined. He cut the sandwich into quarters, ate only one French fry at a time (although he ate them continuously), and sipped the Pepsi through a straw without once making a slurp or sound. While chewing, his face was all pleasure. It had been a long time since he'd eaten food, and the tsunami of sensual delights—hot, gooey, pungent, crisp, aromatic, sweet, salty, carbonated—held him in thrall.

Patterson still had not said a word. He was staring out the window at the parking lot. A family came through the front door. Mrvic saw them, wiped his lips with a paper napkin, and dropped it on the plate. "Hey."

Graham turned from the window.

Mrvic pointed to the family now walking toward an empty booth nearby. Mother, father, three kids around the same age. To the big man's surprise, Patterson didn't flinch, jerk, or show any surprise other than a widening of his eyes in the moment he recognized these people. The family passed by and sat in a booth several feet away, kids on one side, their parents on the other.

The famous photographer put both hands around his coffee cup and squeezed it. "Did you do this?"

Romeo shook his head. "No, *you* did. That's what I was going to tell you."

"They didn't recognize me. None of them did."

Romeo smiled. "Of course not. Because none of them back then knew you when you were in your fifties."

"But it's my *family*. It's me when I was, what, ten?"

"Eleven. Your parents were in their late thirties. Why would any of them recognize a fifty-year-old man they'd never seen before?"

After all that had happened to him since getting the breakfast tattoo years before, very little surprised Graham Patterson, including encountering his family and himself age eleven at a roadside diner outside Hallet, Nevada.

"You don't remember, do you?"

"Remember what?" Patterson wanted to look at the family, to stare at them, drink them all in. But his back was to them, and he knew he needed to hear everything Mrvic was saying.

"The day you ate here with your family."

"No way!"

Romeo threw up his hands in mock exasperation. "You just *saw* yourself walk in here with them when you were eleven years old! What more proof do you need? All right, all right—remember the road trip you guys took to Disneyland in California in your father's new car?"

Patterson gasped. "Oh my God, that's right! Dad had just bought—" He twisted around to look out the window again. Seeing something in the parking lot, he pointed at it excitedly. "—*that* puke-green Dodge station wagon. It was the first new car we'd ever owned. Mom told me later we could only afford it when Dad got a big discount because no one else wanted to buy a station wagon in such a horrible color. I learned to drive on that car."

Mrvic shrugged. "I don't care. Do you want to know what's going on or not?"

"Yes." Deflated, Patterson sat back in his seat after a quick glance over his shoulder at the family.

The waitress passed, and Romeo ordered a slice of banana cream pie.

"If anyone waits too long to decide which life they want, something you could call an undertow starts to happen. You do *not* want that to happen."

"What do you mean, *undertow*? Like in the ocean?"

"Yes, sort of. Do you know *exactly* what an undertow is? It's important you do."

Warily, slowly, Patterson shook his head no.

Mrvic spoke in an unfamiliar monotone that sounded like he was reciting a dictionary definition. "Any strong current below the surface of a body of water, moving in a direction different from that of the surface current." Raising his hands, he crossed one above the other moving in opposite directions. "Until now, your life, *this* life, has been moving in only one direction. Obviously. Young to old. But today, starting now"—he pointed to Patterson's family —"it all changes because you haven't decided yet. Your personal undertow has begun.

"On *your* surface body of water, which is today, you came here to take pictures of an old, deserted diner. But as long as you stay undecided, the undertow is going to keep pulling you back to your past and tossing you around between now and then. There's nothing you can do to stop or control this, and it'll only get worse till you make a decision. You're going to be like a swimmer pulled out to sea by an undertow, which is the days of your life all mixed up between past and present.

"You had a small taste of it on Mykonos with the turtle. Then that time with Antheia—one moment you were on a beach in L.A., the next you were back in Crane's View when we were in high school. The same day you met your old girlfriend as a grown woman with children: Patterson's past and future, crossing, pulling you both ways." He did the gesture again of passing one hand above the other in opposite directions.

"Why?"

Mrvic shook his head, not understanding the question. "Why *what*?"

"Why is this happening to me? Why now?"

The waitress brought Romeo's dessert. He immediately stabbed a fork into it. "I already said—because you haven't chosen yet." Cutting off a huge chunk of the beige pie, he slid it into his mouth. His right cheek bulged. While chewing, he waved the fork at Patterson to indicate he wanted to say more after swallowing. "If you'd gone to one of your other lives and stayed years too long *there* without deciding, the same thing would have happened—an undertow would have come and tossed you around the years of *that* life, too.

"Just between us though, why *haven't* you decided? You seem to like the way life has worked out here. You're sort of famous, rich, and can do whatever you want. Shit, all you've got to do is just say the word and these complications will go away. Easy-peasy. Look at how happy Mark Curry is." He shrugged and went back to attacking the pie.

Out of the corner of his eye Patterson saw Minnie Yeggy coming toward them carrying an empty metal tray. She was going to a corner table full of dirty dishes. He looked up and their eyes met. She smiled and exaggeratedly mouthed two words, "*He's lying,*" as she passed.

Patterson whipped his head around to Mrvic. The big teenager was grinning and chewing, having seen the whole thing. He swallowed and took a long drink of soda. "Not lying *exactly*, just leaving out a piece at the center of the puzzle. I thought by now you'd have figured it out, Graham, but obviously not. She just gave you a big shove in the right direction.

"Because I'm a great guy, I'll give you a last hint: Minnie didn't say those words just now—*you* did. How do you think you ended up in this fucked-up place for the *second* time in your life?" He tapped the middle of his forehead with a fat thumb. "Something in here is telling you important stuff—you should *listen* to what it's saying."

———

The next thing he knew, Patterson was suddenly back in the parking lot, standing next to Hillman Moss, who still held photos in his hand. In front of them was the abandoned diner Patterson had seen when he first drove up a few days before and stopped to have a look around. He turned to the old man. "How many years ago did this place close down?"

Moss pursed his lips and thought for a moment. "Ten, fifteen years, maybe more. It was around the time my wife died."

"And when did Minnie Yeggy work here?"

"Oh, now that was a *long* time ago, at least forty years."

After Moss drove off in his big yellow truck, Patterson opened the hatchback of his SUV and pulled out an aluminum folding chair. The rain had stopped, and the sun was beginning to push its way through the remaining clouds. He set the chair up next to the car, making sure to have a good view of Mr. Breakfast and the vast desert landscape stretching out behind it to the horizon, where the Sierra Nevada Mountains loomed up gray, brown, and topped with white.

Out of a small cooler he took the hero sandwich and bottle of lemonade he'd bought at a market next to the motel where he was staying.

There was a sleeping bag and some camping equipment in the car, but he used it only for emergencies or when he was stuck out in the wild and too tired to drive back to civilization. This road trip was a gift to himself after a particularly grueling few months of nonstop work and travel. A week off driving around Nevada and Utah—taking pictures, as always, but mostly just puttering down and around empty country roads with no particular place to go.

Until an hour ago, he thought he'd happened across Hallet, Nevada, and Mr. Breakfast by happy accident. But if Mrvic was telling the truth, his past had led him here like a dog on a leash. He sat down in the chair and unwrapped the tinfoil around the sandwich. He realized his mouth was very dry. Uncapping the lemonade, he tipped his head back and took a long drink.

Lowering his head again, he saw something flying toward him in a kind of lazy, unhurried flap and glide. At first he thought it was a big vulture, or maybe even a California condor. When he was going out with Tera, his second serious relationship since Ruth, she had shown him California condors at the Los Angeles Zoo. But this bird flying toward him now was much bigger than they had been, enormous even in the air at a distance. Its vast wingspan alone made him think of some kind of military drone.

The sandwich unconsciously squashed now in one hand and the lemonade bottle gripped tightly in the other, he stood up slowly so as to get a better look at the giant bird gliding closer and closer to him. The moment he recognized what it actually was, he gasped and dropped his lunch on the ground. Ironically, Graham Patterson was probably one of only a handful of people in the entire state of Nevada who knew what he was looking at, and the impossibility of it being there.

The longest relationship he'd had in recent years was with Theresa "Tera" Soto. They met inside the Page Museum at the La Brea Tar Pits in Los Angeles. Patterson was wandering around the museum alone one Sunday afternoon looking at dinosaur bones, films, and illustrations of creatures that had lived thousands and millions of years ago in this area and died when they got stuck and sucked down into the famous tar pits nearby.

Eventually he came upon the colossal spread-winged skeleton of an extinct *Gymnogyps amplus*, the biggest bird he had ever seen. Was it an actual bird, or some kind of flying dinosaur? How could such an enormous thing fly? He was fascinated. Walking back and forth in front of the display, eagerly snapping picture after picture, he didn't notice the smiling woman standing off to one side watching him. In time she sidled up and said quietly, "Pretty impressive, isn't it? That's the ur-great-grandfather of the California condor. Lived nine thousand years ago and had a wingspan of ten feet. Huge. But there was an even *bigger* bird than him back in prehistoric times, if you can imagine."

"Rodan?" Patterson said without missing a beat.

The woman pretended to clap at his reference to the famous horror film about the monster bird. She nodded appreciation at the joke and touched his arm a moment. "No, not *that* big. The largest bird of all was called *Teratornis, Argentavis Magnificens*. Lived around six million years ago. It weighed at least thirty pounds and, if you can imagine, had a wingspan of between *twelve and twenty* feet. That's at least two times wider than this guy's spread." She pointed to the skeleton in front of them. Walking away from Patterson, she paced off roughly twenty feet and turned back toward him. "Can you imagine flapping wings this big? But the wings were so enormous he probably didn't flap much, just got up on high perches and soared down off them like a hang glider. They think the species might have lived as long as a hundred years because it had no real predators."

Her voice grew louder and louder as she spoke. Self-consciously, Patterson looked around to see if other people were listening. She was all joy and enthusiasm. It was obvious she loved talking about the subject.

"Are you a tour guide here?"

She pulled back a little, her voice dropping to normal, and she smiled embarrassedly. "No, I just come here a lot because these fellows *are* my job. I study ancient birds like this one. I'm what's called a paleoornithologist. Just for a minute think how thrilling it would be to look up in the sky and see one of those beautiful creatures flapping by!"

One of those "beautiful creatures" was now about to touch ground in front of him. Patterson said in utter disbelief, "It's a fucking *Teratornis!*"

He knew it on sight because Tera (who preferred being called that rather than Theresa—because of the bird) had covered one entire wall of her loft with an enormous, extremely detailed illustration of the beast as it must have looked in flight. Often while waiting for her, Patterson sat on the couch and stared at the picture, never quite believing such an animal could really exist despite Tera having shown him other artists' renderings of what the gigantic bird must have looked like, as well as photos of full-scale models and skeletal remains in other museums. On her desk, she even had a nondescript brownish bone fragment from one.

Now the ancient bird landed ten feet away from him and, once on the ground, ruffled and fluffed its airplane-like wings back in tight to its body.

Later, Patterson could never figure out why at that dangerous moment what flashed through his mind was not fear or a desire to run from the mini-Rodan in front of him but what Minnie Yeggy had said as she passed their table in the diner: "He's lying."

He'd said Patterson would now be experiencing *all* of the life he had lived until now, the past and present of Graham Patterson 1 weaving in and out of each other, like it had that day in Crane's View with Antheia and just now in the diner where he watched himself as a child with his family. But that was Romeo's lie.

Like railroad cars clank/coupling together, watching the giant bird settle nearby, what became clear to Patterson was that this was not just his life 1's past and present; maybe *all three* of his possible lives *concurrently* would now come into his reality—so long as he remained undecided. The three possible lives of Graham Patterson would now weave like a braid in and out of his daily life—the past and present all at once of the photographer, the prehistoric reptile, and the husband of Ruth Murphy. The Teratornis in front of him was the only proof he needed of this. It must have lived at the same time as he had when reincarnated in prehistoric times. But here the beast was, who knew how many million years later, in the Nevada desert, staring at him with big eyes as if sizing him up for dinner.

He had no other choice but to quickly say "Pinecone 3" and touch the tattoo before the bird attacked and just hope it wouldn't follow him to his life with Ruth Murphy.

Felek

One of his favorite things was to sit in the kitchen and watch as she prepared their meals. She used the small, ferociously sharp Japanese knife to cut everything with the precision and efficiency of someone who long ago mastered the art of small necessary things—cooking, building, or repairing things that were broken. It reminded him of great waiters who served everything with flair and just the right amount of theater, made even more wonderful by the fact they weren't even aware anymore of doing anything special. If you brought it to their attention, they would be surprised: You liked the way I serve things? That's funny.

The way she cooked, her hands, the twist of her body as she went from cutting board to stove, to the sink and then back . . . All of it done with an almost balletic flow and economy that made him long for her even when she was a few feet away across the room.

"Read a little to me while I'm cooking. You know I always love that."

He still held the boy's book because he'd been reading it to the kid as he drifted off to sleep for his afternoon nap. It was Conor's favorite these days. Patterson had read the story to him at least twenty times, and would probably read it twenty more before his little son's enthusiasm for it waned. When Conor fell in love with something, he was all in for whatever it was, one hundred percent, until something else caught his fancy.

Patterson ran a hand across the cover of the book before opening it. The bright green letters of the title—*A Paper Dog*—were raised and felt nice beneath his fingertips. Conor loved the writer Marshall France's book *The Land of Laughs*. But Patterson had grown tired of reading it to him over and over. So he bought this one by France, the author's last, unfinished work that had been edited by France's daughter Anna.

Patterson cleared his throat and began to read the first page of the book while his wife moved busily back and forth across the kitchen, preparing their lunch of homemade soup and freshly baked bread.

"The dog was made of paper. But that didn't seem to bother the animal a bit. It knew to avoid water and fire. Though it had no bark because it had no vocal cords, its bite was one wicked paper cut."

Ruth smiled and interrupted. "Conor loves that part. I had to explain to him what a paper cut was, but now every time I read it, he giggles."

Patterson smiled, nodded, and continued reading. "The owners bought the dog in a Japanese store specializing in origami pets. They could have bought a smoke-breathing tissue paper dragon the size of a large iguana, or a cardboard calico cat. But the dog was just the right size, its body folds and wrinkled face made it look adorable, and they wanted to start small. The kids picked it out of all the other animals in the store, so that was that."

Ruth turned from the stove and faced him. For a moment, she grinned. Then her eyes widened, and she jerked a hand quickly to her chest over her heart. Patterson froze. In those terrible few seconds, the look between them held, as too often now, so many conflicting emotions—icy fear, love till the end of time, anxiety, resignation . . .

Was this it? The final one, the death blow—here in their kitchen, with wonderful Polish *żurek* soup cooking on the stove, their children asleep in the other room, the boy's book in Patterson's hand?

The man watched helplessly as his beloved wife, his best friend, face terrified, mouth half opened and silently imploring the gods not to let this be the one, this too familiar flawed flutter in her chest. Atrial fibrillation, seven deadly syllables that now beat a rhythmic memento mori into her every day, always maybe any moment away: one last fast furious heart dance before it stopped forever or shot a chunky blood clot like a mortar shell into her brain and took out half her life or more.

Closing her eyes, she waited with her other hand clenched tightly against her chest. Patterson thought what he always did when this happened and he was there to witness it—What would I do? What would I do without her? He knew there was no answer until it actually happened. As always, he stiff-armed the thought away from his deepest hope. She would not die. This moment could not be it.

Loosening her hand, she opened her eyes and looked blankly into space while her untethered soul slowly parachuted back down into her, the day, this room with her worried husband. After a silent inner check to be sure, she said, "I'm all right now. It passed."

"You're sure?"

"Yes."

"Was it a bad one?"

"In between. No, they're all bad. They scare me."

Patterson grimaced. "I hate it. I feel so helpless watching you suffer. And it makes me angry. It shouldn't happen to you. You don't deserve it."

She shrugged and touched her forehead. "The only remedy for me is to say fuck it and move on once it's passed, Graham. Otherwise, it beats me twice. I'm not going to let it scare me to death or govern my life. No. Deserve is a dangerous word. I'd be careful using it, especially when you apply it to yourself or the people who matter to you."

Ruth turned back to the stove, picked up a long wooden spoon, and stirred the soup. "I read an article about a famous photographer who at the height of his fame ruined his life with drugs. For years he slipped down and down, so low that everyone who knew him was sure he would die. But by some miracle, he was able to pull himself back up. Eventually he even started taking pictures again.

"After something like twenty years, he had his first exhibit of new work. He was interviewed right before the show opened in a famous London gallery." She spooned out some soup, had a taste, and said, "A few more minutes and it'll be ready. Anyway, they interviewed the guy right after the show opened and was a big success. He said, 'I've come back from hell after all these years. After what I've been through, I deserve this show.' Guess what, Graham? He dropped dead a few days later. True story.

"Nobody deserves anything, Sweetheart. Life just is what it is. All we can do is work hard and love hard, try to do the right things without letting our ego trip us up, and hope the bogeymen stay away for another day." She tapped her chest. "Including the one doing this to me."

She put the spoon down. "Did I ever tell you my mother's shish kebab story?"

Patterson smiled and shook his head. Still very disturbed by what had just happened to her, he was grateful to hear her talking in an almost normal voice again.

"In the summer when I was young, my family used to have lots of outside barbecues. One of our favorite meals was the shish kebab my mother would prepare and marinate overnight before grilling. Everything about it was precisely done. Slide one big hunk of meat onto a metal skewer, then one vegetable. Meat, vegetable, meat, vegetable—all very orderly, and no cheating. But my brother absolutely hated vegetables and always tried to get away with sneaking them under the table to our dog, who would eat anything.

"Once Mom caught him slipping a tomato down to his partner in crime. She said to him, 'You only want to eat the kebab, but not the shish. It doesn't work like that around here, mister, and you know it. It doesn't work like that in life. If you want to eat the good stuff, you've got to eat the bad, too. You've got to eat your vegetables. That's the deal.'

"Naturally as soon as she said it, my brother frowned and said, 'Shit kebab.'

"Afterward, it became part of the secret language of our family. Whenever something went wrong, like the car broke down, one of us would say 'kebab' or 'okay—that's the shit—where's the kebab?'" Ruth pointed the wooden spoon toward her chest. "This heart thing is my shish. You and the kids are the kebab."

An hour later while she had a nap, Patterson took their son to the park near their apartment. Conor was a quiet, rather aloof little boy. He spent a lot of time standing next to his parents, thumb in mouth, serious faced, watching rather than participating in life. Ruth called him the little philosopher.

In contrast, his older sister Mickey threw herself into life and people like a base jumper leaping off the tallest building in Singapore or a rugby player charging into whatever scrum was nearby.

There was an enclosed playground section in the park full of swings, a teeter-totter, a large complex fort to climb around on, and other structures that kept most of the kids there busy and loud. But not Conor. He stood next to his father for a long time, watching all the other children run, swing, climb, and yell. Patterson gently asked if he would like to go on any of the playground equipment. Conor just shook his head and kept watching the raucous hubbub around them. Eventually he took his father's hand and walked slowly over to the swings, which for the first time since they arrived were empty.

He didn't want Daddy to push him, so the man went over and sat down on a bench nearby. It was close enough to catch the boy if he took a tumble, far enough away that he could feel independent. Patterson took a book out of his messenger bag and started reading, with frequent glances at Conor to make sure the boy was okay.

To Patterson's surprise, he was a very good father. He thought he knew himself pretty well, but the moment his daughter Micah (now Mickey, by her command) was born, the architecture of his heart changed dramatically. His wife was amused and touched in equal measure by the intensity of his feelings. She frequently reminded him of how hesitant he had been about having children and that if it hadn't been for their showdown in Greece, they never would have been gifted with these two beautiful kids. On Mickey's third birthday, he sent Ruth a bouquet of roses and an Irish proverb: "Bricks and mortar make a house, but the laughter of children makes a home."

Now he looked up from the book to check on Conor and saw the boy was once again talking animatedly to himself. This was a recent development. He did it so often his parents had become concerned.

Ruth had a friend who was a child psychologist. He said not to worry—it was probably just a phase the little boy was going through, creating an imaginary friend to tell his secrets to, especially since he was a quiet little fellow anyway. When Conor was older, he'd connect with real children his age and no longer feel the need or desire to talk to his invented "Ghost Daddy," the name the boy had given his invisible friend.

The other Patterson, Graham Patterson 1, "Ghost Daddy" Patterson, was in the room at that meeting with the psychologist. Of course, he was invisible to all of the others. But for some reason, some magical or malevolent reason (he hadn't figured out which it was yet), he was visible to the little boy.

Ghost Daddy Patterson now sat on the swing in the park next to Conor.

"How come my Daddy can't see you?"

They'd had this conversation before. Patterson tried his best to explain in terms a child would understand. But he failed at it more than once, so he just repeated the word he'd used before that appeared to satisfy the boy last time they spoke. "Magic."

Conor silently mulled this over, as if hearing it for the first time.

Graham 1 glanced over at 3 reading his hardcover book. He looked closely at the other's face. He'd been doing this a lot since returning to this version of his life. What struck and touched him deeply was the unconscious expression on 3's face most of the time. Hard to explain, but it was a kind of beautifully sad combination of serene and fully resigned. As if without really being aware of it, 3's face said, This is definitely not the life I dreamed of or hoped for once upon a time, but it's surely good enough and I'm grateful. The warmth and security of family life, an easy loving relationship with his wife, the uncomplicated day to day of working at an okay, half-interesting job that paid decently, a family dog, a newish economy car to fit them all in . . . Altogether an agreeable but invisible life, and by no means special. Definitely not the life he had dreamed of when he boldly set off from the east coast years before in his bright red convertible, only to turn around just outside Kearny, Nebraska, and drive right back east to Ruth Murphy and a fate as neat, good smelling, and sweetly dull as a mown lawn.

So what was better—a special life, or a peaceful one? At this point in his existence, Patterson was famous enough that many of the people he knew and hung around with were famous, too. Truth be told, most of them were either weird, unappealingly self-absorbed, or genuinely messed up. Patterson was a bit more content and stable than them because his fame had come almost by accident rather than his intentionally striving for it. He had wanted to be a famous comedian, but he ended up a professional photographer simply because from the start he was preternaturally good at it rather than driven or inspired. He thought of himself as having accidentally stumbled backward into acclaim rather than marching for years toward it.

He thought about that aspect a lot—how many people would excel at certain things if only they were exposed, taught, or given the chance at some point to experience it: The naturally talented cunning old woman who would have won big playing professional Texas Hold'em poker but was never taught the game. The diffident Welsh plumber with a spectacular tenor voice, too timid to sing except to himself when he was sure no one was around to hear. And others— the Paraguayan young man who'd have been a master pastry chef had he not been raised in a family of nine by brutish parents in a tiny mountain town, fifty miles from the nearest restaurant. Or the young girl herding Zebu cattle on some parched African savannah. She had so much potential to be an important medical researcher if she was educated, but she never would be. Patterson's fame was a fortuitous accident, but it hadn't made him particularly happy or brought him peace, even now with all the acclaim he'd received.

"Do you know that goats eat Christmas trees?"

"Really?"

"Yes, and hippos poop so much in the water sometimes that all the fish die."

Patterson chuckled and shook his head. He thought the kid was making it up. "Where did you hear that?"

"On a TV show. I watch a lot of TV. I like shows about animals. We have a bulldog named Tofu. Do you know what Tofu is?"

Graham 3 checked his son to make sure he was all right on the swing, then dove back into his book. He read mostly thrillers these days, thrillers and crime novels with big plots, cliché characters, and the good guys won in the end, mostly. He didn't read them for escape, but more to jazz up his everyday a little, like putting hot sauce on a good sandwich.

Right now, the hero of his book was in Jordan, riding a horse slowly through a steep canyon that opened up at the end to the famous lost city of Petra, "a rose-red city half as old as time." Waiting for him there was a shady Latvian arms dealer with secrets to sell.

Patterson knew he would never go to Jordan or Petra, most likely never ride a horse—because he had no desire to—shoot a gun, fly first class, ride in a McLaren or a catamaran, take calls on his cell phone from important people, or on any future day in his life have contact with dangerous shady characters with secrets to sell. He was a husband and a father, and a pretty good provider. Was that enough? Yes, at this stage in his life, for him it was. He'd recently said to Ruth he realized he had no bucket list, and he meant it.

He did make lists, though. He thought of the practice as doing pushups with his memory. How many lyrics to Beatles songs could he remember? The complete names of every woman he had slept with before getting married. The TV shows he'd watched as a kid. The names of his favorite candy bars back then: Charleston Chew, Bonomo Strawberry Turkish Taffy, Jujubes, Chuckles, Zagnut, Black Jack, and Beemans chewing gum . . . Patterson's way of daydreaming was usually to think of a specific subject and then make a list about it, either on paper or just for fun in his head, challenging his brain to remember things, mostly from his past. Often the practice dislodged the nicest memories from the far, dust-covered corners of his mind.

While reading now, he came across a name of a character that reminded him of the name of a pitcher on the New York Yankees baseball team. Naturally it detoured his attention from the book to what other Yankee pitchers he could remember from that era. Staring at the page but digging in his mind for Yankees, he did not at first see the woman enter the playground.

Oddly enough she looked sort of hip/chic. She wore brand-new jeans that had recently belonged to a teen killed in a car accident and an expensive-looking puce cashmere sweater full of small moth holes. She had fished both pieces out of a charity clothes donation bin with a straightened metal coat hanger days before. The only things that didn't fit were her sneakers. They were completely destroyed, laceless, and many sizes too big for her feet. She'd stolen those, too, out of a charity bin. Her hair used to look filthy and scraggly, but a barber had been giving free haircuts to the homeless at a shelter. She had asked in her gentle voice for a to-the-skull crew cut. Most striking about her appearance was how good-looking she was despite the gulag-prisoner buzz cut and the dangerous life she'd been living for months on the street.

She was also as crazy as a jar full of flies. Her worried family had been looking for her for months since she ran away. She had been off her meds a long time. Without them, many voices in her head sang to her for much of the day. They sang well, like her own personal heavenly choir, so she was pleased when they appeared, sad when they left for a while, and almost always glad to have them as company. Although sometimes they did tell her to do strange things, which made her very confused. But they were her friend and constant companions. She couldn't imagine them telling her to do something wrong.

A man at a shelter who she'd let fuck her gave her a seven-inch-long Tanto box cutter as a gift after he was finished. It was stuck in her left back pocket. She'd used it once before to defend herself, but since then it was difficult to open and close.

She had found the beautiful old beige brick in front of a busy construction site, the name of the nineteenth century company that manufactured it—Felek—inscribed on both sides. Lifting it out of a full dumpster on the street, she read the name twice, and it made her laugh. She said it over and over—Felek Felek Felek. The way she pronounced the word in her mouth, it tasted like a jolly friend. She knew from the start it would help and protect her at the right time. She carried it always now, like a student with a large book, and she slept with her head on it at night.

Two days before, she'd crushed the jaw of a Rottweiler with the brick. The giant animal had lunged at her while on its walk down by the railroad yard where she had been sleeping. Until a moment before it happened, standing a few feet away, the owner of the dog thought it was funny to see his hound scare the hell out of homeless creeps. Big Pepper never actually bit anyone but sure was terrifying when charging full steam at them, teeth bared and growling like a black and gold demon from hell.

But this time, in an instant Pepper was suddenly staggering around howling in incredible pain, blood streaming out of his broken mouth, bewildered that his life of a moment ago—flying across the ground, ferocious king of the world—was gone.

Enraged at what had happened, the owner—all two hundred and forty-four pounds of him—came jogging over, fully intent on grabbing the woman by the neck and kicking the shit out of her. Seeing him approach, she calmly picked up her blood-covered brick, turned slightly to the right, and threw it as hard as she could at his face. Bullseye.

The man reeled, five drunken staggering steps, thick hands on his already wet face. Dropping to his knees, he howled now, too. His nose was broken, his right eye socket badly damaged.

Cheered by the choir of voices all around the inside of her head, the woman walked over, picked up her brick, and ran away.

She liked having hit the bad dog with the brick. So did her voices. She liked throwing it at the fat man's red face. So did the voices. She wanted to do it again. Her choir said yes, do it again. For the next two days, she looked and looked for someone to hit.

The weather had been mild and clear, so at night she'd been sleeping on the far side of a park on the grass under a large chestnut tree.

That morning she had been walking around the neighborhood for hours looking for things to eat in garbage bins, on the street, and around park benches, where surprisingly she often found good stuff. She returned to her place against the tree after having found a half-eaten cheeseburger in a soggy bun and four french fries inside a damp McDonald's box, a dented can of Red Bull energy drink with a few sips left, and (best of all) two green sticks of Doublemint chewing gum still in their wrappers.

When she had finished her meal, she lay down and took a nap. It was a lovely, quiet day, and for the first time in a long while she had a full stomach. But an hour later for, some mysterious reason, she woke up furious. Her voices were silent, which made things worse. Where were they when she so wanted them to keep her company? They were the only beauty she knew now.

She sat there looking through mad, hooded eyes at other people in the park. A thin beam of sanity slowly cut through her madness for a short, intense time, like sunlight through billowing purple rain clouds on a stormy day.

This only made things worse, though. Because riding that bright beam of sanity was a deep hatred for the others around her. She hated the women—the teens with their stupid copycat tattoos and cell phones, the singles, the mothers, the old ones, the haughty business-women in their expensive suits staring at laptop screens. The playing children, the smelly old couples plopped together on the benches like big peeping pigeons. The roadkill bums over there talking loudly to each other about nothing while sipping shit wine from waxed card-board boxes. More than once she'd been in groups like that, drinking the rotgut along with other skeezy vagrants. But it didn't stop her now from hating all of them. Hating the normalcy and grim gray medi-ocrity of anonymous human beings in a park, faces tilted up toward the sun or down at the books they were reading, kids screaming ev-erywhere, dogs barking and playing fetch with their owners. She just hated all of them and wanted to escape back into her madness where things were better and more to her liking.

Enough. Time to hit out at all of it, all of them, at someone around her here today who deserved to be bashed because they were a willing part of this horrible world in the park.

Brick in hand, she stood up and went looking.

After three complete trips around the park, she began focusing on the little boy alone on the swings. On the first trip, she thought of smashing one of the loud bums because he looked vaguely like her brother. But not enough to really get her anger boiling. Then there was an old woman snailing slowly along on a metal walker, one step in front of death, and probably smelly, like all old people. She hated smelly people. She knew she smelled, too, but it was different. She was allowed to smell. Her voices said it was okay because water scared her now. When she was young she used to like baths and showers, but not anymore. She hid from the rain sometimes when it came down too hard, from fountains, definitely from the river living on the other side of town.

The boy on the swing reminded her of water, but she didn't know why—he just did. She knew water hated her back now and would drown her if ever given the chance. So why not bash in its head and then run away, like she did with the fat man and his bad dog? Maybe water would get scared of how fierce she was and leave her alone afterward. Maybe crushing it with her brick would shock it enough to make it go away for a while. Yes, the boy who was water needed to be bashed by her friend Felek.

Graham 3 was immersed in his book. Conor was swinging and humming to himself. Patterson thought maybe it was time to return to his life and, thinking this all through, make a final decision about where he wanted to spend the rest of his days: a life that was creative, free of most tedious obligations, and almost effortlessly successful versus one where he was loved, mostly fulfilled, and felt needed in all the best ways by wonderful people. The only thing he knew for sure was he did not want to be Graham 2, the prehistoric reptile. Truth be told, this life, 3, despite its beauty, security, and comfort, was just a little boring. He'd have to consider it all very carefully.

Looking up now, he saw a young woman walking determinedly toward them with something very big in her hand. Was it brick? Why was a stranger coming toward them—with a brick? At first she looked normal, decently dressed, upright posture, although it was unusual to see a woman with hair that short. Was she a cancer patient undergoing chemo treatment, or protesting something political? By then he could see her pretty face better, and a moment later her wide-open crazy eyes and half-opened mouth. He grew alarmed. She was walking straight at them, straight at Conor! His other self, Graham 3, still had his head down over his book. She started walking faster.

He said to the boy, "Conor, get up, run! Go over there. Run as fast as you can to Daddy."

Conor looked at him but didn't move. He was clearly confused by his Ghost Daddy's abrupt order.

"Run! Run away!"

"Why?"

By then it was too late. What Patterson did next was entirely spontaneous, without thought. He had no idea if it would work, but it was the only thing he could do: Invisible to everyone here but the boy and powerless, there was no other way to save Conor. And it might not even work. Fuck it—he had to.

Graham Patterson yelled the words he'd been thinking about for years. He touched the tattoo on his arm and said:

"Pinecone 3 here!"

Graham 3, sitting on the bench, suddenly lifted his eyes from the book and saw the odd looking young woman walking quickly toward his son, brick in hand. He stood.

The woman hesitated a moment and frowned. Something suddenly slowed her in her tracks, like a strong hand, a wall, or even a giant wind. Shaking her head, she started to walk again. Though she was close to Patterson now, she didn't look at him. Her face grew enraged, burning mad eyes only on Conor, who was very near. Her arm holding the brick rose, ready. It was clear what she was about to do.

A man came out of nowhere and grabbed the woman by her free arm with two hands, stopping her momentarily. She yanked on her arm to pull away, and she was very strong. Just as she was about to free herself, Patterson hurried forward and hit her as hard as he could in the face with his book. She stopped but did not fall or move. He hit her again and again. She swayed. The book fell out of his hand, so he punched her—in the chest, in the neck. Someone somewhere nearby screamed. The man who had grabbed her arm yelled out a name Patterson didn't catch.

The madwoman fell to one knee but got right up again. Having dropped her brick, she picked it up and swung blindly at the two men. Luckily the swing was wide, and she didn't hit either. They did jump back, and she started forward again. The boy stood staring at her, unmoving, fascinated, his thumb in his mouth. There was still a chance to get to him, she thought, to bash him. She never once looked at the man who hit her, only the boy, only at the water that hated her.

Someone else grabbed her from behind, locked their arms around her chest, and threw her violently to the ground. Together the three men held the woman down. She never stopped jerking around violently, pulling to get free, head raised, neck straining forward, eyes always on the boy. What spooked all of them, besides her great strength, was that she never said anything while they held her, not a single word. Only growls, screeches, and grunts, like a crazed wounded animal.

Nearby, several women were calling 911, their faces horrified at what was happening. Some had seen what took place and told the others in excited, appalled voices. All of them, men and women, thought the same thing: It could have been mine. It could have been my child stalked by this lunatic.

The woman on the ground bit one of the men on his hand. He yelped and slapped her face. Gripping tightly, Patterson looked up at Conor, who was still holding one of the metal chains of the swing.

What would have happened if I hadn't looked up from the book at just that moment? Why did I looked up precisely then? Patterson couldn't answer those questions. He just did what he did, and thank God for it. What would this crazy monster have done to my little boy if we hadn't stopped her?

The police arrived and were told what happened. One of them picked up the brick, weighed it in his hand, and said a long slow "Jesus!" under his breath, thinking of his own little daughter.

He noticed something. "Hey Larry, this brick has dried blood on it, I think. Take a look." He offered it to his partner, who was holding the woman at arm's length. He thought she had calmed down, but a moment ago she snapped her head to the side and tried to bite him. He grabbed her neck and shoved her out in front of him so she couldn't do anymore crap. He'd dealt with loonies before. They could catch you off guard. You had to be careful with these freaks.

He glanced at the brick, but she started thrashing again. He told the other cop to bring it along and they'd check it out at the station house. He told the father to come down there and make a formal statement about what happened.

Someone called out, "What are you going to do with her?"

"For right now, put her in a cell until we decide what's best to do. There are procedures we follow. She'll probably end up in a hospital. At least they'll give her a nice long bath. You can smell her ten feet away."

Conor had gotten off the swing and leaned up against his father's leg, small arm wrapped around it. One of the cops bent down and ruffled the boy's hair. He looked at the father and said quietly, "Close call, eh?"

Graham Patterson, Graham 3 no more, father of two, husband to Ruth, owner of a dog named Tofu, and the only version of himself now and forever, took a deep breath and could only nod.

A Lazarus Glass Soul

"I'm not *blaming* you for what happened, Anna Mae. I'm just not *thanking* you for it either. I don't know what to do now. I don't which life to choose. In every one of them, I'm always attached to him, like with some kind of cosmic umbilical cord. And I have no idea why I was a kidnapper. What did I learn from *that* life?"

The old woman pulled on an earlobe. "The breakfast tattoo works differently on people. You can never predict what will happen. From what I've seen and heard, one of two things usually happens: The first group comes to their alternative lives with exactly the same life experience. For example, all three stole a candy bar when they were kids and got away with it. And today they are shown how identical experiences up till now *could* still lead to their three different lives in the future.

"The second group has it harder. They enter three very different lives because of the different consequences of their earlier actions. Same example—in life one, they stole a candy bar and got away with it. So they continued stealing. In life two they got caught but were let off with a warning. That scared them, and they never did it again. In life three they were caught, turned over to the police, and sent away to a juvenile detention center. They were never the same afterward. Sounds from your experience like you're in that second group.

"Sit down now and have some soup, James. It'll make you feel better."

James Arthur said "I've had enough soup. I thought this experience was going to enlighten me, but it's only made me ten times more confused."

"But it's my mother's tomato soup. I always follow her recipe exactly. You loved it the first time you were here. Besides, it was your hero's favorite. He even photographed it!"

Anger growing, his mouth tightened. "The first time I was here, you tricked me. Ever since then, my life has been on a downward spiral."

"James, don't be dishonest—it's not true, and you know it. You chose that tattoo because Graham had it. Your choice had nothing to do with me. What's happened to you since was because you said 'I want *that* one.'"

The first time James Arthur ate Uschi Collins' tomato soup, he sat in exactly the same chair Graham Patterson had many years before. Anna Mae Collins remarked on it when she sat him down at her kitchen table and told the story of how she'd met the famous artist.

Years before, the biographer entered the tattoo shop in the small North Carolina town, not expecting much. Like Patterson, before going into the place James had marveled at the photographs and sketches by the artist inside that were in the shop window. When he told the old woman who apparently ran the place why he was there, she didn't seem surprised, which surprised him. When he asked if she remembered meeting Graham Patterson the photographer, she said only, "Sure!" Hesitantly, not really believing it could be true—although he *had* been sent by Patterson via Ruth Murphy specifically to this place—he asked the old woman if she had tattooed him back then.

"Yup."

Nothing he had ever read about Graham Patterson, and James had read literally everything he could get his hands on, said anything about a tattoo. He felt a small thrill of discovery about this unknown fact relating to the man he had been obsessing over for a long time. He immediately thought if he could find a picture of the tattoo, it would make a marvelous cover illustration for his eventual book on Patterson.

"Would you mind telling me which tattoo he chose?"

"No."

"Excuse me?"

Anna Mae smiled at him. "No, I won't tell you which one he chose."

"Oh."

She paused for effect, and then touched his elbow with one finger. "But I *will* show you my books and see if you can guess which one. It's in there."

"You want me to *guess?*"

"I don't *want* you to do anything. You asked." She pointed an accusing finger at him.

He didn't know what to say at that point without being either rude or aggressive. He was spared when she stood up and left the room, returning a few moments later with two thick carmine red ring binders, which turned out to be full of photographs of her tattoo work. Plunking them down in front of him, she pointed at the books and said, "Have a look. That's my catalog. I'll get the soup going."

James opened one fat binder to the first page. It took him less than ten minutes to pick out what he thought was the Patterson tattoo. He didn't know exactly why, but he felt in his gut it was the right choice. He wanted to be sure before he told Anna Mae so he went through both books, turning the pages slowly, making sure not to miss any one before going on to the next. He kept one of his business cards in the page with the tattoo he had chosen.

He did not change his mind, even after seeing them all.

On the other side of the kitchen, Anna Mae was heating up her homemade tomato soup and a half loaf of fresh cornbread she'd bought that afternoon at the town bakery. She'd invited James to stay at the bed and breakfast she had taken over after her mother died. He quickly agreed because he had so many questions and wanted to squeeze every detail out of her that she could remember about her time with Graham Patterson.

"How are you doing over there? Made up your mind yet?"

He looked up from one of the books, shaking his head in wonder and appreciation. "Your work is so beautiful. *Really*. I never thought of tattoos as works of art."

"Thank you. I do my best. Do you like sour cream in your soup? I like a little dollop."

He shook his head, not to be distracted. "I don't know anything about tattoos, but these are astonishing."

She closed her eyes and nodded thanks for the additional compliment. "Have you figured out yet which one you think Graham chose?"

"Yes, I think so. I hope so."

Wooden stirring spoon in hand, she walked to the kitchen table and looked down over his shoulder at her book opened in front of him. He flipped to the page where he'd found the one he had chosen. He pointed to it.

"Well, look at you! You're absolutely right, mister. You *do* have a good feel for Mr. Patterson and what he liked. I call that one the breakfast tattoo, for obvious reasons."

"Why?"

She pointed to her mouth. "Don't you see—every one of them's eaten the other for breakfast. They're all in each other's stomach. Except for the lion, of course, who's the king of beasts. No one eats *him*."

Looking at the photo, James had a startling idea. He wanted to blurt it out immediately but knew not to. He wasn't an impulsive man by any means. Usually when a big or important idea, theory, or inspiration came to him, he treated it like a teacher handles a rambunctious student in class: Sit down, Freddy—you have to give others a chance to speak, too. He weighed and balanced things carefully, or *forever,* some of his friends and family said. One frustrated lover said he was as impulsive and spontaneous as a snail. But to be fair, this idea was a *forever* thing, so he felt he needed to be extra careful before acting on it.

Over their dinner of soup and cornbread, Anna Mae Collins told him the whole story of how she had met Patterson and what happened in the two days they'd spent together years before.

"What was he like?"

Anna Mae was only the second person he'd talked to who actually had real contact with the photographer before he became a photographer. Ruth Murphy was different because she'd been romantically involved with him, which obviously affected both a person's judgment and perspective. As far as he knew, Anna Mae had only spent two days with him long before he became famous. She tattooed him at the beginning of his big road trip across America after his career in comedy failed.

When Anna Mae got to the part of the story where Graham ("Gray-yam") ate dinner with her and her mother, she told him the photograph "The Queen of Tomato Soup" was of her mom's scarred hand serving this very soup. It was likely one of the first photos he took that helped establish his reputation.

James Arthur was over the moon with excitement hearing all of this. He took notes furiously in his notebook as she spoke and couldn't wait to bring them all together in coherent order when he was alone again.

"Did he come into your shop intending to get a tattoo?"

"Nah, not from what I saw. He came in because he liked what he saw in the window and was intrigued."

"Me, too. I can understand his curiosity." He bent over to write something down.

"What about you, James?"

Confused, he looked up from his notebook. "What *about* me?"

"Have you ever thought of getting some ink, too?" She said it with a light, dismissive tone of voice, as if she knew it wasn't going to happen but thought she'd throw the idea out there just for fun.

Looking at her, his lips curled slowly into a smile. "How'd you do that?"

"Do what?" She smiled back.

"Read my mind."

She sat back in the chair and folded her arms over her chest. "I thought I saw something in your eyes light up when you were looking at the pictures in my book. I'm pretty good at reading customers' reactions after all these years."

"I was thinking about getting the breakfast tattoo." He said it shyly, as if afraid of her reaction to the idea, as if afraid of the preposterous pretension. Would she sneer at such an unoriginal, copycat idea? It practically screamed, I want to look like my hero! Would she think him pathetic?

Anna Mae nodded, her expression saying nothing. "So you want to join the Graham Patterson club, eh?"

James dropped his head, embarrassed he'd even brought up the idea. What an idiot he was. She was right—it was a completely lame fanboy thing to do.

She saw his reaction and her voice rose. "Look, I say go for it if it's what you want. Life's short and ends ugly. The less regret about things you didn't do that you carry to the finish line, the better."

"So you think I should do it, and I'm not just being pathetic?"

"We're *all* pathetic, James. We each just got our own personal brand of it."

———

That night, he couldn't sleep. He'd sat up in bed going over his notes from the day and thinking about how tomorrow he was going to be *tattooed*. He was actually going to get himself *inked*, for God's sake— something he never in a million years would have even thought about doing until hours before when he saw the breakfast tattoo. The master Graham Patterson had it, too! It was so cool. Just that fact alone blew his mind, especially knowing the same brilliant artist who'd done Patterson would now be working on him. Few people knew about the tattoo, as far as James could tell, which made it even more special. As if in some way he was in secret cahoots with his idol, wherever he was now.

Maybe Patterson was dead. It was likely, after all these years. Maybe he's dead and been cremated, and I'll be the one to carry the breakfast tattoo into the future. He wondered how many other people had it. He made a note to ask Anna Mae in the morning.

Climbing out of bed, he took off the t-shirt he slept in and looked at himself in a large mirror across the room. Turning this way and that, he thought about where would be best to have the tattoo. First thought was on one of his thin arms, perhaps on the bicep? Or maybe on one side of his chest? Smiling, he thought, Maybe I should have it over my heart. Definitely not on my back. I want to be able to see it.

He knew a woman who had the name Elizabeth Thug tattooed across her palm. She said it made for interesting conversation because no one could ever guess correctly what the name meant. The irony was it meant nothing. She created it to make herself more enigmatic and intriguing to the rest of the world. James turned over one of his hands and glanced at the palm. No, he wouldn't put it there either.

Looking again in the mirror, turning this way and that in the reflection, he felt good about his decision. He felt good about himself for having *made* that decision. His friends would be shocked when he showed it to them. He was sure of it. You, James Arthur—a *tattoo*? What did you get? A bee inside a frog inside a hawk inside a lion. Are you out of your mind? They'd say things like that, but secretly go, Whoa, I never knew James had it in him.

Normally he was not a man for dangerous situations. He did not seek out exotic places, people, or even papaya, when he had a choice between that and an apple. No papaya, poblano peppers, or prosciutto on his pizza, thank you (and always with just a plain margarita). No worn hiking boots, ice axe, or motorcycle helmet in his closet. No desire for distant climes where malaria lurked alongside ten-foot-long pythons and people slept in hammocks under mosquito nets in jungles. But look at this—here he was, stepping five miles out of character and getting a tattoo in the morning.

Pleased with himself, James Arthur slipped his shirt back on, climbed into bed, and turned off the light.

—

They had been following him ever since he left New York. It was not difficult to do, in his ridiculous red pickup truck that stuck out in any traffic like an emergency flare. Why would someone so famous who lived in Manhattan choose to own an enormous, gaudy truck with enough horsepower to pull the moon? Was he planning on buying a ranch in Montana, or going off-roading in some remote wasteland, home only to scorpions and abandoned gold mines?

They talked about this as they followed him at a distance in their stolen van. Aaron believed when you're rich, you can create and afford to live whatever dream or fantasy you like, no matter how crazy or farfetched it was. Look at that billionaire who was paying some obscene amount of money to be the first to fly on a commercial jet into space. Or the other billionaire who'd spent tens of millions just to ride a Russian rocket up to the international space station.

As far as Aaron was concerned, famous comedian Graham Patterson had bought the big red truck to live out some fantasy he had, probably about being a macho, rough-and-tumble cowboy.

"When we take him, we could dress him up in a Tom of Finland cowboy outfit with chaps and spurs."

"Our Graham doesn't really have the body type for a Tom outfit," Barbara said over her shoulder while she drove.

They were broke and excited. They had a plan. They were going to kidnap Graham Patterson and hold him for at least a million-dollar ransom. Maybe even more—they hadn't worked out the exact sum yet. They talked about that, too, as they followed him west on interstate highways. They'd stolen the silver van from a street in Bridgeport, Connecticut, driven it down to the city, and hidden it in a garage in Bushwick a few blocks from where Barbara lived. They stole some Ohio license plates off a visiting Chrysler, and then they were ready to go.

They'd been friends for years, having met when all three were waiting tables at the short-lived but wonderful Lean and Bean's Doghouse restaurant in Williamsburg. When the place closed because of the recession, they were laid off. Each of them worked a variety of part-time jobs elsewhere, but there were too many times when all of them barely scraped by.

They never lost touch with each other. James and Aaron moved in together to save on rent, and gradually the arrangement turned into a romance. Barbara said, half seriously, that she was jealous, particularly because she had a history of disastrous relationships that all ended up in the muck.

Sometimes, when they were all a little drunk or high or seriously depressed, they talked about committing the perfect crime and getting a lot of money out of it. Enough money to last all of them for years, if they were careful with it. Nothing violent, of course, but something they would only have to do once to land them on easy street. The subject started out as a joke—Ha ha, know any good banks we could rob?—but over time as their financial situations grew more desperate and job opportunities stayed grim, they looked in each other's eyes one day and knew what was being said about it now was wholly serious.

Barbara came up with the idea of kidnapping someone famous. She was a tech whiz, her great passion the internet. She'd majored in computer science in college and was so adept and well-versed in all the latest developments that for a while she worked as a high-level coder for a tech company before it eventually went bust.

She said the biggest problem with kidnapping was not the actual taking of the person, but getting hold of the ransom money and escaping without being caught. But now there was Bitcoin, which largely solved that problem. She could easily create untraceable Bitcoin accounts into which the ransom would be paid, then be routed all over the place like a pinball so it could never be traced directly back to them.

The next question was *who* to kidnap. No children, obviously. No politician, either, because who the hell would want to pay any kind of sizable ransom for one of those weasels? Pop and sports stars had teams of bodyguards and lived in impenetrable mansions in rich enclaves like Neptune, New Jersey, or grand city apartments with state-of-the-art twenty-four-hour security.

Then one day James saw the comedian Graham Patterson coming out of a cigar store on Greene Street. Patterson was by himself, and making no effort to disguise who he was. The signature Mohawk haircut stood out from his head like a big brown shoe brush. He wore Chelsea boots, jeans, and a red chambray shirt under a beautiful salt-and-pepper tweed jacket. James loved fashion and for a few seconds thought more about what designer had made such a gorgeous jacket than the fact the famous performer was standing five feet away from him, even briefly making eye contact when he lit up a cigar.

New York was the town of celebrities. If you lived there, you would see them all the time doing actual human things like reading a book in a restaurant, hailing a cab in the rain and getting pissed off when it doesn't stop for them, or buying cigars on Greene Street. Later, when James casually mentioned he had seen Patterson earlier in the day, Aaron opened his mouth in surprise, snapped his fingers, and said, "*Him!*" He immediately called Barbara.

She agreed. In less than an hour of snooping and hacking, she discovered Patterson's home address on Perry Street in Greenwich Village. The three of them took a trip uptown one night to check the place out. It was one of those sleek, icy-cold modern buildings, probably designed by some famous architect, with too much glass, exposed girders, exotic wood, and a total lack of warmth or heart. Sure enough, when Barbara searched online on a fact-finding mission about the place, she discovered the condominium had been designed by the renowned architect Harry Radcliffe and was a bastion of security. Out went the idea of taking Patterson where he lived.

However they were going to kidnap him, they needed a van for their plan. On James's suggestion, instead of taking a vehicle off the street in New York, the men took a train to Bridgeport, Connecticut, where Aaron grew up. They stole a perfectly anonymous-looking van after walking around the industrial outskirts of the town for an hour. Thanks to Barbara and her expertise, they learned to hotwire a car's ignition and start it without a key from a dark-web site that gave detailed instructions on how to steal any number of interesting things. Before leaving Bridgeport, they swapped license plates from the van with ones from a banged-up beige Chrysler that came from Ohio— "Birthplace of Aviation."

Speaking of transportation, Aaron read in an automotive magazine at his dentist's office that Graham Patterson, like many other celebrities, had recently bought a Ford Raptor pickup truck. There was a color picture of him standing in front of the tomato red behemoth with arms crossed and a big, triumphant smile on his face. At the end of the article, there was a list of the comedian's upcoming club and concert dates. One of those dates was at Rutgers University in New Brunswick, New Jersey, an hour from the city. They were certain Patterson would drive his new truck to the venue.

They planned to go there and, while he was performing, attach a GPS tracking device to the bumper so they could know where his truck was at all times. They were hoping sometime in the near future he'd go for a ride in the country or somewhere remote where they could snatch him without the risk of being seen and get away with it. As soon as they had him, Barbara would send a text message from an untraceable account to Patterson's agent and make their demands.

But he surprised them, taking them completely off guard. In New Brunswick they found his truck easily enough. They arrived just before sunset, and his big, bright red machine dwarfed all the other cars in the parking lot outside the theater where he was performing.

They attached the magnetic device to the inside of the rear bumper and then went for dinner at a cheap Hungarian restaurant off campus. When they got back to the parking lot, the red truck was gone, much earlier than they had expected. Barbara said it was no problem and, while Aaron drove, booted up the app that would track the truck. She said to think of this as a trial run to see if things worked the way they had planned.

To their growing dismay, Patterson did not drive back to New York after his performance that night. He got on the New Jersey turnpike and headed south toward Philadelphia.

Barbara sat in the passenger's seat with the laptop open on her lap.

"What do you want me to do?" Aaron asked, his eyes on the road.

Watching the computer screen, she said, "What the hell—let's follow him for a while and see where he goes."

James was sitting on the pile of four sleeping bags in the back of the van. Their big plan was to kidnap Patterson and just drive him around until the Bitcoin ransom was paid. If they stopped or stayed in

any specific place while waiting for the payoff, they were more likely
to be caught. But if they kept moving around the country with their
prize in the back, how was anyone to know where they were?

The first night after his performance at Rutgers, Patterson drove
as far as New Hope, Pennsylvania. He stopped at an inn where he
had stayed not long before with Ruth for a romantic getaway weekend
after his last tour. They both remarked on what a lovely place it was
and how they wanted to come back some time. The inn was still on his
phone's speed dial. He called while driving fast down the turnpike. Of
course there was a room available for Mr. Patterson. They were thrilled
to have him back.

After arriving and checking in, he ate dinner at the Blue Moose
Restaurant. Although other diners recognized him and smiled when
he looked their way, no one bothered him. He took a walk by the
canal after dinner and felt fantastic. On the spur of the moment, he
had decided to play hooky from his hectic life for a few days and just
drive who knows where. Already he felt clearer in his head than he
had in a long time.

Once the prospective kidnappers knew where Patterson was staying, they found a camping place nearby and settled into their sleeping
bags in the back of the van.

In the middle of the night, James got up to go outside and pee.
While standing there watering a bush, he had a strong panic attack.
One very loud inner voice wailed, What the *hell* are you doing here?
Why are you doing this for God's sake? Are you out of your mind?
In truth, there really were no good sane answers to those questions,
other than to say I'm tired of worrying about money and tired of fail-
ure and tired of looking at every third person I pass on a New York
City street and being envious of them, even though I have absolutely
no idea of who they are or what their lives are like. It scared him that

both jealousy and despair were growing like twin tumors in his soul. When you're jealous of a stranger you encounter and pass by within seconds, then you know you are one fucked-up kitty. Something toxic and deadly was eating away at his life. He shoved this scared James out of his thoughts, pulled up his zipper, and returned to the van.

The next morning after breakfast, Graham Patterson got back in his new truck and started driving west. This was cause for alarm inside the stolen van, still following him at a discreet distance. Where the hell was he going—California? Between the three kidnappers, they had a grand total of two hundred and seven dollars plus a couple of almost maxed-out credit cards to pay for everything—gas, food, whatever else. Patterson just kept driving.

In the van's glove compartment were four plastic zip ties and the Umarex XBG pellet gun Barbara had bought, used, on Amazon for $28. It was a damned scary looking thing. Particularly from a distance, it looked like a real pistol for sure. Probably only an expert or gun nut checking the weapon would see it wasn't the real thing, although it would certainly hurt if you were shot with it. Most importantly, it was good enough to scare the shit out of someone if it was pointed at them. Two hundred seven dollars, a few zip ties, and a $28 used pellet gun to pull off a million-dollar kidnapping.

Fifteen hours and nine hundred miles later, they got their chance.

On the third day, Patterson pulled off the interstate highway at a rest stop to stretch his legs and make some phone calls to people to let them know he was okay, but AWOL for the next few days.

He called Ruth, his agent Ginger, and his best friend Steven Bergman, who had given him the biggest scolding for just disappearing without telling anyone why. Patterson rubbed his Mohawk haircut and smiled sheepishly while his friend ranted at him for being such a selfish, thoughtless asshole to those who cared about him.

After the phone calls he sat on the picnic table breathing deep and slow, realizing he was done with driving for the day and wanted to stop soon. He looked up a travel website on his phone and discovered a college town close by that even had a comedy club. Patterson had written some new material recently about Evangelical Christian weight-lifters but had not tried any of it out yet on an audience. This college comedy club sounded like the perfect place for a dress rehearsal.

The kidnappers followed him into the town and watched as he parked in the club lot and went inside. He came out a few minutes later and drove to a nearby motel. There was no sign at the club announcing he would be performing that night, but they agreed there was a good chance he would, and that's when they started making plans.

He was really good. There was no question about it. Graham Patterson could definitely make you laugh out loud. He said hilarious lines, anecdotes, and stories that sounded completely spontaneous, like they'd just popped into his head a moment ago, but were so bright, insightful, and relevant that you were his willingly captive audience from the get-go. He did one bit about sex toys for aliens that made a guy at the next table laugh so hard, beer shot out of his nose.

James and Aaron sat in the middle of the room, nursing beers they'd bought two hours before, both of them totally enjoying the show even though they knew in a little while they were going to kidnap this funny man and hold him for ransom. The irony of the situation made James smile nervously while he sat there, part of the captive audience. Right now we're his audience, later his captors.

Their plan was to wait till Patterson left the club and went back to his truck. As soon as it happened, James was to call Barbara, waiting in the van parked a few miles away. She was the best driver of the three and would need to keep a steady hand on the wheel for the next few hours.

Next, James and Aaron were to follow the comedian out to the lot and, after introducing themselves as big fans (with fake names), keep him occupied making small talk until they saw Barbara coming. She would stop just outside the lot to let them say goodbye to him and go back into the club. It was better they be seen in there again so later, if things went wrong and they were suspects, eyewitnesses would say they saw the two men in the club when the kidnapping took place. As soon as they went inside, Barbara would come flying up in the van, pull next to Patterson, point the gun, and tell him to get in or she'd shoot him. She would rendezvous with the men down the street from the club, and then they'd all be off.

Their plan worked perfectly. Even they were surprised at how easily and fluidly everything went. Patterson seemed pleased to chat with these two gay strangers outside the club while he smoked a post-performance cigar. He even asked them how they had managed to stay together for so long. On the spot, James adlibbed a bullshit story about paper towels that Patterson loved.

Aaron saw the van first and nudged James. They thanked the famous man for talking with them and headed back inside. Patterson stayed there, leaning against the truck while smoking the last of the cigar, at total peace with the world.

Moments later, Barbara drove in, picked him up, and sped out of the lot. As far as she could tell, no one had witnessed the snatch. A block down the street she waited for the men, pointing the gun at

Patterson the whole time. She just prayed he didn't try to grab it or recognize it wasn't real. He did neither. And a few excruciatingly long minutes later, the side door of the van slid open, and her partners in crime hopped in.

Patterson turned in his seat, looked at them, and said in amazement, "*You two?*"

Barbara had no idea how much time they had before the police found out what happened and the chase was on, so she drove faster than she should out of town. Suddenly remembering that cell phones can be traced, she told the comedian to throw his out the window and raised the gun from her lap to show she meant business. He didn't protest. He tossed it, then stared straight ahead, shaking his head from side to side. They didn't know if it was because he couldn't believe what was happening or because he thought what they'd done was stupid. He did not appear to be afraid, which made all of them nervous; it felt as if he sensed something they didn't that was going to affect this whole plan.

What happened next probably never *would* have happened if Patterson had kept his mouth shut. Once his initial shock passed and he realized just what was happening, he turned to the woman and asked in a ticked-off voice, "What the *fuck* are you doing?"

"Be quiet." She had the gun in her lap with one hand on it, her eyes on the road. They were out in the countryside somewhere, surrounded by what looked like wheat fields.

"No, but really, what the fuck are you doing—*kidnapping* me? Really? How much do you think you can get? Nine dollars?"

From the back of the van, Aaron piped up, "Try a million."

"Hah! That's a joke. A *million*? You guys are totally nuts. Who do you think is going to pay a million dollars ransom for me, my mother? Who is dead, by the way."

James said, "You've got that kind of money. How much did you get for your last Netflix special? I doubt nine dollars. And if you don't have that much on hand, you know people who do—people who depend on you for their living."

The road was badly lit and narrow. There was a faint light up ahead, which Barbara hoped was a sign for the interstate highway. She wanted to get them on it as fast as possible and far away from here. They'd carefully studied a map of the area beforehand and planned to take this road as part of their escape route, but they never imagined it would be so very dark and badly maintained.

Patterson slid both hands up tight under his armpits. "How do you plan on getting this million-dollar ransom without being caught, if you don't mind my asking?"

"Bitcoin."

Their hostage barked out a loud derisive laugh. "*Bitcoin?* What are you, from Romania?"

All three kidnappers sat up straight and looked at him.

"What do you mean, Romania?"

"Because that's what all the thieves from there and Russia demand as payment when they blackmail poor bastards on the internet. Threaten to broadcast pictures of you jerking off or screwing the wrong people that were stolen from the camera on the schmuck's screen if they don't pay a ransom—in Bitcoin. Now we have you and the Romanians—brothers in crime.

"Fucking Bitcoin—you know it's about as predictable as the weather on Mars. It climbs and drops ten times an hour in value. More often than not, that big, fat-ass Bitcoin fortune you had yesterday? Poof! Suddenly today it's worth zip. Zilch. Zero. My kidnappers want to be paid in *Bitcoin.* That is so adorably lame. You're the gang that couldn't shoot straight."

Barbara, whose idea it had been to use Bitcoin for ransom, kept swiveling her head from eyes on the road over to Patterson, who now held them in thrall with his scalding monologue. She was both frightened and fascinated by what he said. She knew Bitcoin could be extremely volatile. What if it *did* collapse right after they were paid?

"*Plus,* my new friends, I've now seen all your faces. I assume you're not going to kill me, so what happens—"

They had driven up to a rural railroad crossing that had no descending gate or blinking red light to warn cars not to cross the track without looking carefully both ways. Totally distracted by what Patterson had just been saying, none of them did look.

An express train bound for Chicago roaring along at eighty miles an hour blew its horn at them, but way too late. Seconds later it slammed into the van broadside, killing everyone inside instantly and driving their vehicle almost a quarter-mile up the track before it came to a complete stop.

The final irony came later in a detailed obituary about the comedian Graham Patterson in a prominent newspaper. It said he was killed while riding "with friends" in the Illinois countryside. It is not known where the group was going at the time.

———

"Tell me about the bird."

James Arthur glared at Anna Mae Collins as if she were to blame for everything that had happened to him. He took a long drink of Dr. Pepper, his angry eyes never leaving her face. She was trying hard to suppress a smile. He saw, and it didn't help his fury.

"You think it's funny? You think being killed by a speeding train is something to laugh about?"

She held up a finger to stop him. "No, James, not at all. But I do think the way you're tellin' the story is funny. You're so *indignant*. Why? This miraculous opportunity has been given to you, but the only thing you're focusing on is you died after committing a crime? Look, did it hurt?"

His eyes narrowed. Her answer was not what he expected. He answered hesitantly, "No."

"Did you know what hit you?"

"The last thing I remember is the train whistle blowing, and it sounded this close." He put a hand up inches from his ear.

She counted the next points off on the fingers of a raised hand. "So let's summarize all this: In just one of your three possible lives, you died painlessly while committing a crime that's a capital offense in some states. You were a kidnapper, probably sure to get caught eventually and put in jail for who knows how long—because your plan was ridiculous, I must tell you.

"But hey—look at this: Here you are all comfy-cozy drinking ice cold Dr. Pepper in the kitchen with me, none the worse for wear. You just got to watch an interesting scenario starring yourself doing just about the stupidest thing you could, short of drinking bleach. I'd say not only did you survive your very own catastrophe, but you did okay, even though you're not a cat."

"What does a cat have to do with it?"

"Cats have nine lives. You only have three, but that's two more than most people. When they make outstandingly terrible choices like you did back there, they don't get to walk away from them and try on another life. But you *do*.

"As I said before, from what I know about the tattoo, some people who get it start living their alternative lives exactly from the moment they enter them with all they've experienced and accumulated in *this* life, like Mark Curry did. He went to his alternatives, found something there, brought it back to *this* life, and used it to make his fortune.

"Others meet up with their alternatives after those lives have gone in different directions because of personal qualities or previous events that happened to them. For example, if you're a liar it can help you succeed in life, like a politician, or destroy you, depending on what happened in your past.

"Something in your past led 2 to kidnapping. In this life, you ignored that negative thing or overcame it and have done fine. James 2 became a kidnapper because whatever it was from the past won over his better judgment. You said your father died early in your life. *You've* been able to work around it. Maybe James 2 never did and needed your father's guidance to help overcome his tendency for doing bad things.

"So enough of that. Tell me about this bird. I always like hearing these 'after death' stories. You died in the train crash. Then you met a guy named Larry Ivers on the other side. Who was he?"

"My Little League baseball coach. He had a heart attack and died at our championship game the year I played on his team. He was a nice man."

"He was the one who met you over there after you died?"

"Yes. He told me about reincarnation and all it entailed. I was excited and relieved I could return to *this* life or try out the other. He repeated a lot of the stuff you'd already said, but the train wreck really shook me."

"But in the end, you *still* chose to stay with 2 the kidnapper to see what his next life would be like after reincarnation?"

James looked away, embarrassed. "Yes, dumb me. Again." He made a sour face and shrugged.

"And you were reincarnated as a bird?" The smile on her face came back, and this time she didn't try to stop it.

In a sarcastic voice, he said, "Not just any bird either—a Teratornis, the biggest bird that ever lived. A prehistoric bird, no less. When James Arthur goes bird, he goes big. I did some research on it when I came back here from my short trip to prehistory."

Anna Mae leaned forward to hear better. "So you kidnapped Graham, got hit by a train, died, and were reincarnated as a big bird in the time of the dinosaurs. *That* must have been a shock."

He shook his head after taking a sip of soda. "I wasn't there long enough to know. The first thing I saw, I was flying way up in the air, looking on the ground for something to eat. I saw this lizard thing down there and started to dive-bomb down after it.

"As I flew, I could feel my brain going mushy. Thank God I immediately recognized I was about to lose my own mind and get this bird's. I bailed out and came back. The next day I got in my car and drove here again to see you. Because I've got questions, Anna Mae."

She ignored what he said and ventured a guess instead. "I *bet* it was Graham you saw down there on the ground. I bet you were going to eat Graham the lizard." She told James the story of how Patterson 2 had been reincarnated after their train accident as some kind of prehistoric gecko or something, probably back at the exact same time as James the Teratornis was high in the sky, looking for a snack.

"It all makes beautiful sense." She nodded, mostly to affirm what she was thinking. She couldn't help admiring how once again, even when how people experienced their other lives shifted, the pieces of the breakfast tattoo all fit so neatly into place. Every single time.

"It *does?*" He wasn't about to be convinced without proof.

"Yes, it does, James, it does."

"I have another question—sooner or later, do all of the people you've given this tattoo to come back to you with more questions?"

"No, just a few, actually. Graham never did, if that's what you're asking. I saw him only that once at the comedy club to explain how things worked. That was the night you kidnapped his second self. He saw you do it—he saw *your* second self kidnap *his* second self. Perfect symmetry."

"But it's crazy—why *don't* people who get the tattoo come back to see you? I can't believe they have no more questions. How could you *not*? Don't they want to know more before they make their final decision? I sure as hell do."

She reached over and patted his hand. "But that's just you. Some, like Mark Curry, made their decision on their own, which meant both the tattoo and their memory was erased. They don't remember me.

"It's not to say people make the *right* decision with all the information they can get, but that's just life—no matter how many you have. Others, like Graham, seem to want to do it on their own, with no outside help. I respect them. Find their personal answers by just *doing*. Everybody has their own way. I'm here to answer as many of their questions as I can, although as I told you before, my knowledge is limited. Even after these many years of doing it, I'm still in the dark about a lot.

"Now, the technical answer to your other question is so complicated I'd need seven Einsteins with seven years to explain it. But I'll try to spell it out like this. Remember Rubik's Cube? The square twisty puzzle from a few years ago everybody was tormented by and yet was still all the craze?"

"Sure, I had one and hated it—I could never get all the different colors lined up perfectly in proper order. It drove me crazy."

"You and a million others. Well, think of one of those Rubik's Cubes now. As you said, to solve it, you've got to keep twisting all the different colored sections of the cube around and around countless times in countless combinations until you've got them all aligned in rows of exactly the same color, right? All nine whites together on one side of the cube, all nine reds on another, and so on. Only when *all* of them are lined up correctly together on *all six* sides of the cube is the puzzle solved.

"The ones who get the breakfast tattoo are like Rubik's Cubes. Because in all three of your different lives, you will always encounter and be dealing with exactly the same people. For example, in all three of your different lives, you will encounter Graham Patterson in one form or another. Think of yourself as the cube, and them as the different colors that need to all be lined up correctly—red, blue, white, yellow, orange, green. Even when you've been reincarnated in a different time, and maybe as a different species, you'll still be dealing with the same group. Same parents, same friends—who may be friends in this life but enemies in another. You never know what the arrangement is going to be. But it's always with the same people, no matter what. No, correction—not always the same people, because a big *bird* ain't a person. Let's call them souls. In all three life options, you will always be dealing with the same souls, trying to line them up in what's for you the correct order. Got it?"

James nodded slowly, still processing everything she said. "So far, yes."

"All right, then. The next step is choosing the *right* life of the three—"

"There's a right one?"

"Absolutely. But the choice is always yours, and it may be surprising. Years ago, when I was working in London, I gave the tattoo to a Greek couple. After I explained to them how it worked, the man chose to experience his other two lives, the woman didn't. Said she was content with hers the way it was. I distinctly remember feeling jealous of her and her contentment. Lucky woman.

"After visiting his other two, the husband also chose to stay in the life he already had with his wife. To him, to both of them, it was more than enough. He felt blessed. Soon after he made the choice, though, he fell while mountain climbing and died."

"Oh my God! What if he had chosen differently?"

"Who knows? I don't know what he experienced when he went to the other lives. But if he had chosen either of them, he probably would've at least lived longer with the woman he loved so much.

"Anyway, to get back to the Rubik's: You've been handed this cube, these three possible lives for James Arthur. By twisting them into different and varied combinations, you figure out which one to choose. Once you have chosen, to finish the cube, you've got to try and live that life correctly. No easy task. Only then do you have all of your colors aligned and solve the puzzle."

He understood and was frustrated by her answer. "But what do you mean by correct? What's a correct life?"

She answered calmly. "It depends on the person. All I know is what I was taught: There's a light, and you *know* where it is—it's obviously different for each individual—and then you must *try* and walk in it. Of course, the key word there is *try*. You choose the life you think best suits you. Then try your best to live it right. Do that, and it's more than likely to cause some kind of positive ripple out into the universe, and maybe across other people's lives, changing them for the better. You know, it's the butterfly effect.

"When I got the tattoo years and years ago, I chose to stay right where I was and not to experience my other lives. Why? Because I was genuinely happy with what I was doing and believed with all my heart it was the right life for me. But living *this* life has also meant I've been alone all these years. Still, you can be sure I'm always trying my damnedest to make this life I did choose a masterpiece, even if it's a small one that few ever see.

"As to the tattoo itself, I only know the rules for it as they were taught to me by my teacher in Japan, not the reason or the results, except for the times people tell me, like you or the Greek woman. She came here years ago because Graham gave her my address. This was sometime after he disappeared. She asked if I knew where he was. She thought because I tattooed both of them, I would know something about his disappearance or whereabouts. I didn't, and I don't."

James Arthur rubbed his face hard, up and down, as if trying to wipe all the confusion off it. "So in this life, I'm writing Patterson's biography, and it's why I began to see all the photographs from another of his lives that no one else could see but Ruth Murphy?"

"Correct."

"In another life I'm a bird about to *eat* him after having *died* trying to *kidnap* him, and in the third . . . " His voice dropped. He went silent.

Anna Mae raised an eyebrow. "What *about* your third life? You said you haven't seen that one yet."

He moved a hand from side to side as if brushing away a cobweb. "The truth? The truth is after being a Teratornis, I'm kind of scared to go there now. What if it turns out to be the worst life of all? How depressing."

"Then you come back. It's no big deal, James." Anna Mae put a hand to her cheek while she thought about it. "What was the sweet name again of your first dog?"

"Grateful."

"Grateful. That's right—such a nice name. I think you should say 'Grateful' and go see what James Arthur 3's life looks like. At least for a little while. Take a glimpse. No harm in doing that. Why not? You've got your three visits there if you want. If it's terrible, just come back here and write one more off the list. I assume you've already done it with Mr. Kidnapper Big Bird. Maybe if you go visit your third, it'll make your final decision a lot simpler. You'll see the life you're living here now is not only the best, but the only logical choice because the other two are awful."

He started to say something, hesitated, and then said it. "Anna Mae, would you tell me one thing? Just one thing, but be totally honest about it. Please."

His voice was so earnest and pleading. She had no idea what he was about to ask but said to herself that, whatever it was, she would answer honestly to the best of her knowledge.

"In this life we're living right here and now, *do* you know where Patterson is?"

Looking him straight in the eye, she said, "No, I don't. I swear to you, James."

"Wherever he is, do you know if he's alive or dead?"

"No, I'm sorry but I don't. I wish I could help you, but I can't. I have no idea if he's here or in another life."

———

They went to the park because they had been fighting again and needed to get out of the house—move to some kind of neutral ground. The air in there was so charged with negative energy that they even argued about whether to take the baby in her stroller or let her walk there because walking was her new favorite thing to do. Aaron won the battle. Little Ms. Kenyon was plunked down in her orange (for safety) stroller and wheeled out into a pleasant early spring day.

The park had a fenced-in play area for small children. When they got there, they took her squirming body out of the stroller and set her free. There were benches scattered around the space, all of them with a full view of the grounds so parents could keep an eye on their little ones. They sat down on one, both men still tense and grumpy from arguing but glad at least to be out in the fresh air.

They made an interesting-looking couple. Aaron was tall and wide, his hands as huge as cooking mitts, his feet small kayaks. He'd played guard on the Purdue University football team and until recently went regularly to the gym to keep in top shape. His husband James was as short and skinny as a French existentialist, no more than five foot seven.

They'd met one momentous afternoon at a gay bookstore in Hollywood. James was standing near the front desk holding a rare first edition of one of his favorite novels in the world, *The Story of Harold* by Terry Andrews. He hadn't reread it in years, and although it was selling here for a small fortune, he was considering buying it anyway. This was a book that belonged on his shelves.

He stood flipping through the pages, reading and remembering passages here and there with an appreciative grin on his face. A deep voice from behind asked, "Do you know who Terry Andrews really is? I tried for years to find out. It's a pseudonym, right?"

James turned and faced a handsome golem of a man standing not two feet away. James hated and never used the word awesome, but this guy was just that—awesome in size and stature.

"Yes, you're right. Terry Andrews *was* a pseudonym. The author's real name was George Selden. He died years ago, unfortunately. Selden was actually a well-known children's book author, and this was his only novel. Have you read it?"

"It was my best friend in college," said the big man, and James was already a goner.

Aaron Hayes was a defense lawyer with a large legal firm in Los Angeles, but his dream was to be a novelist. James Arthur was a copywriter for a boutique PR company in Santa Monica that was suddenly red hot in the industry after having created and launched a very successful advertising campaign for a young upstart political candidate who had unexpectedly won big in an election against a twenty-year incumbent.

James and Aaron continued talking that first day all the way from the bookstore through to a three-hour lunch of lamb chops and cheesecake at the Musso and Frank Grill on Hollywood Boulevard, and then to bed at Aaron's bungalow in Beachwood Canyon, where a neighbor's dog barked all afternoon, the Santa Ana winds blew, and the first forest fire of the season was started by an arsonist a few miles away.

The men moved in together soon after and were married in San Francisco by a state senator who'd played football with Aaron at Purdue. Two years later, they adopted Kenyon.

Probably because of the many steroids he'd taken as a teenager to bulk up for football, Aaron's heart was damaged. He had his first heart attack at thirty-eight, the second at forty-two, a few months before he met James. It was a sad irony to look at this big imposing man and know inside his broad chest lived a heart as fragile and unreliable as a car with two hundred thousand miles on it.

When Aaron developed an irregular heartbeat a few years later, his doctor prescribed a strong antiarrhythmic drug. But it made him feel sleepy, disconnected and muddled. He hated it. That's when the trouble between the two men began. James discovered Aaron had stopped taking the drug after about a month, soon after the shitty side effects really kicked in and started affecting him in bad ways.

Their discussions about it turned into arguments and, more recently, a few volcanic blowups on both sides. James could not believe his brilliant, normally reasonable husband would risk another major health crisis because of a drug that made him want to take more naps.

"It's not naps, James, I've told you ten times. It's not being clear-headed with my legal work all day long, or when I try to write. I *need* my brain to be fully functional for what I do, but this drug puts it on screen saver whenever I take it. I don't even have the benefit of feeling nicely stoned on it, like with marijuana. It just feels like my life slides into a kind of ugly slow motion."

One night they watched a nature documentary on National Geographic. Among the animals featured was a sloth. Watching the adorably odd creature tread oh so very slowly through a tropical rain forest, Aaron turned to James, pointed to the TV, and said, "He must be taking the same drug I am."

In the park that afternoon, they were watching their young, wonderful daughter waddle here and there, delighted by everything around her. It brought some peace between them, but not enough. Both men wanted to say more, to let all their pent-up feelings out. But they knew if they did, it would likely inflame the already fraught situation.

Too often recently when these arguments occurred, things were said in haste or anger that couldn't be taken back. Grievances, accusations, and reproaches that could very well permanently stain or damage their otherwise very happy relationship. So they held their tongues, which was sometimes hard to do when this subject came up. Right now, an unspoken truce prevailed. They both just wanted to watch as Kenyon marched in her tottering, happy way around the playground.

A few weeks before, Aaron had come back from an appointment with his cardiologist, excited about something he had written on his laptop while sitting in the doctor's waiting room and then finished in a nearby café afterward. James always immediately made room in his day for whatever Aaron wrote and wanted him to read because he knew how important it was to his love.

"Let's see it."

Excited as a little kid, Aaron said, "It just came to me whole cloth while I was sitting in that office. I have no idea where it came from, but I really like it. It says exactly what I was thinking the last few days." He opened his laptop and put it on the table in front of James, then sat down next to him.

"Enough with the introduction, big boy—let's see what you've got here." James put on his reading glasses, squared Aaron's laptop on the table for a better view, and read:

> I was thinking about sea glass and what an extraordinarily good metaphor it is for what we all hope for in life. When it was created and first used, the glass had no value. It was part of a greenish Coke bottle, a cheap brown cough syrup bottle, or an olive oil bottle, or a blue drinking glass. Nothing of importance. Use up the contents, throw the bottle away.
>
> Somehow or other, the glass broke, and the pieces were scattered. This one ends up in the ocean. For a long time, maybe even years, it's tossed and tumbled, flung here and there by the violent whims of the sea. It's not a good life, but it manages not

to break. All the time it's in the ocean, however, its sharp edges are being worn away by the water's constant movement. The violence of storms, the bleaching sun, saltwater . . . all these things transform it.

Eventually the shard gets washed up on a beach somewhere. It is the same glass it once was, but also something new, reborn, resurrected like Lazarus. Call it now Lazarus Glass. The original color has been burned away by the sun and sea, making the glass more translucent, ethereal, lovely. It has no more sharp edges that cut or wound. But without them it has taken on a shape, a new form, singular and truly one of a kind.

Sooner or later, someone walking on the beach comes by and notices it. They bend down to pick it up and are immediately attracted. They love it for what it has become, having no idea of what it once was. Delighted with their find, they'll take it home and, in some cases, even turn it into a piece of jewelry or something else valuable. Something to treasure.

In the park today, stewing next to his beloved partner, James remembered the essay and something new about it struck him. Turning to Aaron, he said in a tight, worried voice, "I want you to live long enough to turn into a piece of Lazarus glass. Me, too. I want us both to. Please take the medicine, Aaron. Do it for all three of us." He pointed to Kenyon a few feet away studying a stick she'd picked up off the ground. When she started to bring it to her mouth, Aaron rose and went over, swooped her up, and swung her around in his arms. A diversion she always loved. James watched, relieved this shift of attention happened so his husband wouldn't feel cornered or compelled to respond to what he'd just said.

Over Aaron's shoulder, James saw the woman for the first time. He thought she was only another young mother with a kid somewhere in the playground. But as she got closer, he saw she held something large in her hand. It looked like a paving stone. No, it was a *brick*. Why? Why bring a brick in here? As she approached, James saw the sick pallor of her face and a frightening madness in her eyes. Alarmed, he realized she was walking with deadly purpose toward a little boy alone on the swings a few feet away. She slowly began to raise the arm with the brick, and it was clear she intended to hit the boy with it. She was going to hit a child with a brick. It was insane.

James Arthur stood quickly and took three steps toward the woman, who was very close now. She did not look at him, despite their closeness, only at the boy on the swing. Instinctively, James grabbed her free arm and tried to hold onto her, to stop her. But she was shockingly strong, too strong, *way* too strong. He managed to slow her for precious moments but could not stop her. As she finally jerked away, he called out desperately to Aaron.

Just then, another man came rushing in from his blindside and hit the woman in the face with a book, again and again, until he dropped the book and hit her with his fist. In response she howled, turned, and punched him punched him punched him so fast and everywhere she could.

Aaron came and, grabbing her from behind, threw her to the ground. No one was stronger than Aaron. The mad woman—and she had to be mad, judging by her actions, her physical looks up close, the wild screams and screeches she made like a furious animal—would not stop twisting and turning in the men's hands. They all knew if they let up for an instant, she might break free. So they held her down with all their strength, but even for Aaron it was not easy. Out of the corner of his eye, James saw several women with phones to their ears. He hoped to God they were calling the police.

Luckily they were, and a few difficult minutes later two police cars, sirens singing, drove into the park and stopped nearby. Four cops got out, took in the scene of three men trying to hold down a wildly thrashing and screaming young woman. Two of the cops, both long-time veterans of the force, actually whistled in their dismay. One of them went back to his car for zip ties, leg restraints, a protective mask, and a brief talk on the radio to his dispatcher to report what was happening.

Three of the police officers took over and picked her up off the ground while holding tight with grips like vises. Despite that, she snapped her head quickly, *so quickly* to the side and tried to bite one of their hands.

The men who'd stopped her from attacking the little boy gave their stories to the officer in charge. He kept shaking his head in disbelief at the craziness of what had happened here. Then they watched as the woman's still-flailing wrists were zip tied, the protective mask was put over her head after the biting attempt, and finally leg restraints were used when she began kicking. All the time this was going on, she never stopped shrieking. They led her to one of the patrol cars and shoved her unceremoniously onto the backseat. One of the cops said under his breath, "Fucking nutty bitch." James bent over and picking up her brick, offered it to one of them. The man looked at it, sighed, and said, "I'll take it with me as evidence."

After the police left, the man who'd hit the woman moments after James tried to stop her turned to him and, to James's great surprise, embraced him tightly.

"Thank you so much. You saved my son's life."

"Hey, you're welcome, but *you* stopped her. I just grabbed her arm. Do you believe how strong she was? I was about to let go. She was so strong I really couldn't hold her."

"You held on long enough for me to get there. It's all that matters to me." Overwhelmed, the man dropped his head to his chest and wiped tears from his eyes.

Aaron put a reassuring arm around his shoulder and said, "Everything's okay now. Nobody got hurt. And Team Us kicked her ass."

The father of the little boy nodded and tried to laugh, but he was clearly traumatized. It was going to take some time for him to come down from the experience.

"Daddy?"

They saw the boy on the swings standing nearby now, looking with concern at his father.

"Hey, Conor, hey. Don't worry—everything's okay. These men are my friends." He pointed to them but was embarrassed now because he didn't know the names of these lifesavers.

James helped. "Hi Conor, I'm James, and this is my friend Aaron."

The boy nodded his approval, as if things were okay now that he knew their names. He walked back to the swings and climbed slowly onto one. His father put out a hand to shake and said to the others, "I'm Graham Patterson. Thank you. Thank you both so much."

James took the hand and said, "James Arthur. Glad we could help."

Then Graham and Aaron shook. The three men stood there looking at Conor, who sat swinging but was no longer talking to himself or his Ghost Daddy friend, and never would again.

—

It was like a normal city in there, and he hated that. Hated the stores on the ground floor selling normal, everyday things—fresh bread, Burger King, dental floss, postage stamps, café latte. There was even a clothing store. Who the hell bought a dress or pair of shorts in a *hospital*? Was it for the healthy ones, or for the patients upstairs who the visitors were there to see—gifts from the life they once knew but hadn't appreciated before now, when they had too much time to long for that past?

Gifts from the stores downstairs in the lobby meant to raise the patients' spirits and make them feel better, to give them some renewed hope that soon they'd be out of here living normal days again, breathing outside air instead of air conditioned, which was always a little too much or too little. Give these poor souls a familiar taste or feel—concrete, material reminders of regular life out there in the regular world where you put on fresh underwear in the morning and not another one of those awful, washed-a-million-times faded hospital gowns that felt specifically designed to humiliate anyone who wore them. Too short, baring your ass in back, and a tie behind the neck you could never get right and kept untying itself.

So here's a new shirt for maybe some time in the future when you get out of here, or some brand-new striped cotton pajamas to actually cover every part of you and hopefully make you feel a little more like a member of the world outside this spirit-drowning place.

Thinking these grim thoughts, James pushed the stroller across the vast hospital lobby while surrounded by multitudes of people passing by in all directions wearing colorful street clothes, doctors, nurses, and hospital aides all in white, patients limping slowly along on crutches, or being pushed in wheelchairs, or walking alone in bathrobes and slippers while hooked up to tall metal IV stands. He'd heard there were thousands of patients in the hospital at all times. Just walking through this busy lobby made the number seem true.

It was almost a thousand steps from the front door to the elevator bank up to the cardiac unit on the sixth floor. The four elevators were very slow. He had learned from coming here so often that the best way to wait for them was to fantasize scenarios for the other people waiting along with him. The young woman in front of him, so flashily dressed, talking loudly on her phone. Who was she here to see, and why dress like that for a hospital visit? Maybe her boyfriend was upstairs, and she wore the outfit to remind him of the good things to come when he got out.

Or the hunched old man, a few days unshaven, carrying a thick book under his arm. Had he brought it to read to the person he was visiting? What would be a good absorbing story to read to someone trapped in this sterile city a long time to help them escape for a blessed little while to an imaginary somewhere else?

"*James*! How are you? So nice to see you again. Hi, Kenyon."

The little girl in her stroller looked up at the man and then back at the pink stuffed cotton monkey she held in her hands.

Graham Patterson had come up on his left side when James was looking at the old man on his right. They hadn't seen each other since that frightening day in the park.

"Are you visiting someone here?" the other man asked.

"Yes, we're here to see my husband, Aaron. He's in the cardiac wing." Was there really anything more he wanted to say about Aaron's condition to this stranger? It felt peculiar seeing Patterson again, so unexpectedly and out of the blue like this. His first feelings were a mix between a kind of intimate connection, because of what happened that day, and distance, because they really were only strangers who'd spent less than fifteen minutes with each other from start to finish.

"Me, too," Patterson said smiling, but it might have been the saddest smile James Arthur had ever seen.

"Excuse me?"

"I'm going up to the cardiac unit, too. My wife is there."

"Oh, I'm sorry."

Patterson put both hands palms up, silently signaling, What can you do, it's life.

An elevator car arrived, and the doors slid open. An old woman lying on a gurney, staring at the ceiling, was pushed out by an attendant. They were followed by a too-thin man walking with a cane. When the car was empty, Patterson gestured for James to go first with Kenyon. A doctor with a stethoscope hanging around her neck and a clipboard in hand got on just as the doors were closing. She smiled thinly at the men, then turned her back to them.

It was a long, slow ride to the sixth floor. Staring straight ahead, both men tried to think of something to say to each other while they rose slowly together toward the ones they loved.

THE END